The Kapellmeister's Daughter

ISBN: 0978736923
ISBN-13: 9780978736927
LCCN 2010927822

PUBLISHED BY
TANNENBAUM PUBLISHING COMPANY
P.O. BOX 117
DOWELL, MARYLAND
20629

FIRST PRINTING, 2010

PRINTED AND BOUND IN THE UNITED STATES OF AMERICA

THIS BOOK IS A WORK OF FICTION. EXCEPT FOR REFERENCES TO THE REAL WORLD MEANT TO SITUATE THE FICTIONAL STORY, ALL CHARACTERS, PLACES, INCIDENTS, AND DIALOGUE WERE INVENTED BY THE AUTHOR AND ANY RESEMBLANCE TO ACTUAL PERSONS, LIVING OR DEAD, IS ENTIRELY COINCIDENTAL.

WWW.TANNENBAUMPUBLISHING.COM

The Kapellmeister's Daughter

HELEN CARSON

To Doctor Beck
Best Wishes
Helen Carson

TANNENBAUM PUBLISHING COMPANY
DOWELL, MARYLAND

Dedication

This book is dedicated to my loving son and daughter,
Howard and Helaine.

The

Kapellmeister's

Daughter

Part One

THE ORCHESTRA

CHAPTER ONE

The room was dark. A light from the hotel veranda filtered dimly through the curtained window. Muted sounds of music, light and lively, drifted in from the establishment's dining room on the farther side of the building. The youngster had been sleeping fitfully, tossing and turning in Bombay's humid heat. Rat-a-tat tat of a drum, and subsequent clash of cymbals, brought her periodically to partial wakefulness.

A subtle jiggling noise, within the room itself, nagged at her consciousness. Her eyes fluttered open. Frowning, she propped herself up on one elbow, ears straining to catch the sound once more. There it was again, only louder, more insistent. The window! Someone was attempting to open it!

Surely her mother had locked it before departing, as she always did. Fully roused, the little girl sat up in the bed, eyes peering into the darkness. The figure of a man, indistinct in the gloom, moved into the room from behind sheer draperies. He crept forward slowly, hovering near the empty beds of her sisters. Whimpering and paralyzed for a moment or two, fear and panic soon erupted in her like a dam of water bursting. Hastily brushing aside the mosquito netting that enveloped the bed, she tumbled pell-mell to the tiled floor, scarcely hearing her own voice shrieking for her mother. Flying to the hallway door, frantically swinging it open, she darted down the hotel corridor, through the deserted lobby, and into the large dining room—white cotton nightdress and carrot-red hair streaming out like a banner in her wake.

Hesitating, she anxiously looked about the room, where her father's orchestra played a spirited tune. She saw the serene face of her sister, Stephanie, on the platform with the other musicians, her violin planted snugly against her chin as she swept the bow expertly to and fro across the strings. Directly behind Stephanie were their brothers—Rudy sitting before his cello, eyes intent on the sheet music on his stand, a lock of auburn hair curled low on his forehead; and Max, tall and blonde, energetically plucking the strings of his bass. At the forefront of the band, imposing and majestic, her father led the musicians in their musical endeavor as though they were members of a symphony orchestra, grandly wielding his baton in a splendid rendition of a Strauss waltz. Hotel guests whirled about in three-quarter time, crowding the dance floor to its limit, seemingly oblivious to the evening's sultry heat.

The little girl gazed about helplessly, not daring to cross the congested floor. Her father would be furious with the disruption she would cause. Her mother, where was her mother? Sobs of desperation escaped as she searched the room for some sign of her parent. The slim, dark-skinned boy named Kumar, dressed in native Indian attire, sat in a corner pulling the cord that operated the *punkah*, a large strip of colorfully patterned cloth suspended from the ceiling. Gliding slowly back and forth, it circulated the air above the diners and dancers. Catching the eye of the tiny redhead, Kumar winked conspiratorially, and pointed to a table by the orchestra. The diminutive three-year-old had become his friend in the short time the family had stayed at the hotel. She was fascinated by his clothes, the exotic turban he wore on his head, and he, in turn, marveled at her coloring. He had never seen such brilliant red hair. They shared no common language—she, German-speaking, and he, the English of the raj—but he was touched by her overtures of friendship. She often brought little gifts of fruits and sweets, shyly smiling as he nodded his thanks. They would, in years to come, cross paths again in a way neither could imagine. Now Kumar watched as the little girl, who seemed to be in distress of some kind, threaded her way among the tables and potted plants.

Finally, she reached her objective, circled her seated mother's waist with her thin arms and buried her face in an ample bosom.

"Mama," she gasped, fear still gripping her like a vise.

"Elena!" exclaimed her mother, "what are you doing out of bed?" She lifted Elena's head to gaze into her green eyes, knitting her brows together in mild disapproval.

"There's a man in my room. A vampire, Mama! He came in the window."

"Vampire? *Liebchen*, you've had a nightmare," her parent soothed. "There are no vampires here. Come, I'll take you back to your room." She smiled, tolerantly patting Elena's slight shoulder.

"No! Mama, no!" Elena wailed, "He's there, I saw him!" She held her mother tightly, resisting any effort to be disengaged. "It wasn't a dream, Mama, I was wide awake."

The orchestra had ceased playing; her cries were now very audible to the diners at neighboring tables. Elena's father approached from the podium, his face flushed and perspiring from the physical effort of directing the band.

"Why is Elena here, Marta?" he asked impatiently. "She is disturbing everyone. Why is she yammering so?" His large reddish-brown mustache, twisted to fine needle-like tips, twitched menacingly as he spoke. His sense of decorum and professionalism didn't allow for even the youngest of his brood to misbehave in public, or in private, for that matter.

"It's nothing, it's nothing, Franz," his wife said quickly. "She's had a nightmare, that's all." In an aside to him, she whispered, "She's upset, I think, with all that's happened." Marta rose from her chair, gathering the youngster to her side. "I'll take her back to the room."

"Please, Mama, please ...," Elena pleaded, pulling away from her mother's grasp. At the same time she stole an uneasy glance at her father, trembling under his stern gaze. How was she to convince them there really was a vampire in her room?

"Elena," her father growled. "Go with Mama." She drew closer to her mother again, her eyes bright with tears.

Max had arrived on the scene from the orchestra platform, Rudy and Stephanie following. Marta realized that Elena was genuinely frightened—disobeying her father would otherwise be unthinkable. It was time for a bit of strategy.

"Max and Rudy, you come along with us," she urged. To Elena, she said, "Your big brothers will chase away the vampire." She smiled at Max, lifting one eyebrow significantly.

"Ah, yes, little one, come," he persuaded, taking his mother's meaning immediately. He folded his sister's small hand in his protectively, and led her from the room. Though still a bit apprehensive, she accompanied him, looking up into his face with trust and adoration as they walked.

"Max," she whispered, "there really was a vampire."

"I'll chase him," he said, "and he won't dare come back."

In the bedroom, Rudy went about searching the wardrobe closet, and made much of thoroughly scrutinizing the undersides of the bed, picking up wisps of dust in his hair as he emerged.

"Nobody here," he said.

"Someone *was* here, Mama," Max interjected. "Did you lock the window when you left Elena? Look, it's wide open now. No wonder Elena panicked, and maybe the robber did, too, not expecting to find a little girl in her bed."

Marta gasped, shaken by his discovery. She took Elena in her arms, caressing her cheek gently. "Oh, my poor Liebchen," she said, "I'm so sorry. I truly thought you had a bad dream. Nothing like this has happened before." She paused for a moment, a twinge of conscience stinging her. "I promise you'll never be left alone again in this room. Yes," she nodded, "it's settled. You'll stay with Lise and Mitzi in the card room until their bedtime."

She turned to Max, who had closed and locked the window. "Max, would you please inform the manager, Monsieur Ferrand, that there's been an intruder here, and that he should have the grounds searched. The man is long gone now, no doubt, but one never knows." She glanced about the room. "I suppose we should see if anything is missing."

The air in the room was already stifling with the window closed. Marta patted her damp forehead with a lace-trimmed handkerchief that she kept handy in her shirtwaist pocket. "Oh, Rudy," she said, as he moved to follow Max, "please tell Lise and Mitzi to come to bed now. Then you had better get back to the orchestra before Papa starts up again. No sense in aggravating him further tonight."

Her heart was heavy as she helped Elena into bed, arranging the mosquito netting about her with tender care. "Poor Liebchen," she thought, "first Emile, and now this frightening incident tonight." She sighed as she seated herself in a chair by Elena's bed. How much could the child endure? Marta couldn't wait until Franz's contract with the hotel expired in August, and the family could return to Bucharest. If it hadn't been for that commitment, she would have insisted on leaving India immediately following her little son's death. The thought brought tears to her eyes. She pictured Emile's angelic face; he had looked so small in the coffin, only two years old. In one day he was gone from her forever.

She heard the orchestra start up again, a polka. Leaning wearily back in the chair, she closed her eyes. So much for being married to a man consumed with a love of travel, she mused.

* * *

On their wedding night twenty-eight years earlier, she had lain in his arms on their marriage bed listening raptly as he voiced his hopes and dreams for them.

"I want to see the world, Marta," he had said. "I want to see all the places I've read about. Foreign lands, new ideas and cultures; we'll sail together to the ends of the earth."

She was fifteen years old then; he, twenty-three. She had cuddled closer to him, dazzled by his ardor, his lively brown eyes, and curly auburn hair. She would have flown to the moon with him if he asked. Young as she was, though, she was still pragmatic.

"I'll follow you wherever you go, Franz," she said, lovingly indulging his fantasies, "but how are we to do all this? It takes money."

"I'll find a way. I have a plan."

Marta smiled.

God had helped his plan along in the beginning. For the first nine years of their marriage, she was unexplainably childless. Thus they journeyed the length of Europe from sunny Italy to the frigid cities of Russia. Franz secured positions as violinist in a hotel here, a restaurant there. They were like gypsies, absorbing the history and culture of each country as they traveled.

That carefree life came to an end when the babies started to arrive, one after the other. Franz became first violinist in the Bucharest opera, necessity demanding he find stable employment to support his growing family. Marta had hoped he would give up his dreams of travel and settle down. She was happy to be back in the city of her birth, enjoying the company of friends and family again. Not so.

"I'm forming my own orchestra, Marta," he had announced one day. "I've contracted with a hotel in India to play dinner and dance music for the summer." He was excited and thrilled at the prospect. She was dismayed.

"What about me ... and the children?"

"You will all accompany me, of course."

It was true that five of her offspring had succumbed to childhood diseases over the years, but there were still seven to be reckoned with. By this time, the older children—Stephanie, Max, and Rudy—were members of the orchestra. They assisted with the packing of clothes and care of their younger brothers and sisters, and Marta had managed to get them all to Bombay without incident. This was now their second stay in India. Previously, they had sojourned to Egypt.

"This is an ideal life for you, Marta," Franz had declared, "a summer holiday with no cooking or cleaning, and native help with the children." She had agreed, until the loss of Emile to cholera, only weeks before, had devastated her.

* * *

The bickering of Lise and Mitzi interrupted her reflections; they scampered through the open doorway, prancing about their mother like fledgling ballerinas.

"Rudy said someone stole into our room, frightening Elena to death," Lise said. "Is that true, Mama?" Her hazel eyes blazed indignantly, as though she proposed to hunt down the intruder herself. "He said Elena will stay in the card room with us from now on. He's teasing, isn't he? We're allowed to stay up later than Elena because we're older than she is. Isn't that so, Mama?"

"Yes, yes," Marta said. "We'll talk about it in the morning." Elena was already asleep, clutching a frayed and worn toy bear to her chest. "Tell me, Lise, who's been filling Elena's head with stories about vampires?"

"Her friend, Poldi, at home. Poldi's grandmother visits from the family farm and tells us about them. Vampires have terrible powers, she says. They come into your room at night and drink blood from your veins. They are the undead, she said … what is that, Mama? Could that happen to Emile?"

"Uh, the superstitious old crone," Marta said, ignoring the reference to Emile. Mitzi's large and luminous brown eyes, which seemed to overwhelm her entire face, widened greater still in dread as she listened to her sister's words. Marta drew Mitzi to her side comfortingly, smoothing wavy dark hair back from her brow, and recalled the old tales of vampires in Romania that had terrified her during her own childhood. "Peasants, just peasants' stories," Marta's mother had said disdainfully. "Pay no attention to them." Easy to say when one is young and impressionable, she thought.

"But, Mama," Lise insisted. "Rudy makes it even worse. He teases Elena, and says 'the vampires will get you!'"

Marta rolled her eyes to the ceiling in frustration. "Oh, that boy! That's why Elena was so frightened. Seeing a man come into the room, she thought it had to be a vampire." She shook her head despairingly. "I can't tell Papa, he's sure to use the strap."

"He should," Lise said. "Rudy's always in trouble."

"No, I'll have a talk with him, he gets thrashed enough as it is. He still has a scar on his forehead from the last beating. Papa isn't careful where he lands a blow when he's angry; though heaven knows he has cause sometimes, Rudy can be so mischievous." She prepared to leave the room with last-minute instructions. "Get yourselves to bed, girls," and as an afterthought before she closed the door, said, "Lise, no tattling to Papa about Rudy, please."

Monsieur Ferrand must provide better protection for the family, Marta vowed, as she swept into the lobby, her petite body ramrod straight under her corset, ready for battle. Where was that servant who usually patrolled the hotel grounds? Asleep again, no doubt.

* * *

As obsessed as Franz was in his pursuit of the far horizons, returning in August to the intensely alive and picturesque city of Bucharest gave him a warm feeling of comfort and enchantment. Romania's four-hundred-year-old capital, in 1901, was vibrant with the strains of gypsy violins rising from the multitude of indoor and outdoor cafés bordering the tree-lined avenues.

The long lovely autumn was ideal for the flourishing social life enjoyed by the populace. Dark-eyed women dressed in the latest Paris fashions and men with Roman profiles strolled in parks and along the thoroughfares, mixing nonchalantly with barely clad gypsies and beggars. Romanians were a people who celebrated earthly pleasures. Business transactions came to a halt from noon to afternoon's end, and dining was delayed until late in the evening. As a musician, Franz was stimulated anew, refreshed by the city's Parisian-like ambiance. The gypsy music, intermixed with centuries-old national folk melodies, greeted him on every street corner as he walked to his work at the opera house; they set his creative juices flowing, inspirations for his own musical compositions dancing in his head.

Marta's mourning for Emile was put aside by the responsibilities of her household duties. She threw herself into the tasks needed to blow away the dust of summer and, in the process, helped to sweep away the clouds of despondency that had plagued her in India. Daytimes, at any rate. Elena's recurring nightmares, suffered for weeks after their return, brought her own grief to mind again as she lay abed nights, unable to sleep after lulling her little daughter back to her slumber. Elena was high-strung and overly sensitive, she thought. Her experience in Bombay had been a traumatizing one, especially the break-in of her room. Perhaps it had been a mistake to include her in Emile's funeral services and burial, but there had been no one to care for Elena, certainly not the *ayah* who was responsible for taking Marta's little son to her village, thus exposing him to cholera.

After a firm lecture from his mother, vampires were now a forbidden subject for Rudy, but teasing his younger sister continued unabated whenever his parents were out of earshot. He relished the tearful reaction his teasing elicited from her. She seldom complained of his actions to her mother, which inspired him to further torment her. His sister, Lise, on the other hand, would have none of his bedeviling. Her tongue was sharp and stinging.

"I'll tell Papa if you don't stop, Rudy," she threatened, punctuating her warning with a stabbing poke to his shoulder. She was solidly built, ready to physically pummel him. He laughed nervously, skipping away just out of her reach. The placid Mitzi stayed quietly in Lise's shadow, so Rudy took little interest in her.

Elena's saviors were the thirteen-year-old Max and nineteen-year-old Stephanie, who took pleasure in her inquisitive mind and sweet nature. Stephanie was the eldest of the Linden children; several of her siblings had perished both before and after her birth. She took her responsibilities seriously, helping her mother with household duties, and shepherding her brothers and sisters through daily activities until bedtime. Elena treasured her time with Stephanie while the others attended school, trailing behind her sister and mother as they worked, full of questions, which they answered with amusement and patience.

"You'll make a wonderful mother someday, Stephanie," Marta said, thinking how much she would miss her assistance when she married.

Stephanie teased. "You think I'm getting old, Mama? That I'll never marry?"

"Of course you will. The right man must come along, that's all."

Elena had picked up on their conversation with anxiety. "Stephanie isn't going away, is she, Mama?"

"Not ever," Stephanie said. "How could I leave my special girl?" She hugged her little sister wildly, ending with a tickling session that sent Elena into spasms of delight.

* * *

Deep snows of winter that had enveloped Bucharest started to melt as the warm breezes of April whispered across wooded plains. Months had passed swiftly; Christmas had come and gone. The house fairly shook with the boisterous goings-on of a lively family as friends and relatives gathered in the small parlor for music, fun, and frolic during the social season. Elena had turned four in March, and the coming of spring was a revelation for her. From the kitchen window she saw the green buds emerging on the willow tree that decorated the narrow strip of garden in the rear of their house; they strained to burst forth into graceful sprays, like a fountain of emerald tears. Excursions with the family into the countryside revealed a lush and fruitful Romania. The willow trees grew along mountain streams and served as fences around individual farms. Max executed a small sketch of the elegantly shaped tree for her, which she stashed away in an empty bonbon box that held her other little treasures.

"Will Oma and Opa be here for Easter Sunday, Stephanie?" Elena asked. The two were seated in the kitchen shelling peas for dinner, the little girl popping several of the green orbs into her mouth, then channeling the rest of the pod's contents into a pot on Stephanie's lap. Her sister smiled faintly, catching Elena's motion with a sideways glance.

"Yes, they'll be here after Mass at St. Joseph's, no doubt laden with cakes and pastries as usual."

Elena smacked her lips in anticipation; her maternal grandparents' visits always included treats for the children. Oma Stagen, tall and willowy, towered over their mother, generating many jests in the family regarding the origins of Marta's parentage.

"She can't be my daughter," Oma would protest. "She must have been left on our doorstep by the gypsies." Her oft-repeated words always gave rise to much giggling by her grandchildren. Now Elena's thoughts turned to her father's parents.

"Where are Papa's mother and father?"

"Umm ... let's see," Stephanie said, setting aside the peas. They would be added later to the fragrant stew simmering on the wood-burning stove. "Papa came from a small town in Germany called Erding. His father, your other Opa, was a watchmaker. He had his own shop, and trained Papa to be a watchmaker, too."

"Why did Papa leave?"

"Oh," Stephanie's face took on a bemused expression. "Papa is ... well ... a rare breed of man." Seeing that Elena didn't understand, she continued quickly, "He left Germany to see the world, Elena. Besides," she said, smiling, "if he hadn't come here to Bucharest, he wouldn't have met Mama." She rose from her seat, patting Elena's shoulder. "I'm due in the parlor now. Papa is giving Lise and Mitzi their violin lessons and I must practice with Max and Rudy. Why don't you find Mama? I think she is going over the summer clothes we'll need for our trip to the hotel in Alexandria next month."

Elena shuddered involuntarily as Stephanie hurried away. Hotel ... The image of a man entering her Bombay hotel bedroom flashed across her mind. Her mother had promised she wasn't to be left alone ever again. She wondered where Alexandria was. Max said it was in a country called Egypt. Perhaps her Indian friend, Kumar, would be there to work the *punkah*, if there was a *punkah*. His features had blurred in her memory, but a picture of the turban he wore remained.

CHAPTER TWO

Alexandria

"Papa wants us all up on deck now," Lise announced to her siblings, occupied with playing board games in the steamship's wood-paneled salon.

"Why?" Rudy asked peevishly.

"Let's go," Max said. "You know why he wants us."

"Oh, no ... that guide book again," Rudy groaned. "I suppose we'll have to listen to a lecture on the 'wonderful history of Egypt,' just like the 'fascinating religions of India' last year."

"Stop your kvetching," Stephanie said good-naturedly as they rose from their seats. "Someday you'll appreciate how fortunate we are to have a father who takes the time to try to educate us."

"Humph," grunted Lise, for once in accord with Rudy. Brisk and energetic, she found it tortuous to sit at length while her father lectured.

As the children settled in deck chairs facing Franz, he twirled his mustache tips with his fingers, waiting several minutes for them to be quiet. "Traveling, as we are doing, even as a means of earning a living," he started, "gives us a wonderful opportunity to gain an education."

Rudy raised his eyes to Max's, flashing him a sardonic grin. Seated nearby, Marta's practiced fingers darted nimbly in and out as she crocheted, her mind obviously elsewhere. Elena had never seen her mother sitting idle; her hands were always busy. She was like a human machine, constantly turning out knitted woolen sweaters, mufflers, mittens, and stockings in the winter, or crocheting doilies, tablecloths, and bedspreads during the rest of the year. Mysteriously, she was also capable of carrying on conversations with friends and relatives, not dropping a single stitch.

"'Alexandria was founded by Alexander the Great more than two thousand two hundred years ago,'" Franz continued, reading from his guidebook. He had discovered Karl Baedeker's publications several years before, and thereafter they became his valued companions on his travels.

Before long, Lise and Mitzi began to squirm in their seats, tiring of a narrative they found boring. Franz paused, bestowing a warning stare in their direction. They were instantly still, fearful, eyes lowered; a slap or a spanking was sure to follow should they persist. Their brothers were more likely to be on the receiving end of the dreaded shaving strap when misbehaving, Rudy more often than Max. For the girls, the mere existence of the strap hanging on a hook back in the kitchen in Bucharest was enough to discourage any misconduct.

As Franz's voice droned on, his displeasure that had been directed so eloquently towards her sisters was not lost on Elena. She sat quietly next to Stephanie, gazing out over the ship's railing to the Mediterranean Sea beyond. Her mind wandered to an account of an escapade involving a younger Rudy and Max at home. Stephanie, who enjoyed a dramatic talent for spinning tales, especially those that demonstrated a moral lesson, had been the narrator.

* * *

The four sisters had been alone in the house one afternoon, and Stephanie proceeded to cast her spell over the girls as they sat by the tile stove in the parlor.

"It was wintertime," she started, "and the snows were deep that year. Rudy and Max had taken the long way home from school, through the woods. Mind you, they had been warned by Papa to come straight home, not dally and play. He had read in the newspaper just the day before that wolves were very numerous and hungry in the forests, coming closer to town and attacking small children who were foolish enough to wander from home."

"Eating them?" Lise asked.

"Yes, I'm afraid so. Rudy was small and pudgy at the time. He would have made a good meal." She smiled, and the girls giggled.

"Boys being boys," she continued, "your brothers dawdled along the path; laughing, chasing, climbing trees, each attempting to outdo the other in athletic prowess. They didn't notice the early dusk of the winter season that was rapidly descending on them. It was then they heard the howling of wolves behind them ...."

Mitzi drew an agonized breath. "What happened?"

"The boys exchanged frightened glances," Stephanie said tensely, "and started running. 'Hurry, Rudy, hurry!' Max urged as they raced along the trail, his long legs carrying him further ahead of his brother.

Shadows of night fell over them, black as coal; trees and bushes became indistinct, their faces were struck by leafless branches and twigs as they fled in panic." Elena, Lise, and Mitzi were mesmerized, their eyes round in rapt attention.

"They could hear the wolves were much closer. Looking back quickly over his shoulder, Max caught sight of gray furry shapes with red eyes as he and Rudy managed to clear the woods. The animals were gaining on them, only separated by yards, when the boys spotted buildings of the town outlined by a bonfire. They headed for the blaze with renewed speed. 'Help, help!' they cried. Rudy suddenly tripped and was flung headlong to icy ground, his schoolbooks scattering to the wind. Max turned back to help him. The wolves were now almost upon them ...."

"They're going to be eaten up!" Elena screamed, caught up in the tale as though it were one of the ghost stories Stephanie told on stormy nights.

"Not to worry," Stephanie said. "Astonishingly, all about them were shouts and bellows as several men came out of the dark, advancing towards them, brandishing flaming torches. They drove the wolves back to the tree line, cagily dropping bits of food to distract them from their prey. Hasty thanks were offered to their rescuers by the breathless and shaken lads; they were eager to get home as quickly as possible.

"Meanwhile, Papa sat at the dinner table in the house, waiting. He removed his watch from his vest pocket at intervals, checking the time, his face darkening as the minutes ticked by. The family usually ate early. Papa, ready to leave for the opera by seven, was dressed immaculately in his black suit and tie. He was no doubt feeling both worried and angry."

"Uh, oh," Lise said, "they're going to get a beating."

"But the boys were almost killed," rationalized Mitzi.

"Because they disobeyed. Max and Rudy knew explanations were useless," Stephanie said. "I saw them come in the door. Their faces were scratched and bloody, clothes torn, and schoolbooks lost ...."

* * *

Franz's authoritative voice intruded on Elena's reflections regarding the complexities of crime and punishment. "So that's all for today. We arrive in Alexandria tomorrow morning. Mama and Stephanie will help pack your things this evening after dinner." Lise and Mitzi and the boys jumped from their seats, relieved, but Elena made no effort to move.

"What ails you, Liebchen, are you seasick?" Marta asked.

Elena looked up at her mother frowning. "Mama, does Papa love us?"

"Of course," Marta protested. "What put that thought into your head?" This little one was deep indeed, she thought.

"Then why ... why is he so ...."

"Strict?" Marta prompted. She smiled, answering softly, "He is strict because he loves you, Elena. Someday you'll understand."

* * *

So this was Alexandria, Elena thought. Wide grid-planned streets, restaurants, casinos, clubs, foreign schools, businesses, and banks flashed by as she sat with her parents in the carriage carrying them from the ship to the hotel.

"See that elegant building over there?" her mother asked, nodding as they passed. "Wait until you see the interior. Last time we were here, we were invited there for dinner and a ball, the entire orchestra, no less. You won't believe your eyes ... ornately decorated rooms, huge sparkling chandeliers. It was beautiful." Marta's eyes gleamed in remembrance. A ball. What was a ball, Elena wondered? Whatever it was, it wasn't something her mother attended very often.

Alexandria had become a Europeanized city as a result of the British refusing to formalize their presence, both there and in Cairo. Consul-General Lord Cromo was the defacto ruler of Egypt with absolute authority in both internal and foreign affairs. In 1902, when the Linden family arrived for their hotel engagement, Alexandria was one of the foremost cities of the Mediterranean basin, thriving under the immigration of Greeks, Italians, Germans, French, English, and Belgians. Middle-class Arabs adopted western-style clothes. Cotton had been introduced as an export early in the nineteenth century, and the port prospered. In winter, the town was a playground for the aristocracy of Europe, and summer found wealthy inhabitants of Cairo flocking there for the cooler climate. It was a luxurious life they enjoyed, one that was to disappear with the clouds of war in a few short years.

Later, Elena explored the airy rooms of the Hotel Alexandrie and the spacious, meticulously groomed grounds surrounding the classically designed building. Other members of the orchestra, whom Franz had under contract, were housed in various rooms and apartments nearby. The French and Arab staff was friendly toward the Linden children, finding them well-mannered and helpful. A stern lecture from Franz at the outset of their stay was potently effective.

Stephanie, Rudy, and Max were soon busy with orchestra rehearsals in the late mornings, and performed dinner and dance music until two o'clock in the morning. In addition to sharing mealtimes, the family spent Sundays and weekday afternoons together touring the town or enjoying the garden. In a remote area of the garden, the management had provided rough-hewn wooden chairs and tables for the family's use. Lise, Mitzi, and Elena could then run and play without disturbing guests. Seventy-foot tulip trees shaded the area, with the evergreen leaves complementing the brilliantly scarlet flowers.

Marta gazed up at the trees one afternoon as she sat with Stephanie. "How pretty the trees are, Stephanie," she said. "Look how the red flowers are outlined on the edges with yellow, so exotic-looking."

"Hmmm ... it's cool here, Mama, an ideal spot for the girls." She watched Lise and Mitzi as they sat playing a card game, squabbling occasionally over the outcome. Elena sat in the grass by Stephanie's chair, fascinated by the progress of a garden snake slithering by. "Don't touch the snake, Elena," Stephanie warned. "It might be poisonous. Yesterday, it was toads you handled."

Max approached, sketchbook in hand. "Elena," he called, "come with me to the pond. I think I saw gold-colored fish in there the other day." He had been out sketching various places of interest in the city. Elena sprang to her feet and accompanied him, skipping happily by his side. Marta gazed after her son with pride that was difficult to suppress. She tried so hard to be fair to all the children, but Max's love and devotion to her struck a chord to her very inner being. Mature beyond his years, he had completed his schooling at fourteen and was ready to make his way in the world. Franz was impressed by his older son's intelligence and earnestness; he could discuss current events seriously with him, and they enjoyed games of chess when there was time.

Marta sighed. If only Rudy were like Max. Then she chuckled, a letter from a cousin of Franz's in Germany had given her some insight into the reason for Rudy's rascally behavior. The cousin had reminisced about her childhood.

"I always remember Franz as being an active boy," the cousin had written. "He teased me unmercifully, and was constantly in trouble because of his pranks and monkeyshines. He was regarded by his uncles and aunts as a bad boy, and was told as much. Yet look how wonderfully he has turned out, so talented and respected as *Kapellmeister*."

Marta had slyly mentioned the cousin's remembrances to Franz, but he had pooh-poohed any similarity between Rudy's and his own roguish boyhood. We must give Rudy time, she thought; he has his good points, too, just different from Max.

Elena came bounding across the lawn, well ahead of Max, carrying large, round, greenish-brown flowers in spikelets. They were mop-headed, on small grassy stems.

"We're going to make paper, Mama," she said spiritedly. "Max said this is a paper plant."

"It's papyrus," he explained as he neared them. "I told Elena the Egyptians used the plant to make paper, so now, of course, we must make some. Elena, take the plants to the table, while I get out my pocketknife. You see, it's the stems we use. We cut them into strips and press them together while they are still wet." Lise and Mitzi abandoned their card game to watch the process with interest.

* * *

One afternoon after rehearsal, Stephanie appeared in the garden with a young man in tow. His manner was solemn and polite, and he was noticeably shorter in height than she. Most ominous to Elena, he followed her gentle sister's every movement with adoring eyes. She perceived him as a threat to her close relationship with Stephanie, and was unsmiling in his presence. "You must be nicer to Monsieur Papas," admonished Marta, observing Elena's continued attitude after several subsequent visits.

"He has eyes like a cow."

"What a thing to say! I don't want to hear any more. He is a pleasant man, and Stephanie likes him. He has graciously invited the family to dine with him next week at the restaurant he owns. Isn't that so, Stephanie?" she asked her daughter, who had listened to the exchange with some amusement.

Stephanie hugged the troubled Elena, so obviously jealous of her admirer. "You'll always have a special place in my heart, Liebchen," she comforted.

André Papas continued to call on Stephanie throughout the rest of the summer. He sat in the hotel dining room every evening as the orchestra played, his "cow eyes" fondly watching as she performed. Some afternoons, the couple walked leisurely along the seashore, Stephanie's parasol hiding the occasional kisses he stole.

Elena, wary of André, was unable to relax until her mother started packing the trunks for the return trip to Bucharest. Franz journeyed alone to the interior of Egypt for a week or so, marveling at the splendors of Luxor and Karnak, and the pyramids in Cairo. He returned, his face beaming. Walking in the steps of the ancient pharaohs had transported him back in time to a world long gone but not forgotten.

CHAPTER THREE

A Taste Of Singapore

Elena stroked her father's freshly laundered dress shirts, neatly arranged in rows on her parents' bed. Pleats and ruffles intrigued her, resembling little pristine snow-covered hills and valleys; she followed each depression and rise lightly with her fingertips.

"Don't touch!" her mother said, "I don't want to wash and iron the shirts again."

"When are we leaving?" Elena asked, hastily hiding the offending hand behind her back.

"Very soon now." Marta's patience was wearing thin.

"Where are we going?"

"Singapore, Elena, Singapore. You've asked me that ten times, at least, in the last half hour."

Singapore. The five-year-old felt the excitement and anticipation building in the Linden household. Preparations for the trip had started in early spring. Marta and Stephanie had industriously laundered and pressed summer wardrobes, and now all was ready for packing in the steamer trunks sitting expectantly in her mother's bedroom. Singapore was a new destination for the family. Max traced the route the ship would take on the upright world globe in the parlor.

"This is the way we go, little one," he said to Elena. "We sail through the Mediterranean Sea, the Suez Canal, into the Red Sea and the Indian Ocean." He paused a moment, charmed by the serious attention she paid to his explanation, then continued. "Now, we then sail into the Strait of Malacca, along the Malay Peninsula to Singapore." He tapped Singapore's location smartly.

The fact that the world was round mystified her. In the fall she would be starting school. Perhaps the knowledge she sought would then unfold before her, like the delicate lace fan that Oma Stagen used to cool herself on warm days.

* * *

With a captive audience once more, Franz took the opportunity to enlighten his brood with a description of Singapore. Out came the Baedecker guidebook from his pocket, and the family again encircled him on the ship's deck in the warm sunshine. Musicians Hans Schenck and Karl Deigelmeier, members in the orchestra the summer before in Alexandria, joined the group on this voyage.

"We're happy to have the opportunity to join the orchestra again," Schenck said to Max at breakfast that morning. "Your father's competence as Kapellmeister is unequaled in Bucharest." Max, several years younger than the energetic and genial musician, had warmed to him from their first meeting the year before. Tall, lean, and modest Deigelmeier, on the other hand, seemed to fade away into nothingness. All one noticed was a small mustache under pale eyes when he spoke, which was seldom.

"'Approximately eighty years ago in 1819,'" Franz began, "'Singapore— the name derived from the Malay, Singa Pura, meaning Lion City—was founded by Stamford Raffles of the East India Trading Company, making the most of its strategic position and natural harbor.'" His flair for teaching gradually drew his listeners into his narrative in spite of themselves. Even Lise and Mitzi sat quietly as he painted vivid pictures in their minds that would stay with them throughout their lives. Elena sat next to Stephanie on a footstool borrowed from the ship's salon. Her father's words made little impression on her; she enjoyed the closeness of her elder sister, and was content to bask in the sun's rays and brisk breezes for the moment.

* * *

Their residence for the summer was the Grand Continental Hotel. There was nothing grand about the structure, but when Elena first caught sight of the two-story building, she adored it. Tall shuttered windows, decorated with filigreed ironwork, stood open to the humid Singapore air. Shaded verandas beckoned the dusty traveler to a temporary rest. Smaller, more intimate than Egypt's Hotel Alexandrie, the interior exuded a comfortable, informal atmosphere that persuaded guests and workers alike to feel very much at home. Trees and tropical plants of the surrounding grounds were less lush, less well-tended than the Alexandrie, especially the sparse grass that could hardly be called a lawn, but again, it seemed to add to the gracious unpretentiousness of the hotel.

The lively entourage invading the cool lobby from the shimmering heat outside that first morning consisted of the Linden family, the two young musicians accompanying them, and several jovial porters. A handsome, dark-haired woman stepped forward to greet them.

"Madam Rosenbaum?" Franz ventured.

She smiled warmly. "Welcome, welcome," she said, embracing Marta and her daughters, giving Franz a firm handshake, and extending a friendly nod to Max and Rudy, who were carrying their bass and cello themselves, not trusting the porters to handle them carefully. "We have been waiting for your arrival," she added. "Several members of your orchestra came yesterday—the drummer and others—so you are all here now." Acknowledging Franz's introduction of Deigelmeier and Schenck with equal friendliness, she then gave instructions to the hotel staff to deliver luggage to their respective rooms, and invited all to her suite for refreshments. It was an auspicious beginning to a strong friendship.

In the ensuing days, Elena watched Madam Rosenbaum's erect corseted figure striding through the corridors of the hotel, directing staff in their duties, consulting with the Chinese cook over the day's menu, and attending to the needs of hotel guests with competence and a rare good humor. Compassion and genuine thoughtfulness shone from her large brown eyes, and she always had a pleasant word for the Linden children.

"Madam Rosenbaum is a shrewd businesswoman," Elena's father said to her mother at lunch one day. "She wears the pants in the family, I think. We never see her husband anywhere, only on the first day we arrived, in their suite. Where does he keep himself?"

"I know where he is," piped up Elena. She had discovered the slightly built man secreted away in a shed while exploring the grounds. "He let me see his collection of bugs and butterflies in his little house. He eats all his meals there, too."

"Butterflies?" Max asked. He and Rudy looked up from the fast-disappearing food on their plates, ears perked up in interest. "Elena, show us where he is after we finish eating."

Herr Rosenbaum's watery blue eyes sparkled from behind his spectacles when the boys entered his insect world, as he liked nothing better than displaying his tropical collection to visitors. Rudy and Max were so intrigued with his work that he soon found himself offering to teach them the proper techniques of entrapping and chloroforming insects. "With appropriate mounting," he said, "specimens will be of particular interest to museums and collectors. I can help you learn, but you must pay attention.

It is a delicate, exacting task." The boys readily agreed and their summer became a stimulating and productive one.

In a further exploration of the garden, Elena discovered friends who would be her summer comrades. To her great pleasure, she came upon a tame young doe nibbling the grass, friendly and receptive to her petting and soothing words. She gasped in surprise as a ram repeatedly butted her rear, obviously seeking to gain her attention. Scratching him between his ears until he contentedly started to graze, she then cautiously backed away. As she retreated, she almost collided with two cages, each housing a young monkey. Her approach started a furor of screeching by one of the long-limbed animals; he bounced back and forth furiously against the bars of his prison. But the other studied her intently, extending his white forepaws through the bars in supplication. Fascinated, she sat down, legs crossed under her on the grass, examining the primates at length, in complete absorption. Herr Rosenbaum's voice broke the spell.

"These monkeys are called gibbons," he said. "They are skillful and highly intelligent. They come from Siam. That friendly rascal there is Chekki."

"Does Chekki ever come out of his cage?" Elena asked, jumping up from the grass to face Herr Rosenbaum.

"Well, little lady, let's take him out, and you can hold him awhile. I'll have to collar and chain him, though, or he'll be off and running." After opening the cage door and slipping the collar over the animal's head, he lifted him and placed him in the delighted little girl's arms.

Chekki and Elena gazed into each other's eyes, an instant rapport developing between the two. He fingered her red hair, the blue ribbon sitting atop her head, and the gold locket encircling her neck. Then he dropped to the ground, held her hand, and led her about the garden, chattering all the while. Herr Rosenbaum shook his head, marveling at the sight of the small child and her new simian friend walking and talking together. At all other times, when freed from his confinement, Chekki had fled, never to be seen again for days at a time. Secure in the knowledge the monkey would not bolt from her, having found a true companion, the hotel owner interrupted them only briefly, instructing Elena how to lure the animal back into his cage later with fruit. His trust was not misplaced; the two were inseparable from then on.

* * *

Hot summer days flowed dreamily one onto the other, and, when it rained, Elena, Mitzi and Lise escaped outdoors to the cool of the garden.

Luxuriating in tepid showers falling from gray misty heavens, they opened arms wide in joyous abandon, smiling faces tilted upwards to the sky above. Round and round they circled, like fallen leaves and soft petal blossoms caught in a manic whirlpool, white skirts twirling around slim ankles. Then all was still as raindrops ceased their incessant patter. The doe raised her head from the grass to gaze about her. Oppressive humid air closed in again about the enchanted youngsters; only the repeated calls from their mother brought them back to the hotel, breathless, drenched, but elated.

Occasionally, on days when Elena released Chekki from his cage, she and her sisters raced about the garden with him, playing games that reached a high degree of merriment and excitement. On one such day, a stimulated Chekki scampered about with them, then nimbly entered the hotel's rear entrance, the girls laughing and shrieking behind him.

"Catch him, catch him!" Elena squealed. "He isn't allowed in here."

Chekki sprinted through the building's corridors and into the dining room where their father was rehearsing the orchestra. Pandemonium erupted as musicians rose hurriedly from chairs to avoid collision with the agile monkey and the screaming girls following him. Music stands and sheet music went flying in all directions. Rudy's mouth dropped open in disbelief, and Max and Schenck exchanged amused smiles.

"Out, out!" Franz shouted, waving his baton threateningly. The animal swerved in circles to evade capture and finally exited the room, the sisters in close pursuit. On through the hallways they chased, into the lobby where guests scrambled from lounge chairs in alarm at sight of the now frenzied creature and his exhilarated pursuers. Ultimately, they darted through the kitchen and out into the garden, with Chang, the cook, shouting Chinese obscenities out the door after them, waving his knife in the air.

That evening, the girls stood still, eyes lowered, as Franz delivered a lecture. "How could you behave so," he demanded, "in our place of employment? Madam Rosenbaum will never invite the orchestra to return next year."

"You're fortunate you didn't get a spanking from Papa," their mother scolded at bedtime.

It was that impish monkey, Franz told Marta later after they had gone to bed. He couldn't deal out corporal punishment when his daughters were only attempting to capture the animal. Marta smiled wryly; he wouldn't admit the incident had struck his funny bone, just as it had everyone else in the hotel, including Madam Rosenbaum. He turned away from her so she couldn't see the twinkle in his eye.

"Chekki's sick, Mama," Elena said as she approached her mother sitting on the veranda several days later. Marta looked up from her crocheting, frowning.

"Where is he?"

"Herr Rosenbaum has him in his little house." Her eyes were bright with tears. "He made a bed for him in a box ... I think it has something to do with what happened yesterday."

"What happened?" Marta was suspicious. "You didn't let him out of the cage again, did you?"

"No, no ... I know he's only allowed out when I can be with him. Herr Rosenbaum said the clever Chekki had learned to open the latch himself. And then he had a party in the room where the laundry things are kept ... that's when I saw him." She laughed suddenly. "Mama, he looked so funny! He was running and hopping in the grass ... and he was hiccuping."

"Hiccuping?"

"Yes, he was hiccuping. With each hiccup, blue bubbles flew into the air after him ... and then he went around in circles, blue bubbles flying all over the place."

"I don't understand."

"Herr Rosenbaum said he must have eaten powdered soap, then drank something called bluing. That's what made him so sick."

"I'm not surprised," Marta said, shaking her head. "Don't you worry, though, Elena. I'm sure the little beast will be fine. Herr Rosenbaum is so good with animals. He'll have Chekki well in no time."

Elena brightened at her mother's comforting words, and went off to visit the ailing pet, most likely for the tenth time that day. How patient Herr Rosenbaum was, thought Marta. Animals, children, they were his world; though perhaps one his wife made possible for him because of her diligent work.

* * *

Remaining weeks of the summer passed too swiftly for Elena. Her mother was already preparing clothes for packing in the steamer trunks. Elena sat on the bed, watching as Marta carefully folded garment after garment.

"I don't want to leave Chekki, Mama," she said. "Can't we bring him home with us? I'll take care of him."

"You know better, Elena. Chekki belongs to the Rosenbaums. School will be starting soon—your first class—and Papa must return to the opera."

As Stephanie walked into the room, Elena sighed tragically, gave her sister a hug, and skipped through the doorway.

"What is it now?" Stephanie asked, laughing. "Is the monkey sick again?"

"No, she wants to bring him home with us." Marta continued her work, but then paused and drew an envelope from her pocket. "Oh, I forgot to give you this letter. Madam Rosenbaum said it came in the post this morning. I think perhaps you've been waiting for it." She smiled as she handed it to Stephanie. The return address on the letter was Alexandria, Egypt. Stephanie clasped it close to her heart and went into the garden to read the love letter in private.

CHAPTER FOUR

Marriage For Stephanie

E lena tagged along behind Rudy and her sisters on the first day of school as they headed towards St Joseph's convent. She was tingling all over with nervousness and anxiety. Her siblings chattered, as they walked, of school-related subjects she didn't yet understand. In fact, she heard nothing but her wildly beating heart and the threatening rumble of her stomach. She had only managed to swallow a breakfast consisting of a roll, cold meat, and a weak brew of coffee, under her mother's watchful eye, and now prayed she wouldn't disgrace herself by bringing up her meal in front of nuns and other students.

Her apprehension increased dramatically at the sight of the teaching nuns clad in flowing black habits. Formidable though they appeared, their soft gentle voices sounded like angels in heaven to her, and she soon eased into a routine of classes and making new friends. By the end of the school week, her fears had flown. Months passed swiftly and the holiday season arrived. Students fashioned little gifts for their parents, and performed the reverent pageants depicting the Christ child, touching all with their innocence.

Christmastime was especially joyous for the Linden family. Franz's usually unbending demeanor was cast aside as he threw himself into celebration of the season. Faithful to childhood memories of Christmas festivities in Germany, he bought small gifts for the children and vigorously supervised the tolerant Marta in her shopping and preparation of Romanian and German holiday foods.

On Christmas Eve morning, he closeted himself in the parlor, closing the pocket sliding doors from little eyes, and proceeded to decorate the fir tree his sons had felled in the woods the previous day. He delighted in unwrapping fragile multicolored glass ornaments, stored from years past, and hung them on the tree with an artistic eye. Candles sat regally on the branches. Franz relished watching the children's awed expressions when the candles were lit at midnight. "Like stars, moon, and sun, all shining in the heavens together," Mitzi had sighed.

"Oh, not to forget," Franz said, after his work was done in the parlor and the doors shut until visitors would later arrive. "The corn, Rudy, the corn." Rudy had been given the task of climbing to the roof of the house, spreading kernels of corn about for the birds, another German custom Franz observed seriously. Rudy was more agile than Max. One year, Max insisted on performing the chore, only to freeze in fear once he was on the roof. Rudy had eased him down again.

December's snowfall of 1904 had been a heavy one. The sharp, metallic clip-clop of horses' hooves on the road in front of their house now sounded muffled. Bells attached to the animals' harnesses jingled musically as the sleighs shushed by. An automobile chugged along at intervals, but vehicles were still a novelty in Bucharest, with only the wealthy able to afford one.

The children's excitement intensified as the day wore on. When grandparents and various aunts and uncles finally arrived, bundled up to their eyes in scarves and furs against the piercing winds, they were greeted passionately by the sisters with hugs and kisses. Numerous packages they carried would have fallen helter-skelter to the floor except for Max and Rudy's quick rescue.

"Girls, girls!" their grandmother laughed. "What a reception!" She and their warm, unassuming grandfather were much loved by the children; having been gentle and indulgent to Marta, they treated the youngsters with even more leniency and generosity.

It was an evening of magic. Elena found it almost impossible to contain herself, wiggling and squirming in her chair. She managed to sit through the concert of Christmas musical selections being played by Franz, Stephanie, and her brothers. Violins, cello, and bass sweetly ended the program with "Silent Night, Holy Night." The family sang along softly, eyes made damp by the beauty of the music.

Midnight was the signal for great rejoicing. Candles on the tree were lit, transforming the parlor into a shining wonderland. The children opened their small gifts; a wooden toy, a cloth doll, or hairbrush and comb. Products of their mother's industrious knitting—a muffler, cap, pair of stockings—would inevitably be included in the packages.

Screams of delight followed as Franz, dressed as St. Nicholas himself, burst into the room showering all with fruits, nuts, and candies. "*Froliche Weihnachten!*" he cried gleefully. Then quickly departing, he casually reappeared in a moment or so as Franz the father, professing great regret that he had missed St. Nicholas' surprise visit.

Christmas Day was then celebrated with a sumptuous buffet table laden with cold meats and salads, molds and puddings, bread and rolls, pastries and melt-in-your-mouth decorated cookies, all washed down with wines and *braga*, the popular sweet drink of Romania. Soon after, the young sisters, having been allowed to stay up past their bedtime, began to nod off. Stephanie gathered them together, leading them to bed under protest.

"How are we going to get up in the morning for church, if we don't go to bed now?" she asked.

* * *

"I can't believe how fast time flies," Marta said, as they were again laundering and pressing, preparing for the upcoming trip to Egypt. She laid one flatiron on the wood-burning stove in the kitchen, then picked up a second that had been heating on the stove, and continued pressing her husband's shirt, first testing the temperature with her tongue-dampened finger.

"Too quickly, Mama." Stephanie had discovered buttons missing from a shirtwaist and replaced them with incredible speed, her needle flying in and out. "There is yet so much for me to do." She sat by the kitchen table, her mending basket sitting on the floor beside her.

Stephanie's talent lay in sewing. Much of the family's feminine wardrobe was created by her diligent use of their sewing machine and finished by fine hand tailoring. Over the winter months, for her approaching marriage to André, she had produced a trousseau of exquisite beauty, eclipsed only by the pièce de résistance, her lovely wedding ensemble of silk and French lace. Marta had contributed snow-white linens on which she had embroidered delicate designs, then crocheted handsome borders. Additional items included elegantly crocheted tablecloths and a bedspread decorated with pink satin rosebuds and ribbons.

Marta paused from her ironing for a moment to gaze pensively at Stephanie. Egypt was so far away, she thought. She hoped Franz would be successful in securing an orchestral contract again next summer in Alexandria. If not … she shook her head, better to think happy thoughts. Like how beautiful Stephanie would look on her wedding day. Besides, it was time for someone to tell Elena that Stephanie was getting married—a chore she dreaded.

Surprisingly, Elena learned the plans the very next day, and her reaction was quite different from what Marta had expected. Franz had been away that gray morning. There was no school, and Rudy was indulging his younger sisters by playing a game of hide-and-seek. They screeched excitedly when he found one of them. Silly girls, they weren't really worth his attention, he thought. He was almost grown up now, but he enjoyed the frolic nevertheless. Lifting the muslin cloth cover on the dress form to hide beneath its folds, Elena then discovered the wedding gown.

"Mama," she asked, when the fun and games were over, "what is that pretty dress for in Stephanie's room?" Her sister was always working on some type of clothing resting on the dressmaker form, but this lily-white gown was eye-catching—the pleated bodice, lace yoke, and banded collar were so handsomely designed.

"Umm ...," Marta hedged, taken unaware by Elena's question. "Well ... when we go to Alexandria next month ... Stephanie and André are to be married." She hurried on. "Do you remember the wedding we attended a few weeks ago, when Cousin Sophie was married—the beautiful church ceremony and celebrating afterwards?"

Elena's eyes widened as she pictured the scene. The romantic idyll that most girls shared concerning a church wedding, and the prospect of being a bride herself, thrilled her, young as she was. Her eventual separation from Stephanie was forgotten, for the moment anyway. She seemed to accept the idea as preparations for departure continued, shedding no tears. Marta surmised that Elena was now emotionally distanced from Stephanie. Her little girl's world had broadened since her attendance at school and the making of new friends.

* * *

A profusion of candles burned brightly in every corner of Alexandria's modest-sized Roman Catholic Church, bathing the assembled guests in golden flickering light. Stephanie was radiant as she walked slowly down the middle aisle, her gloved hand resting lightly on her father's arm. Hazel eyes gazed calmly from beneath her wedding veil, though she permitted herself a sly wink and a half smile as she passed the soulful Elena. André, acutely aware of the disparity in their sizes, drew himself up to his fullest height as they exchanged vows. Stephanie was not tall, yet her shapely figure, erect carriage, and lofty pompadour hairstyle made her seem so. She could, however, command a topside view of her new husband's head. Later, as the couple posed for a marriage portrait, the photographer, with much fussing and darting about, diplomatically seated Stephanie on a chair, leaving André to stand stiffly by her side

The reception was held in a private room of André's restaurant. The wedding party gathered about an elegantly set table decorated with fruits and flowers as the restaurant staff bustled to and fro serving appetizers and wines, eager to please their employer on this important occasion. Family, friends, and orchestra members enjoyed a fine dinner. Frequent toasts to the bride and groom and the inevitable ribald jokes caused the reserved André to blush again and again.

"Guess it doesn't matter that he is the mouse, and she, the giraffe, when they are in bed together," Schenck jested irreverently to Deigelmeier. The men took up their violins to entertain after the meal, Rudy and Max joining them, bringing an even more lively and zestful atmosphere to the party.

Elena and her sisters bubbled over with excitement as they watched the festivities. The vision of Stephanie's loveliness and her happiness on her wedding day moved them deeply.

"When I get married," Lise vowed, "I'll have a wedding just like this with all the family together, and I'll have a beautiful dress just like Stephanie's."

Mitzi and Elena nodded their heads agreeably, like flowers blowing in the summer breeze. It was well they couldn't envision what the future had in store for them, for fate would intervene, making their hopes a dream never to be realized.

* * *

Tears finally came for Elena. Farewells were being said as Stephanie, André, and the family gathered on the wharf by the steamer scheduled to sail for the Romanian port of Constanza within the hour. From there, the Lindens would board a train for Bucharest. Summer had passed with lightning speed, the pleasant hours spent with Stephanie in her new flat were too brief, and here they were already saying goodbye. In the midst of the hustle and bustle of hurrying passengers boarding the ship, and overburdened Arab porters following with bags and bundles, Elena stood, suddenly alone, desolate in the realization of her loss.

"I'll never see you again!" she wailed, thin arms encircling Stephanie's waist in desperation.

"Oh, Liebchen," Stephanie said, her voice trembling. Hers was a bittersweet effort, her happiness with a new husband intermingled with the heartbreak of separation from loved ones. What had been a gay and cheerful

"Auf wiedersehen!" now sank into tears and embraces by Marta and the sisters. Elena's pain had become their pain. Franz and André gazed at each other helplessly, murmuring assurances of an early reunion in the future.

Franz's heart was heavy, though, with the knowledge that it would indeed be a long while before they would see their daughter. There was no new contract with the Hotel Alexandrie for the next season. Traveling home to see her family would be financially prohibitive for Stephanie; André was already supporting his mother and an aunt. Any children coming along would be an added expense for them.

As he stepped from the gangplank to stand by Marta on the deck, Franz released a melancholy sigh. Waving her handkerchief vigorously, her eyes red from weeping, Marta said mournfully, "Stephanie is the first to leave us. It's to be expected, I guess. We left home, too, when we were young."

"Hmmm ...."

"She will write."

"Hmmm ...."

Tucking her arm in his comfortingly, she thought how difficult it was for her husband to display his feelings. She knew there was a gentle, loving heart beneath his rigid exterior. Impatient, blustering, and ill-tempered at times, he was yet not much different from other men of his generation. A pity the children usually saw only the stern, uncompromising disciplinary side of him. Well, someday they would understand, but would they forgive ...? Marta pondered a moment, envisioning each child's personality and their reaction to Franz's strict training and punishments. Some would, and some wouldn't.

CHAPTER FIVE

Romanian Times

Several years passed uneventfully. To Franz's deep disappointment, his efforts at obtaining summer employment in Egypt, India, or Singapore were unsuccessful. He reluctantly accepted an offer to accompany the opera orchestra on its summer tour of Europe, unhappy at the prospect of separation from his family.

Max and Rudy performed nightly at a popular restaurant, joining Deigelmeier and Schenck as a quartet. Franz relied on Max to be "the man of the house" in his absence, a role his son carried out with serious attention, following his mother's every directive with patience and humor, much as Stephanie had done.

He adhered strictly to the schedule his father laid out, emphasis rigidly placed on musical practice for himself and his siblings. Marta's heart glowed with affection as she watched Max go about his chores. All she could fault him with was his casual attitude towards the matter of dress. Handsome and tall, his image was one of untidiness, a rumpled look about him. Each evening as he prepared to depart for work in the restaurant, he appeared before his mother with tie comically askew and the collar of his shirt unbuttoned.

"Oh Max," she would say, hastily straightening and buttoning. Then, kissing her cheerfully on her cheek, he would carry his bass out the door, on the heels of his fastidiously well-groomed brother.

The meticulous care Rudy took of his appearance was of little consequence to Max, but it irritated Lise. As the eldest daughter at home, she was now elected to iron his dress shirts.

"Rudy," she stated one morning, dropping several of his shirts in his lap. "Here, do them yourself. I'm tired of your complaints." She eyed his pressed and brushed clothes that hung neatly in the wardrobe closet he shared with Max. "I'm so sorry I don't do your shirts to your liking. His Majesty King Carol himself wouldn't be as picky as you are," she said, referring to Romania's reigning monarch. She completed her household duties diligently and energetically, but pressing clothes was nothing more than a cursory exercise for her, something to be executed as quickly as possible.

Rudy had been sitting on the bed polishing his black dress shoes to a brilliant shine. He glared at his sister, his mouth drawn to an ugly gash. He held his soiled hands out helplessly before him, hesitant to remove the shirts, lest they become smudged with shoe black.

"Lise," he roared, as she strolled out the door. "Take these shirts away!" When she didn't answer, he called, "Mama!" He was relieved when the accommodating Mitzi came to his rescue, lifting the shirts from his legs.

"I'll do them," she said, smiling at his nod of thanks.

Sixteen years old, Rudy's mischievous nature had lessened considerably, replaced by a tendency toward curt criticism and a hot, red-headed temper when provoked. His interest and ability, however, in repairing and maintaining the house they lived in inspired his mother's hopes for him. Rickety chairs were strengthened, walls were trimly painted, and miracle of miracles, Elena's dolls, that a few years before had seen rough treatment in his hands, now had their frizzy wigs glued carefully back onto frightful-looking bald heads. Most encouraging of all was the dedication Rudy displayed in playing the cello.

"That boy has great talent," Franz said to Marta, impressed. "With further study and practice, he will be an artist, not just another musician."

"Ah," Marta crowed, "and there he will surely shine."

* * *

At this time, when the Linden family resided in Bucharest, the Kingdom of Romania had been independent for thirty-two years. King Carol the First, formerly the penniless Prince Karl von Hohenzollern-Sigmaringen of Bavaria, Germany, had wrought a miracle in accepting the challenge offered him by Romania's parliament to assume the throne. A country that had been invaded first by the Romans; then the Goths, Huns, Bulgars, Mongols, and Tartars; and, finally, the Turks, after the collapse of Byzantium, now had a German prince as ruler. He had faced what seemed to be insurmountable odds and triumphed.

The young Catholic Prussian officer set about the task of governing this immensely beautiful, yet primitive, land of mountains, mighty rivers, and fertile plains. Undaunted by the state of the country, within a short time he had reorganized the ill-equipped and undisciplined army, built a network of railways, reformed law facilities and police, and secured his throne. Despite what had been a half-starved peasantry, an empty treasury, and wealthy nobility who mocked him, King Carol was instrumental in improving business and commerce with the outside world that knew little of Romania.

"Somehow," Franz said to Marta, "in spite of the fact that the Romanians considered the king a usurper—and a German one at that—who didn't speak their language or share their Orthodox religion, I think his calm and resolute dignity nevertheless inspired a confidence in the people that seems to have assured him a long life on the throne."

Marta laughed. "Well, maybe so, but it's been an uphill battle for him. He's done much to raise the moral standards in the country; a real feat, considering how easygoing and indulgent the populace has always been." She had been reared in the tradition of virtuous German morality, and thought the Romanians to be much like the uninhibited French.

"I saw him," Elena said. "I saw King Carol when we went to the opera last month, didn't I, Mama?" She was sitting quietly by her parents in the parlor, seemingly involved in working a puzzle. Her sisters were out visiting friends, and Rudy and Max were practicing cello and bass in the girls' room.

Marta's eyebrows lifted in surprise, sometimes forgetting how attentive their youngest was to adult conversations. She must remember that in the future. "Hmmm ... yes," she said, "we saw the King, and Queen Elisabeth, too."

"But you called her another name, Carmen ... something."

"Ah ... Carmen Sylvia ... that's her pen name," Marta explained. "She writes books. 'Pen name' means she doesn't publish under her royal name."

Elena digested this awhile. She'd been thrilled to attend the opera that evening with her mother. Franz had obtained two passes for a performance of *Hansel and Gretel* especially for Elena, deciding she was now mature enough to sit through an opera.

She had sat restlessly in the plush, red velvet seat next to her mother, observing the sophisticated and elegantly dressed audience surrounding her. An air of anticipation and excitement abounded. The hum of conversation began to rise in volume in the house, until suddenly it ceased, all eyes riveted to the royal box. Applause erupted from the audience as the king and queen entered the box, nodding serenely, acknowledging the homage being paid them.

Elena peered at the royal couple closely. On the ride to the opera house with her parents, her mother had gossiped that the ruler had no sense of humor and little charm, and the queen was eccentric and sometimes unkind.

They resembled her grandparents, Elena thought, but decided her mother's description of the royal ones was far different from her loving Oma and Opa.

As the houselights dimmed, the audience grew quiet, and the music commenced. Elena, spellbound by the sights and sounds enveloping her, searched for her father in the orchestra pit. It seemed odd to her that he wasn't standing at the podium directing the orchestra.

* * *

"Not again, Elena," her father said gravely as he perused the report card she had handed him, her knees weak with fear. "I see you have done well in reading, grammar, and music. But arithmetic?" He paused, gazing at her with accusing eyes. "That's a failing grade. You're evidently not working hard enough. I thought Max was helping you, isn't that true?"

"Yes, Papa."

"Then why hasn't your work improved?"

"I don't know. I just ... I don't understand numbers."

Franz studied his youngest daughter contemplatively. She was nine years old. Slim and freckle-faced, she was an active, earnest little girl, eager to please. Sometimes, he thought, she was too easily intimidated by her siblings. Yet, perhaps the tide was turning. Just lately he had been startled by a temper she had displayed when embroiled in a quarrel with her sisters. She had held her ground against them, body tense, rigid, green eyes flashing, voice strong in protest. He had smiled. Good for you, Elena.

"I expect you to try harder, Elena, you must at least pass the subject."

"Yes, Papa," she said, relieved she had been spared physical punishment.

Aside from her poor showing in mathematics, Elena otherwise enjoyed her days in school. Her sweet nature had garnered her a spot in a circle of friends who were busy with games and play in each other's homes as well as in school. There was Martha, Poldi, Frieda ... and Mina, with the dancing blonde curls, who had invited Elena several times to stay the night at her home.

"Please, Mama, please," Elena pleaded. "May I go?" She twitched and fidgeted at the delicious prospect of sleeping over with her friend, a daughter of the wealthy Turda family.

Finally allowed to visit, Elena was awed as she entered the house, a large building surrounded by an extensive garden and high walls. Madam Turda was on her way out for the evening; cool and elegant, she was dressed in a chic Paris gown and fur cape, presenting a far different image in Elena's mind from her own ample-figured, affectionate mother. A maid, aping her employer's nose-in-the-air demeanor, gingerly took Elena's coat and worn overnight bag, a look of distaste spreading over her face as though a grimy, homeless waif had wandered in.

Mina, oblivious to Elena's feelings of inadequacy, gaily took her by the hand and led her through the house. Drawing and dining rooms were expensively furnished in a fashionable mixture of Byzantine and Second Empire styles—heavy red velvet draperies, carpets deep and plush that one sank into like a fluffy cloud, and papered walls impressively adorned with huge oil-painted portraits in gilded frames. Elena felt as though the subjects in the paintings looked down on her disdainfully as she passed.

"Mama said there's a light supper in the kitchen for us," Mina said.

Elena was struck by the contrast between the kitchen and the other rooms of the house. It was bare of any decoration, only a plain wooden workspace and sink, a black iron stove, naked windows, and simple wooden chairs and table in the middle of the room. Shelves harbored dishes and staples on one entire wall. "Kitchen" to her meant the German word *gemütlich*—a cozy friendly place with cheery lace curtains on the windows, potted plants, and a kettle and coffee pot warming on the stove.

"We don't usually eat here," Mina said, noting Elena's puzzled expression. "We eat in the dining room." I've eaten in hotel dining rooms, thought Elena, more elegant than hers, but she said nothing as Mina continued. "After we eat, we'll go to my room and play with my doll family. They have pretty bisque heads; my aunt brought them from France for me, you know, as an *Etrennes*, a New Year's Day gift."

The dolls were exquisite, so beautiful that Elena was at first hesitant to touch them. Some were like miniature Minas, shining blonde ringlets and enormous blue eyes—like angels. She fingered her own carroty-colored head; angels didn't have red hair, she thought. Innumerable changes of silk and lace costumes, a small leather trunk to hold the doll clothes, a tea set, and a Normandy-style wooden armoire were all certain to occupy the girls for hours.

The haughty French maid, whom Mina called Hedy, breezed into the room later in the evening, turning down coverlets on the bed. She fluffed the eiderdown quilt vigorously while the girls prepared for the night. They snuggled together, giggling as Hedy lowered the gaslights.

"Be quiet and go to sleep," she said as she exited the room. Of course, sleep didn't come easily; Mina was wide awake, whispering and teasing. She never tired of hearing tales Elena told of her family's travels, especially anecdotes involving her beloved Chekki. Eventually they both drifted off—Mina first, then Elena as she finally overcame her sense of being in alien surroundings.

Elena didn't know how long she had slept before she slowly awakened to a sensation of something crawling about her body beneath her nightdress. She felt a sharp sting, then another, and itched all over.

"Something is biting me, Mina!" she cried, sitting up hastily and throwing the covers off. "What is it?"

Mina jumped up, instantly awake. She turned up the gaslights, then pulled the quilt all the way back on the bed. Elena saw, to her horror, small, pincered, beige-colored bugs crawling about the sheet.

"Oh, they're only bedbugs," Mina said. "We get them all the time." She giggled at the sight of Elena's shocked face. Then she collapsed onto the bed, laughing harder and harder as Elena frantically lifted her nightdress, brushing away as many of the bloodsucking interlopers as she could find on her body.

A very subdued little girl returned home the next morning, looking pale and drawn, having spent the remainder of the night sleepless on a chair. When Marta saw the welts on her daughter's skin, she shook her head in disgust.

"They are not clean people, Elena," she said. "Bedding must be aired each week, as we do, and kerosene used on the wood frame of the bed. Those bugs dig in and hide until dark, just waiting to have a juicy meal. Heaven only knows what other creatures there are in that grandiose house. Did you see any roaches? I hope not." Frowning deeply, she inspected Elena's clothes for signs of the dreaded insects.

Elena was still friendly with Mina in school, but invented excuses to avoid any further stays at her house. She reflected on the contrast between their families—Mina's home so richly appointed, yet unclean, and the Linden household, moderately furnished, but immaculate and spotless.

Winter evenings were warm and secure times for Elena. After family members had departed for their work at the restaurant and opera, the sisters gathered in the parlor to play board games or take turns reading aloud in the flickering gleam of the gaslights. From her favorite upholstered chair close by the heat of the tile stove, their mother sat in judgment when arguments arose over the outcome of a game, or she quietly commented on the credibility of a story being read. Her fingers were less nimble these days as she knitted, having become misshapen and painful with the onset of rheumatism.

Nevertheless, the still brisk movements of her hands attracted the attention of Spatz, perched on the armrest of Marta's chair. Gray and black, the striped feline pet of the family watched Marta with great interest as she worked. Occasionally, she dove with ferocious outstretched claws into the heart of the busy needles and vivid-colored wool, as though they were spiny fish sprightly maneuvering through beds of coral in a tropical sea.

"Spatz!" Marta laughed, tapping the cat lightly on her nose. The animal's ears lay back flat to her head as she pulled away, but her gray eyes continued to observe the knitting process, ready to mischievously pounce again.

Affectionate and fruitful, Spatz had periodically produced multiple litters of kittens, delighting Elena with their playful antics until, regretfully, the kittens were by necessity established in new homes. Mousers were always needed. Franz, at one time, had taken two of Spatz's offspring to the opera house where the sharp-eyed stalkers prowled the dark depths of the cellars, padding silently among the costumes and accessories hanging on racks and in boxes stacked up high. The voices of lyric sopranos on the stage above echoed and re-echoed on opera performance nights, like birds warbling and chirping in a perennial spring. The cats would stop briefly to listen, then continue their lonely patrol.

Daytimes would find Spatz sitting by the windows of the glassed-in porch in the rear of the house, dozing, eyes half closed against the weak winter sunshine, yet instantly alert at the slightest movement in the garden outside. Her ears twitched to and fro; then, observing no threat to her well-being, she nuzzled and sniffed the potted plants on the sill beside her and resumed her nap. During the family's absences, their landlady, Madam Balescu, had fed and otherwise cared for her Sometime after the family's return from Egypt, they moved from the rented house to a flat on Calea Plevnei. Spatz, now well into old age, did not adjust well to the change. She took days to investigate her new home, poking her nose into every corner, absorbing unfamiliar scents and odors, telltale signs of previous tenants that only a feline's sensitivity could detect. One morning she was gone, vanished. Elena searched street after street, anxiously calling her pet's name. She feared that Spatz might have fallen prey to unfriendly dogs walked daily by smartly uniformed, army officer neighbors. As Elena passed their former residence, Madam Balescu, now occupying the house, waved the youngster inside. There was Spatz sitting in her favorite spot by the window on the porch.

"Spatz, what are you doing here?" scolded Elena, relieved and annoyed at the same time. "You don't live here anymore," she said, and carried her wayward pet back to her new abode. Several days passed and Spatz was missing again. This time Elena headed straightaway for the family's old lodgings, expecting to find the cat there, and so she was, perched nonchalantly on the windowsill. She continued this pattern of remaining at the flat a week or so, then departing for her old home again.

"I guess Spatz is too old and attached to the house," Marta said. "Madam Balescu has agreed that she should stay where she is happiest." Thereafter, the cat lived out her days settled by the porch window, basking in the warm sunshine by the potted plants.

* * *

Alexandria, Egypt, 1910

Dearest Mama and Papa,

Thank you for your letter of February 17th, we were so happy to hear from you. Wish you could be with us now, the weather has been very warm and mild, not like in Bucharest, snowy and cold.

Everything is going well with us here; business in the restaurant is good. André says I'm of great help to him, greeting customers and also my work on the books.

We have happy news, we are expecting a baby in the fall, your first grandchild! We hope to rent a house soon, we're too cramped where we are now. André's mother and aunt share space in the dining room as it is.

Papa, will you be coming here to Alexandria this summer? We miss you all so much. Tell Lise and Mitzi I'm waiting for a letter from them. Give my love to Rudy and Max, and of course, Elena too, she must be getting very big now. Stay in good health.

God be with you,
Your loving Stephanie

Poor Stephanie. Franz read her letter for the third time, shaking his head regretfully. The Linden family would not be going to Alexandria this summer, for the singular charms of Singapore had called to Franz, luring him as surely as Germany's siren Lorelei had called Rhine River sailors to their destruction. Perhaps Madam Rosenbaum was his Lorelei; in offering him a contract for the orchestra, she unknowingly presented him with a choice that would forever change his life, should he accept. Letters went back and forth between Singapore and Bucharest, the last containing a contract for the orchestra, which Franz signed eagerly and returned to Madam Rosenbaum posthaste.

"We'll leave in June," he announced to his family, assembled in the parlor amid music stands and instruments that had been in recent use for practice. Just one glance at his radiant face was enough to signify the importance of the news he was about to impart. His voice alone betrayed an emotional undercurrent of anticipation impossible for him to conceal. "We go to Singapore, this time not just for the summer," he said, "but perhaps for several years, as long as Madam Rosenbaum has need of the orchestra."

Several years! The reaction to his words was immediate, and a happy one. Elena beamed, her face flushed with excitement; Lise, Mitzi, and the boys exchanged jubilant smiles. Franz relaxed; there was no opposition to his plan. He smiled, not that he would brook any objection had they protested—the orchestra was their livelihood.

"But what about school, Papa?" Lise asked.

"Madam Rosenbaum has recommended the convent school of the Cathedral of the Good Shepherd for you and Mitzi and Elena."

"That's where we went to church each Sunday on our last visit, Lise, remember?" Marta said. "It was a short walk from the hotel on North Bridge Road."

Marta was silent while the children conversed animatedly over the prospect of a long stay in Singapore. Franz had discussed all aspects of the move to Singapore with her beforehand. It was her husband's work that was most important, she'd concluded; leaving her mother was unavoidable. Her father had died the year before, but he'd amply provided for his wife and she was able to live comfortably. Still, Marta's heart ached with guilt. It wasn't as if Franz couldn't obtain work in Bucharest. The plain truth was that a life in the tropics beckoned to him as though he were under a magician's spell.

God help her, she couldn't deny that his enchantment had held her equally spellbound in the past. Now she was older, however, and they would be away a longer time. She sighed and shifted her weight in her chair. The pain in her back and knees had been severe this winter. Rheumatism, the doctor had advised on her last visit; an ailment, he said with a sly wink, that would be greatly relieved by a stay in a hot climate. She frowned; she would be fifty-two years old next month, and going through the change. She was getting old.

* * *

Tasks had to be attended to; they were to be away for several years. Packing clothes was a chore that fell to Marta and Lise. Max and Rudy were responsible for the sheet music, which was to be sorted, labeled, and stowed away in boxes. Elena and Mitzi scurried about doing little jobs as needed. Furniture, linens, winter clothing, and kitchen utensils were to be stored at Oma Stagen's home since their flat was to be vacated.

As time drew near for departure, younger family members grew subdued. They felt euphoria at the prospect of returning to Singapore, but, at the same time, regret at the thought of leaving beautiful Bucharest and close friends. Franz seemed oblivious to the mood of his children, being busy with organizing the orchestra and arranging steamship passage, but he had a surprise for them. Several days before leaving, he ordered all to dress in their best and accompany him on a stroll. Mystified, they followed as he led them along Calea Plevnei, Strada Buzesti, and onto the tree-shaded Soseaua Kisseleff, a broad avenue.

"Papa," Lise said, "where are we going?"

"Tell us Papa," Elena said, skipping between cracks on the sidewalks. "Where are you taking us?"

"I would like to know, too," Marta said dryly. "One would think you could at least let your wife in on this big secret."

Franz smiled, shaking his head. He took pleasure in keeping his family guessing. Marta became uneasy as he threaded his way through the poorer quarters of town called the Devil's Slums, situated on the banks of the Dambovitsa, a small river running through the city. The sights and sounds about them were similar to noisy Asiatic souks. An open market teemed with bargaining customers clustered around hawkers of squawking chickens and ducks; loads of vegetables, pistachios, sweet pastries, *halvah*, and yogurt; and the honey drink, *braga*. Street vendors carried traditional wooden yokes supporting baskets of seasonal fruits.

Max and Rudy cast appreciative glances at the beguiling black-haired gypsy girls who squatted, barelegged, over wicker baskets of flowers. The girls flashed brilliant smiles at the young men passing by, thrusting colorful nosegays in their faces. Max flushed a deep red, embarrassed.

"Watch your billfolds, boys," Franz murmured, maneuvering his way through the crowd until they left the bustling throng behind and emerged onto a small side street. He continued walking, his retinue struggling to keep up with him, until he came to a small restaurant. He opened the door wide, and ushered everyone in.

"The best café in town," he said to Marta. She rolled her eyes.

Once inside, they spied Oma Stagen seated at a round table, smiling and waving at them. Schenck, Deigelmeier, and two other men rose from their seats to greet the family.

"Marta, I want you to meet Herr Braun, the violinist I spoke of, and Herr Rauschner, our drummer," Franz said. "I thought this dinner would be a good way to get acquainted." Marta saw that Braun was young and rosy-complexioned, eyes a deep blue. Rauschner was middle-aged, round-faced, and wore a brown toupee noticeably darker than his own gray-brown hair showing beneath. The men nodded, "Frau Linden," they said, almost in unison.

"How much is this costing you, Franz?" Marta whispered in his ear as they sat down at the table.

"Your mother's treat," he whispered back

She turned to her mother seated on her right, and embraced her. "How good of you, Mama," she said. "I'm feeling so bad about leaving you. This time it's not just for the summer, you know."

"It's nothing, it's nothing," Oma Stagen said. "You must go where your husband goes, Marta. I wanted us all to be together before you leave. So, drink up, everybody," she said, raising her glass to all seated. "A toast! A toast to everyone embarking on your new adventure ... if I were younger," she said, laughing, "I might just go with you."

That speech set the tone for the gathering. Menus were brought, and soon they were cheerfully dining. Conversation was gay and lively, wine glasses clinked together again and again. As the party rose at the end of festivities, the men exchanged hearty handshakes, and fervent kisses mixed with tears were showered on Oma Stagen by Marta and the granddaughters. They exited the restaurant in good spirits, ready for their forthcoming journey.

All but Marta. The family walked back slowly to the flat, Marta in deep thought as the others chattered. She mulled over her mother's words, relieved that she seemed to understand the situation and had not reproached her. Yet, it was more than a reluctance to leave her aged, widowed mother that troubled Marta. A brooding sense of finality weighed on her breast, like a cloud of doom. I will never return to my lovely Romania, she thought. I know it, I feel it.

Franz looked up from an earnest conversation with Max, noting her bleak expression. He raised questioning eyebrows, the silent language between spouses, and she smiled wanly. How melodramatic of me, she mused. I'm already homesick, that's all. It took several days for her mood to lift, last-minute preparations eventually crowding the dejected thoughts from her mind.

On the twenty-eighth of June, the family and company traveled to the port of Constanza on the Black Sea and boarded a ship for Singapore.

CHAPTER SIX

Singapore Revisited

When Elena saw the familiar building again, potted plants sitting in irregular rows on the verandah, rattan chairs ready for guests to relax in, she couldn't restrain herself. She jumped ecstatically from the rickshaw that bore her back to her tropical paradise, and raced up the stone steps to blissfully embrace one of the four white pillars that graced the first floor of the hotel. Before her father could voice disapproval, she had already darted through the open doorway to the lobby within. Franz shrugged his shoulders and gave Marta a secret smile.

Lise noted his leniency with annoyance. "The youngest gets away with everything," she grumbled to Mitzi.

Elena's happiness was shared by all the family; they felt they were coming home. Madam Rosenbaum welcomed them with open arms as they entered the lobby, her smile as expansive as a vast sweeping ocean.

"Oh, Marta, you haven't changed a bit," she said as the women hugged each other affectionately. "But look at the children! How they've grown!" She bussed the three exuberant girls encircling her heartily on each cheek, and bestowed additional kisses on all around her, including the retiring Deigelmeier, who blinked his eyes in surprise. Everyone spoke at once then, producing a lively commotion. Braun and Rauschner were introduced, and Herr Rosenbaum joined the group. He had emerged from the insect world of his shed in honor of the Linden family's arrival. Rudy and Max pumped his hand vigorously, a friend they were especially delighted to see again. Pleased by their cordial greeting, Herr Rosenbaum brightened. "How tall you've gotten," he murmured. He'd missed their engaging youthfulness during the past years, and now here they were again, grown almost to manhood, sons one could be proud of. He envied the Kapellmeister.

Elena roamed through every public room of the hotel the next morning, satisfied that all was as she remembered. The sisters again shared the large marble-floored room at the rear of the building, adjacent to a smaller chamber occupied by their parents, while Rudy and Max shared quarters in a separate building with the other single musicians. The furnishings of each of the rooms were much the same, consisting of scrolled and carved teak wardrobe closets, rattan chairs, cedarwood chests, and simple teak-wood bedsteads with mosquito netting gathered overhead. On each chest, usually against the wall with an oval mirror over it, rested a ceramic basin and water pitcher.

One lavatory in the hall served the family, water being released from the commode's overhead tank. A separate bathing room next to the lavatory, ten-by-ten feet, featured a concrete floor with a drain in the middle. Wooden benches lined the walls; hooks held clothing, towels, and robes. A water spigot released warm tropical water into available buckets or containers. Elena recalled with particular clarity how her mother had used them to pour a welcome shower over her after a thorough soaping of her body. Primitive, but effective. Sometimes, a Malay servant girl helped the ladies in their bathing ritual; a boy served the men. Each person used the bathing room four or five times daily, the oppressive Singapore heat and humidity necessitating a frequent change of apparel. Clothes were more easily maintained and laundered if perspiration was not allowed to be absorbed by the material.

For that reason, early mornings found Marta and her daughters washing their shirtwaists, dresses, intimate undergarments, and men's white shirts in a tub at the rear of the hotel, and laying them out on the grass where they dried within the hour in the hot sun. Having the laundry done by the Malay servant girl proved to be a mistake, as Marta had discovered during their previous stay. The girl had not only scrubbed, but beaten the clothes against the rocks of a nearby stream so that they had almost disintegrated. No amount of reasoning could change the girl's methods, a custom that reached far back into her country's traditions. Ironing the clothes was the worst of chores for the women in Singapore's muggy atmosphere, especially the ongoing task of pressing the men's ruffled evening shirts. Fortunately for Marta, the men's white dress jackets and trousers, and also their daytime wear—consisting of white tunics with mandarin-style collars and plain trousers—were sent to the Chinese laundry man, who also laundered the hotel sheets, tablecloths, and towels.

"Well," commented a perspiring Marta, as she surveyed her handiwork baking on the grass in the morning sun, "at least we don't have to cook in broiling heat of the kitchen, as Chang does."

That afternoon Elena peeked into the kitchen where Chang prepared the daily curry dishes, inhaling the aroma with remembered fondness. Chang looked up from his work and smiled at her. She hoped he had forgotten her escapade with Chekki years before, but he raised his knife menacingly and winked. She turned quickly and scooted away from the swinging doors. Evidently, the monkey's race through the hotel that day had become a humorous tale—recalled and retold many times by Madam Rosenbaum and the staff.

In the garden, Elena had been elated to see that the mature Chekki recognized her. He danced about his cage in a frenzy at the sight of her, then reached white forepaws out through the bars. The excited monkey leaped to her shoulders after his release, nuzzling her neck affectionately. She giggled, dropped to the grass, and they rolled wildly over and over together. Elena lay back happily, identifying each remembered plant in her mind—the hibiscus, frangipani, bougainvillea—while Chekki proceeded to pick at the roots of her hair, just as he would groom his own furry relatives. A Siamese kitten, newcomer to the hotel, approached the two cautiously, circled them carefully, then settled into Elena's lap. Chekki transferred his attention smoothly to the interloper, finding a profitable new field for grooming.

In the days to follow, Elena communed with nature in the garden. She was fascinated by the teeming insect life, as well as small animals, snakes, and frogs, irrespective of Stephanie's warnings of warts and poisonous reptiles in Egypt. Sometimes she trapped an unfamiliar bug in a jar, taking it to Herr Rosenbaum for identification. He would carefully examine the specimen, then peruse one of the many books in his library. When the insect was found listed in a volume, he answered her questions, thinking all the while how unusual it was that a female found nature so interesting. Back in the garden again, she amused herself with imaginative games surrounded by her menagerie—Chekki and the kitten by her side, but also the doe and ram of former times, who grazed contentedly nearby.

* * *

Lise and Mitzi, now young misses, passed the summer in more adult-like activities. Their father had included them in morning orchestra rehearsals, and they were feeling very grownup as a result. Their appearance now of primary importance, they fussed with coiffures, matched shirtwaists and skirts in profound absorption, and sewed ribbons and bows to hats and dresses. Gone were the little girls who had circled wildly in the warm rain a few years back. Gone was the innocence of childhood, now replaced by giggles and knowing smiles, intrigue and romantic novels uppermost in their minds.

As their intellect had grown, so had their bodies matured. Lise's features were similar to Stephanie's—wide cheekbones, hazel eyes, determined mouth—but unlike her older sister's abundant crop of hair, hers was scanty, a hot curling iron only causing frizz. Of average height, her figure already showed a hint of the plump shape she would gain in maturity, much like her mother.

Mitzi was rapidly becoming the prettiest of the Linden sisters. Her oval-shaped face, with its small, finely sculpted nose, full sensuous mouth, and large brown eyes, was crowned by a head of wavy dark hair and complemented by a well-proportioned figure. She saw the humorous side of everything, was amiable with friends and family, but absolutely drove the competent and impatient Lise to distraction by her unhurried approach to life.

"Mama!" Lise wailed, "Mitzi is still locked in the bathing room. How am I supposed to get dressed if she dawdles so? She is so slow! And Mama, why can't we wash together, I'd like to know? She's so bashful about being naked in front of me. You'd think she was a queen or something."

"Now Lise," Marta said, "not everyone is as open-minded as you; there's nothing wrong with being modest."

"Yes, well, then she should be quick as well as modest."

"I'm sorry I took so long, Lise," Mitzi said good-naturedly, sauntering from the bathing room. Her sister rolled her eyes upward and brushed past her, disappearing through the doorway and locking the door with dispatch.

On another day, the sisters walked around the hotel grounds together, as close as peas in a pot, whispering in each other's ear, parasols shielding them from the brilliant sun overhead.

"That Braun," Lise said, "his eyes follow your every move, Mitzi, as though he's going to devour you. You should tell Papa. Don't answer the fellow when he talks to you."

"How can I not speak to him, Lise, when we all sit together at the noon meal? It's as though we are all family, anyway. The musicians are just like our brothers."

"He doesn't look at you as a sister."

"If he gets fresh, then I'll tell Papa."

At that instant, Elena raced by in a great rush, Chekki and the cat in close pursuit.

"Elena!" called Lise, "Mama wants you to wear a hat outdoors. Where is it?"

"On the veranda," answered the twelve-year-old, slowing down not a whit. "It makes me too hot."

"You're going to freckle again terribly without it, maybe even suffer sunstroke."

"Later," Elena called over her shoulder. "I'm going to see Herr Rosenbaum. Max and Rudy netted some butterflies, big as birds, and they're going to mount them now. I want to watch."

"Bugs, butterflies, ugh," Lise grimaced, as Elena disappeared from view.

"The butterflies are unbelievably beautiful, Lise," Mitzi said, "all the colors of the rainbow. Rudy and Max have been paid well for specimens they sent to museums in England and Germany."

"They're going to come down with some fever or other, tramping around with their silly nets in the rainforest," Lise said disapprovingly.

"They earn spending money that way."

"Yes, and Rudy spends it all on that camera of his, eternally taking photographs of flowers and plants. This morning he told me he wants the family to pose for a picture later, and you know what that means. We must sit stone still until he's finished."

Mitzi smiled and sighed.

Occasionally, the Malay and Chinese servants of the hotel brought their children to play in the garden while they worked. The kindhearted Madam Rosenbaum then instructed Chang to provide a simple lunch for them. Elena joined in, taking the opportunity to befriend the children and acquaint herself with the Malay language. One eleven-year-old girl, named Mei-Ling, enjoyed tutoring the inquisitive Elena, and they became fast friends.

"Where do you live?" Elena asked the slender, petite girl. They were lying in the grass, their heads bent companionably close together. The glossy sheen of Mei-Ling's long black tresses contrasted dramatically with Elena's unruly carrot-red hair.

"Our family lives in a *kampong*. That's a small village on the Singapore River," Mei-Ling said. "My father is *khektow* on the bumboats carrying rice and rubber to market."

"What's a *khektow*?"

"He's head man,"

"My father is head man, too, he leads the band in the hotel. We come from a place called Romania. It's warm there in the summer, like here in Singapore, but in the winter it's cold, and it snows."

"What is snow?"

"Hmmm ... I guess it's like a soft white frozen rain." As Mei-Ling looked puzzled, Elena said," Come with me to my room and I'll show you a picture I have."

They walked through the hotel hallways, Mei-Ling's sandals clattering noisily on the marble floor. It was still early in the morning, and Elena's older sisters were dressing as the girls entered the room.

"Out, out, out!" the sisters ordered, waving their hands at the two, and they made a swift retreat, but not before Elena quickly collected a picture calendar from the wall. Mei-Ling studied the pictured snow scene with interest as they slowly made their way back to the exit doors. Elena described how small flakes of the snow fell into huge amounts, and how her brothers made balls of it, throwing them at each other, and at her and her sisters, too.

As they passed Madam Rosenbaum's suite, Elena heard her mother's voice in conversation with the hotel owner. The door stood ajar. Elena, eyes shining mischievously, motioned Mei-Ling over and they peered into the room. The ladies were intently inspecting a corset held by her mother.

Madam Rosenbaum was a full-breasted woman. Elena admired her erect figure held tightly in at the waist by a corset, which adult women wore. She thought, however, that the garment had to be terribly confining, almost like a suit of armor, and also suffocatingly hot to wear in the Singapore heat. It was no wonder her mother sometimes complained of faintness.

"This is the latest model, Marta," Madam Rosenbaum was saying, "I had it sent from Paris. It has whalebone ribs. Let me show you what I do. You can assist me, lace it up for me."

Madam Rosenbaum was wearing a simple white chemise, her back to the doorway. She slid her hands lightly over her torso, then changed her stance, so that the girls saw a side view of her figure. Elena was astonished. A sizeable stomach was now in evidence on the lady's front; it quivered as she spoke, like the bowl of jelly always on the breakfast table each morning.

"You see, Marta," she said, "I start pulling up like this," and she wheezed as she proceeded to lift the fat of her abdomen as far up her rib cage as possible. "Ugh ... now!" she directed through clenched teeth, holding the fleshy mass in place as Elena's mother quickly encircled her waist and hips with the corset. Marta adjusted the front clasp—called a busc—then tightened the cross-laced drawstrings with great energy, emitting little grunts as she worked.

Miraculously, before the girls' wide eyes, there appeared a svelte, trim-waisted Madam Rosenbaum, her stomach fat now nestling with her breasts at the top of the snug-fitting foundation garment. She smiled in satisfaction at her image in a freestanding oval mirror, as Elena's mother exclaimed delightedly over her transformation.

Elena and Mei-Ling exchanged incredulous glances. They clapped their hands over their mouths to avoid snickering, and tiptoed away from the door. Further down the corridor they collapsed into hilarious laughter, mimicking Madam Rosenbaum's slimming efforts with elaborate hand motions. Finally they fell into each other's arms, helplessly expelling uncontrollable whoops until the tears came.

"I'll never, ever wear a corset when I grow up, if that's what ladies do," Elena stated emphatically when the two reached the shade of the garden. But, of course, she did. Her sister Lise made it very clear as she reached maturity that proper ladies must wear a foundation. It wouldn't do, she said, to have one's body flopping about for all to see. Only whores did that, because they wanted to attract men.

CHAPTER SEVEN

Growing Up ... Rites Of Passage

"Hurry, Elena, hurry." Franz's voice, growing abrasive with impatience, called from the hotel's lobby. "We're ready to leave now. Where are you?"

On most Sundays that summer, the family went sightseeing. After church services at the Cathedral of the Good Shepherd, and then the noon meal at the hotel under their belts, Franz gathered his brood together for forays into town. These were hot and humid days, but later in the year, from November to the following February, the wet season would be in effect, making traveling about in the heavy rains less appealing.

"I'm here, Papa," Elena said, running breathlessly in from the hallway. "Mama said I should make one last visit to the lavatory." She saw her father standing in the open doorway, straw hat and guidebook in hand. He motioned with his free hand to the outside, where rickshaws were waiting. Lise and Mitzi were already climbing into the two-wheel carriers.

"I think Elena can sit with us, Franz," Marta said. "She weighs hardly anything."

"Yes, but we weigh a great deal more than her sisters. She had better sit with them."

Lise made a face as Elena promptly squeezed herself between the two. "Papa," she said, "please let Elena sit with Rudy and Max; she wiggles around so much, our dresses will get all wrinkled."

"She's fine where she is," he said.

Lise was the only one of the children who had dared voice any opposition to her father in the past, usually using her feminine wiles to achieve her goals, but this time she sat back in silence, her lips drawn tightly together. She also knew when the subject was closed.

The rickshaw men took off, rounding the hotel's horseshoe-shaped driveway at breakneck speed, and entered the teeming traffic on North Bridge Road. The coolies were racing each other like reckless Roman charioteers, Franz thought, glancing back concernedly at his daughters. Elena, however, looked exuberantly about as the rickshaw bumped along, her face alive with interest at the passing landscape.

Although automobiles now appeared on the roads, rickshaws and trams were the main means of transportation in Singapore. The easy-going Malay inhabitants preferred a life of agricultural pursuits and fishing, so it was the imported and ambitious Chinese coolies who pulled the rickshaws, worked in the tin mines, and subsequently improved their status by taking part in the various trades and industries in Singapore and the Malay Peninsula. Rickshaws were everywhere, covering the island like so many colonies of busy insects.

The coolies, wearing blue linen tunics and trousers, seemed barely winded when the family alighted in the city's center. They nodded as Franz dropped the few coins they'd earned into their outstretched hands; the small sums would supply their entire families with perhaps a few days' rations of rice and fish.

The British Crown Colony of Singapore was indeed an exciting and fascinating place to visit; to be able to actually live there for an extended period of time was simply splendid. Franz took full advantage of his time that afternoon—and many afternoons to follow—to explore, study, examine, and, ultimately, to learn. The island enjoyed a wealth of diverse cultures: Chinese, Indian, Malay, and European. Churches, temples, and mosques co-existed side by side. All flourished in the atmosphere of East-West relations in the trading center under the watchful eye of the British, who had capitalized on Singapore's favorable location for use as a military base.

Not every excursion included the family as a whole. The ladies sometimes favored a shopping trip; the males, a visit to Chinatown or a stroll along the quay of the Singapore River to watch the busy traffic of bumboats ferrying a multitude of commodities up and down the waterway. Another day, the Raffles Hotel drew Franz's attention; he curiously inspected the lobby of the expensive hostelry, then, on leaving, shrugged his shoulders, unimpressed. "There is one thing much nicer at the Grand Continental," he remarked to his sons. "Our orchestra."

Visits to the Botanic Gardens were a particular delight for Elena. There the family sat on wooden benches and listened to British military band concerts. The musicians, clad in red uniforms, brass buttons shining brightly, were ensconced in an octagonal-shaped bandstand situated at the highest point of the gardens, a nice breezy spot. On each visit, Elena watched her father with great amusement, waiting for the inevitable to happen, and it always did. When the band played a rousing Sousa march, Franz began to rap his fingers on his knees in cadence. The toes of his shoes were then set afire with motion, vigorously accompanying his dancing digits. Soon Rudy and Max joined in. Tapping, tapping—fingers and feet in perfect tempo— the three mentally played every note as they themselves would perform the piece. Elena giggled to herself, but Lise and Mitzi cast embarrassed side-long glances at their father and brothers.

"Pretend we're not with them," Lise whispered to Mitzi, and they moved slowly to another bench.

After one such concert, Max and Elena strolled back together to the entrance of the gardens, admiring the stunning blooms of an orchid display along the path. Set against the backdrop of tropical foliage, the flowers presented a sweeping floralscape that took one's breath away.

"Really exotic," Max said. "We see nothing like this in Europe." He pointed out rubber plants to her. "Rubber is in great demand for automobile tires; planters are planting the crop all over the Malay Peninsula. 'Mad Ridley' wasn't so mad after all."

"Mad Ridley?"

"He was director of these gardens. Papa said the poor man was soundly criticized for planting rubber plants in every nook and cranny of the place, but now planters are mighty happy that he did; he has supplied them with plenty of seeds for their crops."

Elena had never ridden in an automobile. "The autos are so noisy and smelly, Max," she said, "I like the horse and carriage much better, especially the horses."

"Well, girl, they are on their way out as a means of travel." He was suddenly animated. "The world is changing so rapidly, Elena. I've read about the flying machines the French and Americans are experimenting with. You'll see, we'll be flying from city to city; never mind automobiles."

"Really? I wonder how the world looks from up there." She gazed up at the azure sky above. It seemed unending, infinite.

"Pretend you're a bird, swooping and gliding about; that's the view you would get." He swept his arms in wide circles to illustrate a bird's movements.

"I'd get sick."

"You'd be thrilled. Lise and Mitzi are becoming ridiculously feminine, but you ...," he smiled, "you would soar to the heavens in delirious delight, loving the wind blowing through your hair." He paused a moment, studying her earnest freckled face. "At least you would now, young and eager as you are, but heaven knows you may become like your sisters in a few years."

"Oh no," she protested, "no, I won't, Max. Promise me we'll fly together when the time comes." She was transported in her mind to the skies, envisioning the two of them flying through the clouds, like noble eagles.

"I promise," he said, giving her slim arm a little squeeze.

* * *

In September, the three sisters started classes at the Cathedral of the Good Shepherd convent school. Madam Rosenbaum assured Franz the school was one of the best in Singapore. Lise had but six months to complete eighth grade, and Mitzi, one year.

The church and school buildings were set close together on North Bridge Road, a fenced-in enclosure between the two forming a play yard. Both stucco exteriors were painted a soft sand color; the wooden window frames and doors, a chocolate brown. The cathedral was a large formidable-looking structure, with a cross so high atop the steeple Elena had to crane her neck way back to see it.

The girls spent mornings and afternoons in class, five-and-a-half days a week. Chang delivered a box lunch to them each day at noon, which they ate either in the play yard, weather permitting, or in their classrooms. The food containers overflowed with steaming hot rice dishes topped with bits of meat or fish, hard-boiled eggs, and fruits such as pineapple, papaya, mango, or bananas. Mitzi asked Chang occasionally to include a serving of the *durian* fruit she was so fond of.

"That is the worst-smelling fruit in the world," Lise complained. "How can you eat it? It's nauseating. Go to the corner of the yard, away from us, to eat it."

"It's indescribably delicious," Mitzi said, laughing, "once you get past the bad smell."

An alarming contrast existed between Sister Ursula's severe, exacting manner and the indulgent, soft-spoken nuns of Bucharest. In her voluminous white habit, the large pendulous silver cross resting on her bosom, and the starched white wimple framing a startlingly moist, rosy-pink face, the nun presented an awe-inspiring figure in the eyes of Elena and her classmates. She stood before the children on their first day of school, ruler in hand, and spoke to them in a quiet, measured tone.

"Since you are living on an English-speaking island, it will be beneficial for you all to learn the language. We will also study the history of Singapore, in addition to the regular subjects of German grammar, reading and writing, mathematics, and sewing and embroidery, which are essential arts for young ladies to master."

The sewing and embroidery class proved to be Elena's undoing, though she enjoyed the work itself. Sister Ursula demanded absolute neatness and delicacy in their projects, and Elena one day failed the stern nun's expectations miserably.

Unfortunately, sewing class had followed afternoon recess. By that time of day, having been forced to restrain her lively, energetic nature to concentrate on serious subjects, Elena ran and played hard with the other students in the play yard, perspiring heavily in the heat. Reluctant to return to class, she remained in the yard well after the nuns had rung the bells, and had no time to wash her hands before entering the classroom.

"What is this, Elena?" Sister Ursula stood over her, ruler in hand, icy blue eyes boring into her brain as she sat embroidering. The formerly snow-white material she worked on was now soiled and wrinkled from damp, dirty fingers. She was struck dumb with fear and apprehension.

"Why is your work so messy," the nun demanded angrily. "Answer me!"

"I … I …," Elena stuttered, "I … forgot to wash my hands. I was late." Her last words were uttered shakily, weakly. The sound of her heart beat like a drum in her ears. She was sure everyone in the room could hear the thumping sounds.

"I see. Play was more important," Sister Ursula said. Addressing the other students, who were following the conversation with fascinated interest, she added, "Class, I want you to remember what punishment will be administered when rules are ignored. Elena, stand up and put your hands out before me." The ruler she held was at the ready.

Humiliated, Elena hesitatingly extended her trembling hands before the nun, eyes half closed in anticipation of the agony to come. Sister Ursula immediately struck her palms hard several times, first one hand, then the other. It took all Elena's willpower to keep from crying out; she gasped, tears welling up in her eyes. She bit her lip until blood flowed. Searing pain flashed up her arms and through her entire body. Worse was the shame she felt when she sat in her seat again. She closed her eyes against the stares of the students, their amusement and gloating, or so she imagined.

Lise and Mitzi did their best to comfort the weeping Elena as they walked to the hotel after school, having been on the receiving end of punishment from uncompromising nuns themselves.

"Please don't tell Papa what happened," Elena pleaded. "You know he will spank me, or at least a slap for being late to class. I know he will." Her flushed face was streaked with a mixture of perspiration, dust, and tears.

Mitzi was soothing. "We won't tell, Elena." She examined the poor swollen red hands in pity. "That nun is known for her harsh discipline, she hits too hard. Papa should be giving her a spanking, not you." She paused, smiling, "Just get yourself washed up when we get to our room, and I'll ask Chang for some ice to put on your hands; that will ease the pain."

"Next time, don't be late for class," Lise added, unable to resist voicing a hint of criticism, "and don't let Rudy see you; he'll tell Papa."

Rudy spotted the unhappy girl, as luck would have it, before she could get to the safety of her room.

"What's with you?" he asked, noting her red-rimmed eyes and inflamed and bruised hands. She belatedly attempted to hide the hands behind her back. He smiled snidely. "Ahaa ... so the nuns gave you some whacks. What did you do, wet your pants? Is that why you were rapped?"

Brushing past him, Elena seethed with anger and chagrin. This had to be the worst day of her life, she thought; he would now surely tell her father in his hateful, amused, bantering fashion, and she would be punished. Why was she the one he always teased, and not Lise or Mitzi? She was relieved when her father said nothing to her at the dinner table. Engrossed in conversation with Max and Herr Schenck, he also failed to notice her swollen hands. Rudy, however, continued to flash knowing smiles, rubbing his hands together suggestively.

Lise, seated next to him, watched the tormenting of her sister for several minutes, then obviously having enough of his nonsense, she delivered a well-aimed kick to his shins. Her new pointed-toe shoes sent a shock of pain through his leg and thigh. He gasped in surprise and indignation.

Their father gazed from one to the other, eyes narrowed, but Lise stared at him innocently while Rudy concentrated on his dessert plate of fruit and cheese. Lise and Mitzi shot triumphant smiles across the table to Elena, and she smiled back, hiding her telltale hands beneath the tablecloth away from her father's gaze.

The days passed swiftly, and though Elena was ever in a state of dread and anxiety when Sister Ursula called upon her to recite, she eventually settled in, doing well in all subjects, save for her nemesis, mathematics. The nun drilled her relentlessly, but by the end of the term, she was forced to give her a barely passing grade. Her father, as a man of his generation, believed that education for a girl was wasted since her life would be one of marriage and babies. Elena's failure was not considered to be a disaster.

English class was where Elena would shine. Within a short time, she was conversing with British patrons in the hotel, sometimes translating for Franz when he desired to communicate with interesting guests, or perhaps quiz British officials on some matter or other. Learning the language came easy to her; just as she had become adept in Malay, with Mei-Ling's help, she worked diligently during the next two years in school to acquire a serviceable vocabulary. Her pronunciation was excellent—she showed little trace of a foreign accent.

Elena was surprised to discover that Rudy had also acquired knowledge of the English language, burying his nose in novels in his free time. She had to admit that when she overheard him in conversation with a British musician, he spoke confidently and fluidly. Perhaps fate was intervening in the lives of brother and sister—the English language would someday be important to them both. Relations between the two had warmed somewhat in the interim. She was older, less vulnerable to his teasing, and Lise made it clear to him his behavior was not to be tolerated. As they all matured, he accepted the situation, though this facet of his character never ceased.

* * *

At fourteen years old, Elena was well acquainted with the history of Singapore. Sister Ursula had provided a map for the class, outlining the coastline and featuring the enormous, almost uniformly flat, natural harbor. Much of the tropical rain forest was rapidly disappearing as immigrants from China arrived, almost a quarter-million of them by 1912. Rubber plantations took over the land, spreading to Malaysia as well, just as Max had predicted to Elena that day in the Botanic Gardens. Trade with the rest of the world ballooned.

Sister Ursula hadn't elaborated on the huge Chinese immigration into Singapore and what changes that had wrought. That information came from a conversation between her father and Herr Rauschner, overheard by Elena as she sat nearby, apparently absorbed in a study of English grammar. "That was a good meal, today," Herr Rauschner said. The two were seated in the garden, her father fanning himself vigorously with a fan shaped like a palm leaf. The air was heavy with the humidity of threatening rain showers.

"Yes, Chang is a good cook. Madam Rosenbaum said his father was indentured to a *gonsi*. You know—a company paid his passage from China. He worked off what he owed, then became a hawker selling cooked food on the streets. Chang learned from him."

"They are hard workers, the Chinese," Rauschner said. "Too bad they are so tyrannized by their secret societies. That's brought all the horrors of China to Singapore: the slave trade, opium dens on Pagoda Street, and prostitution. I've been to Chinatown," he hesitated nervously, "just to look around, you understand." Franz nodded, a slight smile on his lips. "Everything is freely open; I feel sorry for the girls, many brought here against their will, I think." He glanced covertly about, then lifted his hairpiece, quickly wiped his hairless head, shiny with perspiration, with his handkerchief, and swiftly replaced the wig. Franz caught movement from the corner of his eye but ignored it, patting his own balding pate and the ring of curly reddish-white hair surrounding the lower part of his cranium. At that point, the heavens opened suddenly, and rain fell in impenetrable sheets. The men scrambled to the safety of the hotel.

Elena had picked up the word "prostitution," having a vague idea what it might mean. She related the men's conversation to Mei-Ling the next day as they sat in the garden. Her friend was wiser in the ways of the world than the innocent teen. Lise and Mitzi had tittered over any mention of sex; she was too young to know about such things, they said. She wondered if they really knew so much. Perhaps they had learned from reading their romantic novels, but after slyly acquiring one of the books, she gleaned nothing, only a story of inflamed emotions and torrid kisses. "Your father and Herr Rauschner were speaking of the girls in Chinatown who sell their bodies to any man who wishes to have sex," Mei-Ling said, and she proceeded to enlighten Elena as to the mechanics of the act, and the possible consequences.

"No!" Elena was aghast, certain it couldn't be so. It was a graphic explanation she hadn't bargained for.

"Yes, Elena." Mei-Ling nodded firmly. "That's where babies come from."

Elena turned this startling information around and about in her mind for the next few days, eyeing her prim, correct parents, trying to imagine their engaging in the activity Mei-Ling had described. No, it's not possible, she had decided, not at all. Yet ... twelve children ... she really couldn't continue to believe her mother's story about being found by the gypsies.

* * *

When Lise and Mitzi had finished their schooling, they joined the orchestra, performing dinner and dance music each evening. Under Franz's
watchful eye, the novice violinists labored until he was satisfied they had
become professionally competent. Elena had taken for granted that she
would also be included in the orchestra once her school days were over,
but her father made no effort to see that she received musical training.
She pouted, complaining to her mother that he assumed she lacked talent
because she was the baby of the family. But, in fact, her ear for music was
extraordinarily keen.

A small room in the back of the hotel contained a piano, apparently
tucked away because it was not used for the orchestra. The lovely polished
wood instrument seemed to call to Elena. Day after day she would open the
door and peek in, gazing at the black and white keys with intense interest.
One afternoon, the door stood wide open, and she was startled to see Herr
Schenck seated before the piano, playing a lively tune.

"Oooh," she said, after he had finished the piece, "I didn't know you
could play the piano."

"Well, Elena, there are a good many things you don't know about me,"
he said, his eyes twinkling with good humor. "I'm a very versatile fellow. I
don't just play the violin, you see. Piano-playing makes me the life of the
party, if I could ever find one around here," he joked. "But never mind, sit
down and listen; keep me company." He moved to make space for her on
the bench.

He began playing slowly, softly, glancing occasionally at her; she
seemed mesmerized by the rich sounds he was able to create. She watched
his fingering of the keys intently. Responding to her apparent fascination, he switched to lilting waltzes, exciting rhapsodies, and perky polkas.
Throwing his whole stocky body into the faster tempo, he pounded the
keyboard so forcefully that the piano bench rocked perilously under them.
Once, Elena had heard her father berate the violinist for his passionate gypsy-like performance; now, Schenck gave himself free rein, and she felt his
fire coursing through her entire being. She felt exalted, thrilled, as though
she walked on air.

After he had finished his impromptu concert, he gave her shoulder
an understanding pat and left her to experiment on her own. Her fingers
picked out the melodies he had played, the music still resounding in her
brain. It was the beginning of a love affair with a musical instrument that

filled her heart with devotion. Each day thereafter, she stole into the room, sat before the ivories, and slowly, methodically, taught herself to play piece after piece. Her musical ear uncannily and accurately searched out songs and the accompanying notes. Schenck, astounded and delighted by her progress, stopped by often to help her form chords that better suited a tune.

"Herr Linden," Schenck said one day as they passed in the corridor, "come with me, I want you to hear something."

He led Franz to the room where sounds of Elena's musical efforts flowed, soft and appealing. Schenck opened the door and ushered him in. Franz stood listening, his face a study in surprise and disbelief. That it was his own Elena playing was apparent. He saw the back of her young figure topped by the burnt-orange hair as she sat at the piano, her fingers caressing the keys with a sure light touch. He was transfixed as she moved effortlessly from one selection to another. Then suddenly she ceased playing, her hands dropped to her lap and she turned her head, some sixth sense perceiving the presence of others in the room. When she caught sight of her father, her eyes widened and she gasped. She expected some displeasure on his part, but relaxed when she saw the expression on his face. Admiration and astonishment were reflected in his eyes as he walked toward her.

"I should have known," he marveled. "Well done, Elena, well done." He patted her head and smiled affectionately.

"Do you think she could have lessons, Herr Linden?" Schenck asked craftily. "You see she is very talented." Elena's face brightened hopefully at the suggestion, wanting nothing more dearly.

"No ... no, no, Herr Schenck," Franz said quickly, "I'm afraid not. The orchestra does not need a piano player." The good of the entire ensemble was always uppermost in his mind, but then noting Elena's crestfallen reaction to his words, he said, "You can keep playing for your own enjoyment, daughter. I'll speak to Madam Rosenbaum about your using the piano. You should have asked for her permission, anyway."

"Yes Papa."

Elena saw Herr Schenck raise his beetle brows in sorrow for her as her father turned to leave the room. She mouthed the words "thank you" with an added smile and returned to her music, disappointed but relieved she hadn't been forbidden to further touch the piano. Schenck continued to offer help now and then, joking about her lost opportunity to become a famous pianist. They both would have been amused at the time had they known what destiny had in store for her.

CHAPTER EIGHT

Music, Music, Music

Alexandria, Egypt 1913

Dear Mama and Papa,

Oh, how I miss you all! I wish you could see our Conrad, he will be three years old in a few days, a sweet intelligent little boy, just like his father. I've enclosed a photograph taken of him recently, you can see for yourself how handsome he is. I know you would adore him, Mama.

All goes the same; our restaurant is doing good business. The tourists are still vacationing here. André, though, has been gloomy lately; he reads the newspapers from top to bottom each day, predicting that there will be a war in Europe. I said to him there is always a war somewhere, and still the world turns. "You don't understand," he says, "this fracas could be very bad for business." I'm sure he worries needlessly, and you most certainly will be safe in Singapore, far away from Europe's troubles.

I was sorry to hear that Oma Stagen passed away in Bucharest, Mama; she was a wonderful lady. You will miss her, as we all will. I imagine cousin Sophie will take care of her house until you return to Bucharest.

So, Elena writes that the drummer, Herr Rauschner, was taken mysteriously ill and returned to Germany for treatment, and she has taken his place. What happened to him? I was impressed by her letter written in English; she said she wanted to practice, knowing that both André and I speak the language. I can't believe she is fifteen years old now.

I hope this letter finds you all well. Write soon.

God be with you … Stephanie

Marta and Franz refrained from offering any explanation to their daughters regarding the "illness" that had afflicted Rauschner.

"It isn't something you talk about to young girls," Franz said to his wife, "though I've used the example of his misfortune as a warning to the boys."

"Madam Rosenbaum said contracting syphilis from an Oriental woman is disastrous, impossible to cure."

"Hmmm ... I've heard that. It's well that Rauschner went to Germany, better doctors there. Our problem was getting another drummer ... but Elena is coming along nicely. She has a good ear."

"I told you so."

Any interest Elena might have shown in Rauschner's illness was overshadowed by the fact that his departure left a vacancy in the orchestra that she had been elected to fill, and she was terrified. After only several days of lessons from her father, she found herself seated before the drums and cymbals. The responsibility of maintaining the correct tempo for the ensemble was hers; somehow, she must manage to keep her eyes on the sheet music and Franz's baton at the same time.

"Watch me," her father said, as they practiced each morning. "I'll give you the beat, just watch me. Later, I'll show you the rolls and ruffles." The slightest mistake she made during her first public performance brought a sharp glance from him; her hands shook so, she despaired of ever getting through that frightful evening.

"Papa's eyes are on you," Rudy teased, as the orchestra members put their instruments away. "Now he won't pay so much attention to the rest of us."

She knew that to be untrue. An error made by any of the Linden children while playing brought an immediate flash of disapproval from their father. Ever the perfectionist, he followed with a lecture after the performance, and extra practice was imposed on the unfortunate the next day without fail.

The compassionate Max sympathized with Elena, having witnessed her nervous tension, feeling great pity and affection for her. "You will be fine," he said later. "All you need is practice." His sensitivity and understanding did much to calm her, and she soon found her niche in the orchestra. In fact, it wasn't long before her pragmatic turn of mind focused on the possibility of some compensation for her work.

"Ha! Don't dwell on that idea," Lise said, laughing. "I haven't seen any money since I started with the orchestra." She was lounging on the hammock in the garden. "Papa says this is a family endeavor, our orchestra, and he will feed and clothe us and see to our health care, but there is nothing extra to pay wages, only some spending money. Of course, the other musicians have a contract with Papa."

Elena silently pondered her sister's words. She and Mitzi sat on garden chairs, the Siamese cat perched on Elena's lap. The feline emitted a deep yowl, rubbing his head against her body in search of affection and she complied absentmindedly, petting and fondling.

Lise cast a jaundiced eye at the two; any proximity to the animal caused her to itch all over. She noted that Elena occasionally fingered her cheek gingerly as though it were painful to the touch, "You went to the Chinese dentist on Bras Basah Road yesterday, Elena?"

"Yes," Elena groaned, "the gum is still sore around the molar he filled with gold. I think he drilled deep enough to find oil."

Mitzi smiled. She observed Elena thoughtfully. Her bright red hair had deepened to a beautiful auburn as she matured, and her slim adolescent figure had recently begun to fill out into feminine curves. So, too, had her face flowered. Full and soft in the bloom of youth, her regular features were complemented by a radiantly clear, fresh complexion, marred only by what she considered a fatal flaw, the multiple freckles sprinkled indiscriminately on her countenance. Better than the blemishes Lise and I are plagued with each month, Mitzi thought. "You must stay out of the sun, Elena, or wear a hat. You freckle so easily."

"I know, I'm trying," Elena said, sighing. "Herr Schenck told me about a facial cream he saw at the chemist's; it's advertised to bleach the skin. Ummm … Stillman's Freckle Cream, I think he said."

"Be careful," Lise warned. "It might burn your skin."

Elena was initially very tired. It took some getting used to, this orchestra business. The hours were long; she wasn't used to staying up late. Dinner music, gentle and soothing, commenced at six in the evening; then there was dancing afterwards from nine to one in the morning. As an added attraction, Madam Rosenbaum suggested a Sunday afternoon concert of semi-classical selections. Franz missed his sightseeing time, but managed to tour on other days of the week; the enjoyment of playing music they might not otherwise have the challenge of performing was too tempting.

Electric ceiling fans cooled the dining room and its circular-shaped dance floor, but the musicians nevertheless perspired profusely in the unrelenting humid heat of the island. It was hard work, but music was in their blood. Franz had once rhapsodized on the effect it had on their daily lives. He sat on the veranda, his fan ventilating the sultry air about him.

The family members were seated in various positions around him, some in chairs and others on the steps.

"As a musician, you find that music is a part of you. You eat and sleep with it all your life long, whether you are performing, listening to a concert or an opera, or watching a lively military band go marching by." His eyes lit up, glowing with emotion. "It's exhilarating! Your fingers and feet tap in time to the stirring drumbeat. You thrill to the very sound of the music. Your mind's eye follows the sprightly dancing notes on an imaginary musical score, and you mentally play them whatever your instrument. Your whole body is alive with song—you can't help it."

Elena recalled the concerts at the Botanic Gardens, how she giggled at the finger- and toe-tapping of her father and brothers. Now she understood their involvement. She was transported into the heady, exciting world of melodies and rhythms as she participated in the orchestral performances night after night. Her expertise as a drummer improved dramatically in the following months. She threw herself enthusiastically into the learning of each new selection: waltzes, marches, rhapsodies, overtures, all the music of the ages whirled through her brain morning and night. And she knew ... she knew she would forever be held captive to what the American poet, Longfellow, had referred to as "the universal language of mankind." That's what music was, Herr Schenck had told her. It was no matter that the orchestra played in a small hotel, nowhere near as grand as the prestigious Raffles Hotel on Beach Road. Music was the thing; it was her family's life, and the Grand Continental was their theater of existence.

Franz was aware of the passion Elena felt; he knew it was a feeling only she, himself, and Rudy experienced. From his earliest youth, Franz's gifted musicianship had inspired him to compose original works, and here, too, in Singapore, he devoted afternoons, whenever able, to that purpose. On one such day he sat at the desk he had purchased in town soon after their arrival, ostensibly working, but the notes he searched for eluded him. He lifted his pen from his manuscript, his train of thought turning more to contemplation and daydreams than creative ideas.

Pleasantly familiar sounds drifted through the open window of his room from all directions of the hotel, like a musical play in progress: the mellow tones of Rudy's cello as he practiced, the *pizzicato* plunk plunk of Max's bass, and Schenck's sorrowful serenading violin as his bow swept the strings. Further magic ensued as his daughters strolled by on the garden path, their voices raised in song—Mitzi and Lise's strong sopranos soared in harmony with Elena's rich alto. Franz's heart swelled in admiration, and he listened intently until their lovely sweet songs faded away into the distance.

Surely he was blessed, he thought. God had granted him a talented brood. He mused for untold minutes, reflecting on his happy fortune. Abruptly, the daily mundane sounds of the hotel intruded—Chang bellowing in the kitchen, scolding his helpers, and Madam Rosenbaum striding purposefully by his door, heels click-clicking noisily on the marble floor. He sighed, picked up his pen once more, and, dipping the point into the inkwell, returned to his composition.

"I hope," Rudy said, placing a napkin neatly on his lap, "I hope the British officers don't show up tonight." He sprinkled raisins, coconut, and chutney on the chicken curry dish before him. The orchestra members were seated around a table in the corner of the dining room, eating early, as usual, before the evening performance.

"Yes, Madam Rosenbaum was upset last week when they were here," Marta said. "She told me she had complained to their commanding officer about their ill-mannered behavior."

"Ill-mannered!" retorted Max, his splendid new mustache bristling. "They were as drunk as lords! Was it ill-mannered to insult our sisters, attempting to pull them off the platform to dance? What about knocking over tables, smashing chairs as they fought among themselves? And ...."

"And Mama," Elena interrupted, "don't you remember the other night when they came with bowling balls, and were going to use the dance floor as a bowling alley?"

"Deigelmeier and I will make short work of them if they come tonight," Schenck said emphatically, thumping the tabletop with his fist, sending drinking glasses and chinaware rattling and tinkling. Deigelmeier nodded hesitantly, looking at the impassioned Schenck who had volunteered him as a brave protagonist. Max, Rudy, and Braun leaned forward eagerly; fired by Schenck's brashness, they added threats and heated suggestions for effective strategies to use against the British. The young stallions' blood had been stirred to dangerous levels.

"I want no one from the orchestra to get involved," Franz said, his voice assertive, demanding. "It will only end in a brawl, and other guests will be hurt. Remember also, that our musical instruments could be damaged; they are expensive to replace, if they're even available here in Singapore. No, Madam Rosenbaum will see that order is kept through regular channels. Perhaps their commanding officer can declare the hotel temporarily off limits. I hear the officers don't behave much better at the Raffles Hotel, either; it isn't only a problem here. When I visited the Teutonic Club last week, there was much discussion on this very same matter."

That speech calmed the fevered atmosphere somewhat, and the stimulated young men went back to their meals. They were unsettled at the prospect of an encounter with military guests, but eventually pictured the proposed battle in a more humorous light, ending with flashes of ready wit and jesting.

The Teutonic Club had been organized by German residents of Singapore to be used as an entertainment center, complete with bowling alley. Franz, though not a member, was occasionally invited for lunch, using the opportunity to keep a finger on the pulse of social and political affairs in town. He had heard stories there of the selfsame British officers and their antics in the lobby of the Raffles Hotel. In their drunkenness and horseplay, they had actually demolished a postcard-seller's glass-enclosed booth.

More disturbing to Franz were the undercurrents of war talk being circulated about the city and at the club with increasing agitation. Anger displayed by the young men of the orchestra, as well as his own sons that afternoon, worried him. He had never seen the usually calm and easygoing Max so enraged. It was a reflection of the ill feeling growing between the British and German inhabitants.

* * *

"I'm afraid there's going to be a war in Europe," Madam Rosenbaum said. "The papers are full of stories about tension building between England and Germany." She sat with Franz and Marta on the veranda, her face bleak with foreboding.

Franz nodded. "From what I read, it's not just England and Germany at each other's throats; France and Italy are ready to jump in, too. France wants Alsace and Lorraine back that she lost in the last war; and Italy, territory from Austria. Unfortunately, inside Austria-Hungary is also a hornet's nest of intrigue. The Czechs, Poles, Slovaks, Croats, Bosnians, Serbs, the Ukranians—all want either independence or a larger say in their affairs. And there in the wings the Russians stand, championing the Slavs against Austrian dominance." He shook his head. "It seems as though Europe is descending into an inferno of hell."

Marta watched her husband anxiously as he spoke. "I'm sure it's not as bad as you think, Franz," she said. "After all, these countries have been quarreling among themselves for years." She had never known him to be so troubled.

"Franz may be correct, Marta," Madam Rosenbaum said. "It looks bad."

"Oh, I don't understand it, everything was going along so nicely," Marta said. "Kaiser Wilhelm, Tsar Nicholas, and King George are, after all, cousins—grandsons of Queen Victoria." She threw up her hands in a helpless gesture. "How can they fight each other?"

"It happens in the best of families," Franz said, shrugging his shoulders.

Madam Rosenbaum gazed at her friends steadily for a moment. "You know," she said, "Singapore is not a very good place for you to be, if war is declared. You are German nationals."

"So are you and Herr Rosenbaum," Franz was quick to point out.

"Ah ... but we have lived here so long a time; the British wouldn't bother us."

"I wouldn't count on that. War does odd things to people; tempers get hot," Franz said. "But you do have a point. We've lived in Romania, and the children were born there, but we are registered in the German Embassy as German citizens." He paused to collect his thoughts. "We'll have to think this over; don't want to alarm the family. Perhaps if war comes, it will be short-lived and we won't be involved at all."

"I hope so, for all our sakes," Madam Rosenbaum said," but I want you to know I have a friend in Siam, in Bangkok, who manages the Hotel Europa. I'll write to her; she may be able to use an orchestra. It might be safer there for you." She stopped suddenly, her face crumpling with sadness. "Oh, how we'd miss you, though."

"Oh, me, too," moaned Marta, tears welling up in her eyes. The women rose and embraced fervently, and Franz protested that things weren't that bad yet.

Later, alone in her room, Marta reviewed their gloomy conversation. She felt uneasy, wondering whether world events might make them victims of circumstances beyond their control. Was that why Franz seemed so disturbed? She suspected concern for their military-age sons worried him. She also felt that Madam Rosenbaum was being naïve about her situation; she and her husband were German, too, Jewish or not. It was like a pogrom; they could all be summarily deported, chased from country to country. Her heart grew heavy at the thought; they should have a plan in mind in case of emergency.

* * *

Rudy walked about the hotel, searching for Max. At this time in the afternoon, the public rooms were all but deserted; his sisters were resting before the evening performance, and his father working on his manuscripts. Electric fans turned lazily on the ceiling in the lobby, a cool retreat from the sweltering heat of the city. One guest sat reading a newspaper; he nodded pleasantly as Rudy passed. Where was Max? Rudy was bursting with news. Ultimately, he was found, seated in the garden, a newspaper folded on his knee, seemingly lost in reverie.

"Here you are," Rudy said quietly, and Max started, giving him a wan smile. "I've been wanting to talk to you, Max." He paused to dust off a chair adjacent to his brother with a handkerchief, then seated himself, pulling his white trousers up slightly at the knees. "I've got the job. It's at the Grand Hotel in Yokohama; a letter of confirmation came in the mail today."

"So you're really leaving," Max said, a resigned sadness in his voice. "I knew you wanted to get away, be on your own, but I did hope you might change your mind."

"No, no, it's time. Papa is too strict. He watches us all like a hawk. Everything I do is wrong in his eyes. He keeps saying I could be a real artist, but how am I supposed to be one here in Singapore? I should be studying in a big city in Europe, like Vienna, maybe." His green eyes, so like Elena's, flashed impatiently as he spoke; a wayward lock of his wavy auburn hair fell over his freckled forehead. "This is my chance, and I'm going." He leaned forward, addressing Max earnestly. "You should go, too, Max. I can try to include you in my ensemble."

"No, Rudy. You go, I'll stay with Mama and Papa. They might need me." He tapped the newspaper lying on his lap lightly. "I've been reading about the situation in Europe. There could be a war."

"That's Europe," Rudy said, skeptical. "Even if it happens, it wouldn't affect this part of the world."

"Well, one never knows. Our parents aren't young anymore, and there are the girls to think of. No, I'll stay ... as I said, they might need me."

"I think you're worrying too much, Max," Rudy said, but then he chuckled. "You've always been like that, right? The big brother I could always rely on." He paused, now smiling broadly. "Remember the wolves in Romania? You came back to help me when I fell. You could have saved your own skin. I never forgot that."

"And the beating we got afterwards," Max said dryly.

They gazed at each other; the snowy landscape of Bucharest and the howling wolves chasing them as real now in their minds as it was in their youth. They rose from the chairs, Rudy offering his hand, which Max took warmly in his.

"Good luck to both of us," Rudy said. He gave an encouraging laugh. "I'll be back as soon as my contract is up in Japan, and we'll all be together again in Romania. You'll see!"

Coming world events would change everything … for the brothers … for the entire family.

Part Two

THE WAR

CHAPTER NINE

Siam

Bangkok was a shining, dazzling delight; a never-ending feast for the senses, culminating in a celebration of the mysterious, the exotic. Influenced by their Buddhist religion, the benign Siamese—a cheerful, humorous, and friendly lot—seemed unconcerned with life's problems,.

Elena was fascinated. Each day spent exploring the city revealed another golden marvel, another enchanting glimpse into the lives of an engaging populace. A different world, she reflected, so much more interesting than Singapore, though a part of her heart would always remain there. Siam was truly a captivating jewel of the hemisphere. She wished she were a carefree tourist and could while away the hours of each day without a thought to her duties, but, within a week of her arrival, she was performing with the orchestra nightly in the Hotel Europa's spacious dining room, as well as rehearsing each afternoon.

* * *

Only a short month previously, a whirlwind of frenzied activity in Singapore had followed the news of war in Europe. Elena had studied newspaper articles painstakingly, acutely aware of the effect the course of events had on the adults around her. Her parents and the Rosenbaums, faces grim, had closeted themselves in the Rosenbaum suite for hours. Max paced back and forth in the garden with Schenck and the other young men of the orchestra, deep in conversation. There was an air of uncertainty and excitement abroad, a restlessness that kept everyone in a state of nervous tension. Elena apprehended Max at the first opportunity.

"Max, tell me what's going on," she said, "I've read the papers, but don't quite understand what's happening."

"It's been building, Elena. The assassination in July of the Archduke Franz Ferdinand and his wife was a catalyst—it shocked the whole world.

Then Austria invaded Serbia; Germany invaded Luxembourg and Belgium; and England declared war against Germany."

"But all this happened in Europe," Elena said, perplexed. "Why did Mama say we might go to Siam?"

"Well, you know Singapore is a British colony, and we are German. They could intern us, imprison us all."

"Oh." Her heart skipped a beat at the word "imprison." "Then we would be safe in Siam?"

"Yes."

Several days after their conversation, the family and orchestra members hastily packed their belongings, boarded a ship headed for Siam, and sailed along the coast of the Malay Peninsula into the Gulf of Siam to Bangkok.

The image of Madam Rosenbaum's tear-stained face, her stately figure standing forlornly on the wharf, would remain in Marta's memory for years afterward. She leaned against the railing of the ship as it cruised into the South China Sea, waving her handkerchief in a last farewell, until her friend was no longer visible. She continued to gaze at the blurred shoreline, eyes moist, until Franz tapped her shoulder.

"She's gone," he said.

"Not from my heart, Franz, not from my heart."

* * *

Madam Rosenbaum had professed friendship with the Hotel Europa's manager, Madam Streit, but, in Franz's opinion, the relationship was purely professional—the two ladies being as opposite in character as black is to white. Madam Streit was coolly cordial on their first meeting, businesslike and calculating.

"The Rosenbaums recommended you very highly, Herr Linden," she said. "Your orchestra is competent." Her narrow gray eyes scanned his face closely; he felt she was taking his measure, especially as she continued. "I don't know what arrangement you had with them, but I would like to have the girls of the orchestra dance with patrons when asked. Would that be a problem for you?"

For a split second, a vision of the unruly British officers of Singapore flashed across Franz's mind. He wasn't pleased by her request. He had always been careful that his daughters' reputations were protected through rigorous supervision. But then again, they were fortunate to be in Siam, away from the danger of the British colony in wartime.

"It will be our pleasure, Madam," he said affably, "providing your clientele is composed of gentlemen ... but I might need an extra musician to fill in when the ladies are dancing. Not at my expense, I trust."

"Done," she said. "See me in my office tomorrow morning." She turned abruptly and strode down the hallway, her chin held high in self-importance. Two can play at this game, he thought, watching her fleshless figure disappear around a corner. He had won this round.

The Hotel Europa, as its name suggested, catered to the European element of Bangkok. Guests were attracted by the excellent cuisine, the cleanliness of the simple, but attractively furnished rooms, and now the entertainment offered by the Linden orchestra. Siam had been transformed from a nineteenth-century kingdom of serfdom and slavery to a country striving to take its place among the modern nations of the world. Schools and hospitals had been established with missionary assistance, law courts reorganized, military forces modernized, and young men sent abroad for study. Under the direction of the present monarch, King Vajiraudh, Germany's influence in Siam had expanded considerably, with commercial concessions and lively trade ongoing between the two countries.

Madam Streit introduced an energetic-looking, middle-aged man to Franz one evening during the orchestra's rest period.

"My name is Ethelbert, Kapellmeister," he said, his eyes a startling blue in a heavily lined, bronzed face. He shook Franz's hand heartily. "Won't you join me in a drink?"

After they were seated and had ordered refreshments, he continued, grinning broadly. "I almost didn't make it here to the hotel. Now that Bangkok has some paved roads, instead of all those *klongs*, or canals, the carriage I was riding in was pushed into a ditch by an automobile. The poor driver was so upset, I helped him into the carriage and drove the rest of the way here myself. I need that drink!"

Franz smiled, believing the man capable of anything, so physically fit a specimen was he. His neck and arms were brown as a berry, a person evidently used to working outdoors.

"I don't get to the city often," Ethelbert said. "I like to come here for the good food, even though I stay at the Oriental Hotel. It's been really delightful to hear your orchestra. Reminds me of home."

"Thank you," Franz replied, the name Ethelbert suddenly ringing a bell. "I was talking to your director, Bethge, recently. He gave glowing accounts of your engineering feats constructing the railroad for the Siamese government. I understand it will run from Denchai to …?"

"To Chieng." Ethelbert stopped briefly to acknowledge a waiter serving the drinks. "We hope to have that line completed by the end of next year. I have to say the King's Royal Railway Department has been very supportive, giving us encouragement and all materials needed."

Franz smiled. "I'm sure your success is also a result of your staff being very skilled, Herr Ethelbert. King Vajiraudh is a progressive man— employing German experts was farsighted of him."

They laughed together companionably, and Ethelbert raised his glass in a toast. "To the experts." Franz nodded, meeting the engineer's glass with his own. This was a man he could like, he reflected; working in foreign lands was an adventure they shared, though each approached their aims in a diverse fashion. Thereafter, Ethelbert visited whenever able to take a break from his work.

The idea of his daughters dancing with hotel guests may not have been to Franz's liking, but the three sisters welcomed this new development with pleasure; the social aspect being very intriguing for the healthy, active, young ladies. The opportunity to meet gentlemen under acceptable circumstances, while at the same time performing orchestral duties, brought added enjoyment to their evenings. So it was that they danced waltzes, polkas, and the new American foxtrot, whenever permitted, under the stern gaze of their father. Their mother sat by the entrance of the dining room, on guard, crocheting and conversing with any friendly guests available in her vicinity. The versatile Schenck took up the drumsticks for Elena when necessary, giving her playful winks when he saw her dance by with a particularly aged and infirm gentleman.

It was evident to Madam Streit that the girls were an attraction drawing many to the hotel. Her sales receipts had mounted in the plus column each week since the arrival of the orchestra. She watched in satisfaction as the men came—old, middle-aged, and young; German, French, Italian, American, British, Dutch, and a sprinkling of other Europeans; businessmen, sea captains, architects, salesmen, artisans, military personnel, and German railway construction staff. All those engaged in furthering Siam's plans for westernization gathered at the Europa Hotel for sustenance and diversion.

"Oh, it's hot!" exclaimed Elena, her face flushed and perspiring after an evening of vigorous instrumental performing and dance. "I wish we didn't have to wear these high-collared dresses. Papa must think we'll be ravished by the guests if we bare our throats."

It was after two in the morning, the girls making preparations for sleep in their room. Mitzi, bowl of water in hand, sprinkled pillows and sheets of their beds with droplets of the liquid, striving to create a cooling sensation for their heated bodies at bedtime.

"Much hotter here than in Singapore," Lise said. "Like a hothouse." Brushing her sparse hair with measured strokes, she favored Mitzi with a smile when her sister scattered water in her direction. "More," Lise said, and Mitzi complied, giggling.

Elena slipped on a cotton batiste nightdress, then poured water from a pitcher into a ceramic basin, and bathed her face and throat. Fetching a towel, she patted her face lightly as she sat cross-legged on her bed. "Ahhh ... that's better," she said, and pulled hairpins confining her wavy hair. The heavy red mass fell in rippling cascades about her shoulders. "Now ... what's the name of the new girl Madam Streit hired for the orchestra? When does she start?"

"Camille," Lise said. "A pretty girl, don't you think? Such dark eyes and hair. Did you notice Max watching her?"

"She starts tomorrow," contributed Mitzi. "She was watching Max, too. Took a few small glances in his direction while Papa was talking to her." She smiled mischievously. "You know, we're used to thinking of Max as a big affectionate bear, but you must admit he is rather handsome. A girl couldn't get a better husband." Lise made a face.

"He is kind and gentle," Elena said, her love for her brother unwavering. "Rudy should be more like him."

"Rudy is Rudy," Lise said. "He is clever, always bargaining, getting the best of a deal. He will be rich someday." She moved to arrange the mosquito netting about her bed. "Well, I'm tired, girls; let's get some rest. Mitzi, turn off the light, you're close to the wall switch."

Elena remained wakeful, her thoughts on Rudy. He was clever, to be sure, and very thrifty, to the point of being grasping. Charitably, he could be described as shrewdly economical. In contrast, Max was open-handed, generous to a fault. She had to admit, though, she did miss Rudy, now that he was in Japan. It would be strangely disturbing to see this Camille occupying his chair at meals and performances.

She recalled the times he had been amusing and diverting, after they had more or less "buried the hatchet" between them, and he had ceased his teasing habits. She looked forward to his humorous letters, and was touched when he sent her reproductions of photographs of herself vividly imprinted on gauzy Japanese silk. An affectionate note of birthday congratulations had been tucked into the package. She turned over in her bed, sighing; she resolved to write a warm sisterly letter to him in the morning. She had almost dozed off when Lise's voice, drowsy with approaching slumber, parted the darkness.

"Elena," she said faintly, "who was that blonde-haired fellow you were dancing with tonight? I haven't seen him here before." There was a long pause ere she continued. "He seemed positively captivated by you."

Franz was also sleepless into the early morning hours, his thoughts on the war. Europe's troubles had nagged at him, as a distant, threatening rumble of thunder in his mind. He had sought to keep busy and put reports of slaughter and horror on the continent aside, like a nightmare best forgotten. However, as the days passed and one nation after the other entered the conflict, he became more and more uneasy. So many countries involved: Austria-Hungary, Germany, France, England, Bulgaria, Turkey, Russia, Montenegro, and Serbia. And now Portugal, Italy, Romania, and even Japan were on the brink of a declaration of war against Austria and Germany.

Future historians, he thought, would be hard pressed to make sense of this worldwide conflagration; it was being played out on such a huge scale. The little people, like him and his family, would be wafted about helplessly, innocents caught up in a storm of hate and aggression. Rudy's welfare in Japan was another worry.

Too restless to sleep, he rose from the bed gently, so as not to disturb Marta, and sat in a chair by the window. Crickets chirped loudly outside, calling to each other in the humid night. If the war was still raging, he thought, when the orchestra contract expired, where could they go? What country was left in the world where they could seek refuge?

Perhaps Madam Streit would renew the contract, but perhaps she wouldn't. He sighed deeply. Tomorrow he would pore over his maps again.

CHAPTER TEN

Romance

E lena, still feeling safe in the bosom of Bangkok's religious harmony and elegance, continued to explore the city when time allowed.

"Look, Max," she whispered to her brother as they walked slowly about the interior of the Buddhist temple listed as Wat Benchamaborpit in her father's guidebook. "Another gold statue. There is no end to them here in Bangkok. We meet one at every turn; little ones, big ones, huge gigantic ones. Sitting, standing, lying down." She studied the lofty statue before them with interest. Buddha's golden image gleamed mysteriously in the light of flickering candles that surrounded the base. Gold threads, woven into the tapestry mounted on the walls of the temple, twinkled and glittered their way to the ceiling beams of black lacquer and gold leaf. Trays of cakes and fruits had been placed before the statue, daily offerings by worshipers.

Elena felt a sense of peace permeating the atmosphere. Steady rhythmic chanting of monks, seated cross-legged, clothed in saffron-colored robes, stirred in her a spiritual emotion that was new and exciting. God is here, too, she thought, perhaps the same one. Max smiled as she lit a candle.

After admiring the marble structure guarded by two stylized white marble lions, they reclaimed their shoes from the portico—visitors were advised to remove their footwear before entering temples. Outside, the temple's exterior was equally impressive.

"This Wat is only fifteen years old, according to the guidebook. Built in 1900," Elena said. "It looks so magical, doesn't it, with the sun shining on the golden tiles of the roof."

"A fascinating wonderland, Bangkok," Max admitted, "dazzling golden spires and domes above us, but ...." He stopped in his tracks to lift one foot, then the other, for her inspection, revealing a sticky red substance clinging to the soles of his shoes. "Quite a mess on the ground."

"Oh," Elena grimaced, bending down to examine her own shoes. "That's the betel nut mixture the Siamese chew and spit all over. Ugh ... I hate to see the red mouths and their teeth black from the muck. Well ... better keep our eyes on the ground as well as the heavens."

"It's easy to see where the custom came from, of removing shoes before entering temples and homes," he said dryly, and they walked on carefully.

Elena's world at that time had been a sheltered one; she was confined to the hotel with orchestral duties and allowed sightseeing only in the company of family. Otherwise, she occupied herself with sewing and reading—devouring every book, newspaper, and periodical that came her way, both English and German. With Madam Streit's permission, she was able to play the piano in the hotel lobby an hour each day. The hotel manager noted that hotel guests, attracted by her playing, soon sat in the lobby each day at the appointed time, waiting for the concert.

This familiar routine was interrupted one weekend by the pleasure of a boat excursion to Songkhla, a fishing village a hundred miles south of Bangkok. It was a medium-sized craft they boarded that morning, along with some thirty or so other passengers, plus a jolly Portuguese captain and equally good-natured Siamese crewmen. Refreshments were served as the merry group settled themselves on the deck, with sheets of canvas overhead sheltering them from the brilliant rays of the sun.

Elena was excited by the holiday, released from her responsibilities for two whole days. Cool sea breezes caressed her, sending tendrils of her copper tresses blowing across blooming cheeks as the boat plowed through blue waters. A gentleman, with eyes that matched the blue of the sea, found his attention drawn to the young miss again and again. He watched as she conversed with the females around her. She seemed animated, alive with interest, pointing out places of note along the shoreline.

"Who is she?" he asked of a passenger who seemed to know everyone aboard.

"A member of the orchestra from the Hotel Europa. She is sitting with her sisters and brother, Max," the talkative man said. "I can introduce you, just say the word."

"No, no," the gentleman said, sipping his lemonade. "She's very young."

"Not so young," his companion said. "At least seventeen, and level-headed."

It was late afternoon when the boat reached Songkhla. The party disembarked and dined al fresco, the crew setting up tables on the white sandy beach of the gulf. Palm trees sighed and swayed in welcome as tasty, fresh-caught seafood, vegetables, rice, and bounteous trays of colorful fruits were set before them. Conversation became increasingly jovial and festive as the hours passed. An enchanting spot, a fitting place for a romance to be set in motion, though Elena was unaware of it happening at the time.

When time to leave, the blue-eyed gentleman stood by the narrow gangplank as the ladies stepped daintily aboard the vessel, giving each a helping hand. Elena gave him a rewarding smile as he assisted her. She glanced back at him after gaining the deck, and saw that his eyes were still on her. Blushing, she turned away in an unexplainable confusion. He made an impressive picture in her mind—sunburned face and arms contrasting handsomely with the casually styled white clothes he wore. His blonde hair shone brightly in the waning rays of the sun, like the golden domes of Bangkok's temples.

Attention from the opposite sex was a new and stimulating experience for our young drummer. Every evening there were dance partners—many hesitant and awkward, dancing primarily for the opportunity to social-ize, while others were a delight. They whirled her about the dance floor, performing intricate steps that she was able to follow with ease. She re-turned to her drumming after one such intoxicating swing around the floor so exhilarated that she beat her instrument exuberantly until her father's warning glare chastened her. Occasionally a guest cornered her expressly for the purpose of discussing the war, which was frowned upon by her father. "Keep the conversation on a pleasant social level," he advised, and she be-came adept at changing the subject.

One evening the blue-eyed gentleman appeared. That was the night Lise had sleepily remarked on Elena's new dance partner; he had been "captivat-ed," she said. From that time on, he came to the hotel several times a week, sometimes alone, sometimes with friends. At first shy and somewhat flustered by the attention he paid her, Elena soon began to look forward to his visits. He was natural and humorous in his conversation as they danced; deftly ma-neuvering her about the floor, he held her firmly but decorously in his arms.

"Who is he?" Lise asked, not being put off this time. "He always asks for you."

"Umm ... his name is Lorenzo," Elena said hesitantly. "He was part of the group on the cruise to Songkhla, though I don't think we talked to him then. He is an architect, comes from Italy." She paused, blushing, "He has asked Papa if he can call on me afternoons."

"Oh?" Lise said, raising her eyebrows. "Well, then … he's definitely interested. I think he's a bit old for you, though."

Mitzi grinned impishly. "First Max and Camille, now you and this Lorenzo. Cupid has been busy as a bee around here."

"Max and Camille?" This was news to Elena.

"You haven't noticed?" Lise asked. "They've been mooning around for days. I saw them smooching in the garden last night during the orchestra's rest time. She hasn't wasted any time since she got here."

After that conversation, Elena watched the pair closely as they rehearsed each day, catching the affectionate glances pass between them, even feeling a slight pang of jealousy at losing some of Max's attention. Camille was pretty, Elena admitted. She sometimes sat with the sisters in their room, chatting and arranging coiffures, when Max was practicing. Her luxuriant black hair and dark eyes gave her a gypsy-like appearance.

Lise was hostile. "I don't like her," she stated. "She's sly and secretive, says very little about her past. How did she get to Bangkok, anyway?"

"Oh, you're too nosy, Lise," Mitzi said. "The poor girl has to get used to us. She's probably just shy by nature."

Lise shrugged her shoulders noncommittally, grunting unintelligibly as she walked off, but she wasn't finished with Max's paramour. Things came to a head between the two girls several days later, and after that day, Lise and Camille never spoke directly to each other again.

The three sisters had gathered in Camille's room to admire a length of Siamese silk she had bought from a Chinese shopkeeper in the hotel.

"You know, Camille," Lise said, "if you shop in the hotel, it's much more expensive than going to the outdoor market, where you can get a good bargain."

Mitzi interjected quickly, noting the blush of resentment flooding Camille's face. "Oh yes, Lise, but this is beautiful," she said, caressing the soft fluid material. "The colors are so brilliant, you can make a lovely scarf or shawl from it. Look how lively the design looks next to my white dress." She placed the silk experimentally in different positions over her arm and shoulder.

Lise shrugged, paying scant attention to the fabric, instead searching Camille's countenance critically. "Camille," she said, "you look tired; you have dark circles under your eyes. Are you unwell?" The word "unwell" was a euphemism used to describe the pain and discomfort ladies suffered during their menstrual cycles.

Camille colored slightly, nodding guardedly, reluctant to acknowledge what she considered a private female concern. She had not formed a close enough relationship with the Linden sisters wherein intimate affairs could be shared and also interestingly analyzed, as women are wont to do. In Lise's view, the girl had deliberately isolated herself from their company, even in the free time that she didn't spend with the feverishly smitten Max.

Lise rose from her seat and drifted aimlessly about the room as the others conversed. She stopped before the teakwood bureau and gazed at the usual assortment of items resting on top: comb and brush, perfume bottles, a silver container of hair pins. One drawer was slightly open, as though closed hastily, but not completely. Lise wrinkled her nose in distaste.

"What is that odor, Camille?" she asked. "It's something in this drawer. Have you hidden some snack there and forgotten about it? Something stinks." She slowly pulled open the drawer, lifting out a crumpled pad of cloth. It was darkly stained with what looked like dried blood. Her eyes widened at the discovery, and she held the pad up gingerly for the others' scrutiny, a slight smile on her lips.

"Lise!" Mitzi exclaimed, horrified, but her sister continued her harangue, while Camille's face paled visibly.

"Why do you hide this in the drawer, naughty girl! You know you should soak it in cold water before washing it for future use, as we do. It smells if you leave it around, just as I happened to notice it now." She offered the offending item to a tight-lipped Camille, who snatched it away.

Embarrassed and confused, Camille stuffed the cloth back into the drawer with trembling fingers. She stood for a moment, eyes lowered, gasping for breath, then confronted Lise, her face scarlet with anger and shame. "You have some nerve, Lise, opening my drawers," she cried, her voice shrill like a squawking crow. "It's none of your business what I do, or how I do it!" Tears of humiliation coursed down her inflamed cheeks. "Oh, this is impossible," she said. "Why don't you all just ... leave." She motioned to the open doorway, only to see Max standing on the threshold, his face chalk white. The girls stared at him, transfixed; it was obvious he had witnessed the whole episode, or most of it. Camille dropped down on a chair, hands covering her face. It was bad enough they had been caught in the midst of a quarrel, but the subject of women's monthly trials was a tasteless one to be aired in the male presence. Taboo.

"I was only trying to tell Camille ...," Lise began, but Max gave her a withering glance, turned on his heel and disappeared down the hallway.

Later that day, Elena came upon Max sitting at a table in the empty dining room, gazing dismally into space, his mustache drooping as glumly as his thoughts. He glanced at his pitying sister as she sat beside him.

"I'll never forgive Lise for what she did to Camille," he said bitterly.

"Well, you know Lise. She's always been like that," Elena offered lamely.

"That's no excuse ... to hurt someone like that! What could she be thinking of? And what can I say to Camille? She must be ashamed to talk to me."

Elena patted his shoulder comfortingly. "Oh, I'd just hug her, Max, before you even say a word to her, and she'll know it doesn't make any difference to you."

Max brightened at her words. "You think so?" he said, immediately feeling better. His black mood evaporated. He drew her to her feet and hugged her. "Oh, sweet Elena," he said affectionately. "You are wise beyond your years." Elena smiled as she watched him hurry off, humming happily.

She sat down again, her thoughts on Lise, who had surely gone too far in her treatment of Camille. Her tactics, dictated by distrust of the girl, had the opposite effect from what she had intended, causing Max to come to the defense of his loved one. She wondered whether Lise knew Max had been in the doorway.

Though Max thought her wise, Elena thought otherwise that afternoon. Lorenzo was coming to call. She felt awkward, puzzling over how she should entertain him. "Be yourself," Mitzi advised earlier as Elena dressed, but who *was* she? Lorenzo was educated, an architect, and she was a seventeen-year-old who had only completed eighth grade. She shrugged her shoulders, feeling unsettled, not yet cognizant of the effect an attractive girl could have on a man.

Stepping out onto the veranda, Elena saw Lorenzo sitting with her mother; they were conversing in Italian. His eyes lit up in admiration at the sight of her, and he rose politely from his chair.

"Well, hello. I'm happy to see you, Elena. You look very pretty today."

Smiling uneasily, she said, "Thank you, Lorenzo ... I'm pleased to see you, too."

She had taken special care in dressing, wearing a favorite shirtwaist, a style she knew was becoming, and had her hat in hand should they walk in the garden, no longer careless about the sun. Having secured a bleaching cream in Bangkok, her complexion was fresh and clear of the hated freckles.

Lorenzo was a meticulous dresser, but this afternoon his spotless white suit and tanned, clean-shaven face fairly dazzled Elena. How handsome he is, she thought. Though the two had danced and conversed lightheartedly in the evenings, somehow this meeting was different. They shook hands almost formally, and she was startled to feel an unaccustomed thrill emanating from his touch. She swallowed nervously.

Marta watched the pair with a knowing smile. "Lorenzo tells me he comes from Milan, Elena. Italy is a very beautiful country. Your father and I were there when we were first married."

"Your mother speaks Italian well," Lorenzo said. "It's good to hear my mother tongue spoken again."

"Italian is very similar to Romanian," Marta said. She rose from her chair, wincing a bit from the ever present pain of her rheumatism. "Well, you must excuse me, I have duties to attend to. I hope to see you again, Lorenzo." As she turned to leave them before disappearing into the lobby of the hotel, she added, "Oh, Elena, don't forget to bring in the book you were reading this morning when you come in later—just in case of rain. It's on the table there."

"Let's sit awhile before we walk," Lorenzo said. Curious to see what type of reading interested Elena, he picked up the book her mother had indicated, sat in a chair next to her, and began to peruse the contents. His eyes widened in surprise as he turned the pages. "Insects? Ants? That's what you're reading about?"

"Umm ... yes ...," she said, her face reddening. "Is there anything wrong with that?"

"No!" he said hastily. "No ... on the contrary; it's just that most girls your age read only romantic novels. Actually, I really think it's extraordinary ... though ...," he paused, nodding his head in a sudden understanding of his attraction to her. "Yes, I felt while we danced each evening that I had to know more about you, that you weren't one of these empty-headed females around." His words, upon reflection, flustered him. "Oh, excuse me, I didn't mean to infer that your sisters are."

Her amused laughter interrupted him; she suddenly felt more relaxed in his company. "Sometimes I feel the same," she said. "They are older than I am, but not always wiser." The Lise and Camille debacle that morning flashed through her mind.

"Anyway ...," she continued, "insects have always interested me, ever since my brothers snared butterflies in Singapore to send to museums." She paused, her eyes shining brightly with enthusiasm. "I've enjoyed reading this book so much, Lorenzo—the ants are simply amazing. Have you heard about the marching army ants in the jungle? They eat everything in their path, even humans."

"No," he said, smiling indulgently, like a father watching his child at play; this girl-woman was a delightful mix of youth and maturity. "Let's take a walk in the ants' domain; I'm going to be much more aware of them in the future." As they stepped onto the path, and Elena started to don her hat, he stayed her arm impulsively, gazing at the brilliant reds and oranges of her hair glistening in the sunshine, as though on fire. "I just wanted to … your hair shines so in the sun," he said appreciatively.

"It was carrot-red when I was young; now it's better, darker." She placed the broad-brimmed hat atop her head in a matter-of-fact manner that he found charming, her absence of feminine guile very appealing.

In the garden, they talked of Italy. Lorenzo's descriptions of his home and life there intrigued her and his nostalgia for his homeland was infectious. She responded with a genuine interest as he expressively pictured the glories of Rome and Venice for her, and promised to loan her books so they could discuss the beauties of his country further.

So diverting was their conversation as they neared the hotel again, they barely noticed Franz standing on the path by the veranda. He was shuffling his feet back and forth, fanning himself vigorously. As they came closer, they saw he was stamping down on a broad line of ants, perhaps twelve inches wide. The insects were scurrying along, carrying leaves and other insects ten times their size with little difficulty. Franz smiled sheepishly, indicating his peculiar occupation with a wave of his hand to the parading arthropods.

"Perhaps I can rid the earth of these pesky ants," he said. "They're such a nuisance."

"Papa," Elena said mockingly, "I'm afraid the ants outnumber us by a thousand to one. You're only wasting energy trying to destroy them." She and Lorenzo exchanged conspiratorial smiles as she continued, "Papa, Lorenzo has been telling me about his home in Italy. Mama said you were there years ago."

"Oh, yes," Franz said, "beautiful country, Italy." He paused, regarding Lorenzo with interest. "Perhaps we can talk one day soon, I'd like to learn more about your work."

Lorenzo nodded amiably. "I'd be most pleased, sir."

Elena and Lorenzo continued their walk, finally seating themselves on a bench in the arbor.

"Elena," he said, "I have a confession to make." She raised her eyes to his questioningly; he was joking, she thought, but his face was serious. "I came to the hotel one day on business. You were playing the piano, and I sat down to listen. I hope you don't mind."

"Oh, no," she said, thinking she would have been self-conscious had she known he was there.

"I was very impressed; you play well," he said. "It's a pity you can't play the piano in the orchestra, instead of the drums."

She frowned. "My father needs a drummer, not a piano player. Besides, I play by ear, it would be necessary for me to take lessons to read music."

"Elena," he said, taking her hand in his, "you do very well in the orchestra. You play the drums with admirable energy and enthusiasm. But the piano ...." He paused, closing his eyes. "There ... you played with your soul. I heard it, I felt it ... here," and he thrust his hand to his heart dramatically.

She couldn't help but be impressed by his words, so intensely were they uttered; she was moved, flattered that he felt her passion. No one had understood her love for the piano so well, so perceptively. Perhaps Herr Schenck, but his was always a humorous remark of appreciation for her hard work.

"Well," Lorenzo said, recovering himself. "I didn't intend to be so emotional; it's just that your music excited me. I hope that somehow, sometime, you'll be able to study, realize your potential, you see?"

She nodded shyly, and he was surprised, himself, by his interest in her. She seemed to stir in him feelings he found difficult to define. Fourteen years difference in their ages—foolish of him to think seriously about her, but there was no harm in being friends. She was a refreshing companion.

For Elena, that afternoon was a turning point, from the innocence and security of girlhood to the thrilling, and sometimes agonizing, milieu of love and romance that would be played out in a world torn apart by war.

CHAPTER ELEVEN

Passions Of War

Alexandria, 1915

Dear Mama and Papa,

Again I'm late with a letter, please forgive me. There is always so much to do. This horrible war drags on and on; the amount of deaths and casualties we read about is unbelievable, all those young men being slaughtered. I pray for them. I'm thankful that you're not in Romania now; cousin Sophie writes that all is chaos in Bucharest. King Carol must be turning in his grave. His nephew, King Ferdinand, tried his best to keep Romania neutral, as his uncle wished, but he had no choice; he declared war on Germany. I hear Ferdinand's English-born queen, Marie, was jubilant. We all loved Bucharest so much, Papa; I hope the family will be able to return there when the shooting stops.

I'm sorry to say that just as André feared, the war has affected our business badly. We do get some British customers. There has been buildup of military personnel in Alexandria since Britain declared Egypt a protectorate, but the Europeans are not able to winter here, as in the past, and they were our mainstay. The Arabs don't care much for our cuisine, and if they do come, they are a disgruntled lot; their conversation centers loud and contemptuously around the unpopular Husayn Kamel being made Sultan by the British, and they show even more resentment against the British themselves.

Elena writes that all is the same in beautiful Bangkok; she sent me a picture postcard of the many golden statues, and also a photograph of herself in profile. She looks quite grown up. Who is this Lorenzo she writes of? He seems to be more than a friend.

I must get to the restaurant now; the staff needs supervising. After we train them to be good workers, we lose them to rich

Arab families. I hope this wretched war will soon be over; food supplies are getting hard to come by.

We haven't heard from Rudy. In his last letter he wrote that his situation was uncertain now that Japan has declared war against Germany. You must be worried about him. I hope you are both well.

God be with you, and write soon.

Stephanie

The atmosphere was oppressively close. Marta heard an ominous clap of thunder in the distance as she sat on the hotel veranda, her crocheting forgotten in her lap. Max and Elena had left early that morning for another jaunt into Bangkok, this time accompanied by Camille and Lorenzo. Reviewing the concerns in Stephanie's letter for the last hour, the destruction and human suffering in Europe weighed heavily on her heart, especially the plight of friends and relatives in Bucharest.

News of Stephanie's business downturn was worrisome. And what of Rudy in Japan? His position could be perilous. Then there was Elena. Franz labeled her friendship with Lorenzo as an infatuation. She was young, he said, and Lorenzo was an intelligent and attractive man, one who would seem very fascinating to her. Franz's probing talk with the architect had satisfied him; the man understood the differences in their ages precluded any serious commitment.

Marta was skeptical, remembering her own determination at age fifteen to marry Franz in the face of her parents' opposition. Elena had always been obedient to her father's wishes, but that could change when love came into her life. Marta had observed Lorenzo and Elena together; perhaps the Italian thought theirs was a friendship, or light flirtation at the most, but he might be in deeper than he knew.

Elena's vibrant voice invaded Marta's thoughts as the young foursome stepped onto the veranda. "Mama!" she exclaimed exuberantly, "what a wonderful day we had; you should have been with us."

"Oh, no, I couldn't keep up with you young ones in this heat."

"We saw the Grand Palace; it's really a walled, fortified city, isn't it, Lorenzo ... all that gold again ... and then, Mama, we saw the Reclining Buddha in the Wat Po." Elena's face was flushed, her green eyes shining.

Lorenzo and Marta exchanged amused glances, savoring the young girl's enthusiasm, like a refreshing breeze in the humid air.

"I think, Elena, you enjoyed the boat ride even more," Lorenzo said, then addressing Marta, he continued. "Early this morning, Frau Linden, we came into the market area of the *klong* in time to see hundreds of Siamese in their fruit- and vegetable-filled boats and barges … flowers too. They floated all about us, everything for sale.

"They were cooking on their boats, too," Elena said. "We bought bananas dipped in some kind of batter and toasted over charcoal … umm … braziers, were they, Lorenzo?" When he nodded, she smiled. "They were delicious."

"Ah, but Mama," Max said, grinning mischievously, "I wish you could have seen your Elena as she returned the monks' greetings in the Wat Po, her hands held together, bowing in deference."

"Oh, Max!" Elena said, blushing furiously, "I was only being polite. They are so solemn; Lorenzo says they are not allowed to beg for their food, only accept what is offered."

"Ha!" scoffed Max. "Madam Streit doesn't offer food to the monks when they pass the hotel kitchen. She said to me that not being a member of the Buddhist religion, she had no need to gain merit by her generosity."

"What generosity?" Camille giggled, and they all laughed with her. Madam Streit had proved to be a penny-pinching employer. She watched the orchestra members' consumption of food at meals with an eagle eye, complaining when meals on their plates were left unfinished, or too much fruit (in her estimation) was taken to their rooms for snacks. Oh, how they yearned for the great-hearted Madam Rosenbaum!

Lorenzo soon took his leave, promising to return the next evening. The remaining three tarried, describing the events of the day in more detail for Marta. She oohed and aahed in all the appropriate places until the dinner hour approached.

"It's been a long day," she said. "Why don't you wash up now?" Camille and Elena passed through the hotel doorway, chattering, but Max delayed, sitting next to his mother, his expression sober, lips tight.

"Mama," he said gently, "because we left so early this morning, I didn't have time to tell you that I received a letter from Rudy."

"Oh?" Marta's eyes were anxious. "Is he alright?"

"He writes that his position is becoming uncertain, Japanese officials have asked him to report to the immigration offices."

"Is it possible for him to come here, Max, to Siam?"

"Hmmm ... no, Mama, I don't want to alarm you ... but I think *our* position is ... shall we say, shaky as well. He would be better off elsewhere."

"But where? Almost every country in the world is in this war." She stared at him, her soft brown eyes widening in comprehension as the realization of her family's predicament became frighteningly clear to her. "Not here, too, Max?"

"There are rumors. I think Siam will declare war on Germany soon, very soon. Papa talked to Herr Ethelbert, the railroad construction engineer, and he has heard the same."

"What will happen to us?"

"I don't know," Max said, but then hastened to reassure her. "We'll be fine, Mama, don't you worry." He pressed her hand in his as he saw her eyes fill with tears. An agonizing fear for her sons was already rising in her breast.

* * *

A day earlier, Ethelbert had spoken to Franz as the two sat in the hotel dining room. The man's face seemed more deeply lined than ever; he moved about in his chair nervously.

"It's become a trench war in France and Belgium," he said. "The armies repeatedly advance, then retreat, getting nowhere. Millions of soldiers are being killed and wounded; the poor unfortunates are forced to drop back into the trenches from what the newspapers have named 'no man's land' in between, desperately attempting to escape monstrous artillery bombardments and deadly machine gun fire."

"Gas attacks, too, I hear," Franz said morosely.

"It's incredible."

Franz raised a glass to his lips, sipping ruby-red wine slowly as he reflected on Ethelbert's grim words. "Yes, it sounds bad. Have you heard from your wife?" he asked, recalling that the engineer's family resided in Berlin.

"She writes there are severe food shortages because of the Allied blockade and that rationing will start soon." The mention of his wife seemed to release a torrent of self-condemnation because he rushed on fiercely. "Franz, my work here has left my family alone, defenseless; I feel so guilty. I've tried to get passage, somehow, out of Bangkok, but authorities are uncooperative. I think Siam is ready to declare war on Germany. In that case, we are sure to be interned; heaven knows what they'll do with us." He looked weary, his face pale beneath his deep tan.

"Oh, my friend," Franz said. "You mustn't feel like that. We've been caught up in world events over which we have no control, that's all. I'm sure your wife understands that."

"Maybe so, maybe so ... but that doesn't help her, does it? We are trapped here, and she must suffer the consequences. And it's simply because I yearned to work in exotic countries. I could have stayed in Europe; there was work for me, and I would be there now to help her and my daughters."

The conversation had degenerated into a storm of self-reproach that caused Franz discomfort, striking so closely, as it did, to his own suppressed feelings of guilt troubling him in past days. He gazed at Ethelbert; they were so much alike, he thought, in their desires. Discovery and knowledge. The dreams they shared in walking the paths of history had brought them both to this time and place. He sighed deeply; no sense in condemning himself as Ethelbert was doing. If his family had stayed in Europe, he rationalized, they might be in danger and want, and his sons could be serving in the German army, if not already dead in battle. What would happen to them here in this part of the world was in God's hands.

"Aaah, we can't do anything about it, Ethelbert," he said. "We must make the best of it. Your wife is probably more worried about you. There must be some place she can go and be safe."

The engineer nodded. Yes, admittedly she could go to her sister's farm in the country. He then suggested they have another drink, feeling much better after venting his concerns.

* * *

The insanity of a world entangled in the passions of war was eventually to penetrate the confines of the Hotel Europa. It was the orchestra itself, under Franz's direction, that fostered a melee of gigantic proportions.

Madam Streit had suggested that the Linden orchestra play the national anthems of the nations participating in Europe's conflict at the close of each evening's performance. She reasoned it was proper to do so—every diner present should honor and respect all countries involved, regardless of their private convictions. Franz thought her philosophy was a bit flawed; she had failed to take into consideration the untempered state of human relations in wartime.

The evening had commenced quietly enough. It was one of Bangkok's more oppressively humid nights, and though ceiling fans in the dining room turned ceaselessly in an attempt to cool the muggy air, they did little to make the area comfortable. Perhaps the unrelenting heat helped fire the tempest that followed, or possibly wireless reports from the Western Front, listing deaths and casualties in much greater numbers. Maybe both.

By nine o'clock the room was crowded with the usual mix of Europeans: Austrian, German, French, Italian, a sprinkling of Slavs, and one table of British officers. Lorenzo shared his customary table with friends.

"Papa wants me to dance with others tonight, Lorenzo," Elena whispered as she walked to the orchestra platform. "It's too crowded for us to enjoy it, anyway."

As the evening progressed, a curious unrest in the behavior of the guests became apparent. They were noisy, and wine and beer flowed steadily. Madam Streit stood in the doorway, her face beaming as she surveyed the room. The night's receipts would stuff her cash box. Veiled insults being traded back and forth between tables of German and French patrons escaped her notice. The hostility spread to the congested dance floor when Elena accepted an invitation to dance with a German maritime officer, resplendent in his white uniform. All was well until he collided with a bearded Frenchman dancing with his wife. The resulting foul language between the men appalled Elena. Adjacent dancers joined in, taking sides, then pushing and shoving, spewing forth more obscenities like a river of bile. Elena, dwarfed by the tall, broad-chested men surrounding her, was flung from pillar to post as the group scuffled, until a strong hand grasped her arm and pulled her to safety. She looked up to see Lorenzo.

"Let me get you back to the platform," he said, escorting her through the crowd. "I think it's going to be a wild night."

Franz called a break, and the room quieted momentarily. "No more dancing for the ladies," he stated tersely. As the minutes passed, the unruly atmosphere again began to escalate. The orchestra members exchanged uneasy glances. Madam Streit, now alerted to the possibility of trouble, watched from her seat at the cashier desk, her eyes darting nervously from table to table. The tension rose; drinking accelerated.

Closing time finally arrived, and as the first national anthem was played, the solemnity of the music seemed to temporarily have a calming effect on the diners. On previous occasions, politeness had reigned; all guests had stood in sedate respect as the orchestra performed, but this evening they were obstinate, standing for their own nation's song of allegiance, then sitting down in their chairs defiantly for those they opposed. Germans and Austrians glared at French and British, each barely able to contain the smoldering anger and rage that had been building all evening.

Elena sat behind her drums and cymbals, her attention on her grim-faced father before her. Pulsing fury seemed to be circulating about their heads like the eye of a hurricane. Then it happened. She gasped as she saw several males from nearby tables abruptly rise from their seats and lunge toward each other, furiously pummeling and jabbing. A roar rose from their friends and all jumped enthusiastically into the fray.

Elena struck the cymbals involuntarily in terror; the clanging crash going unnoticed by Franz, lost in the din of the chaos that followed. He frowned, urging the band to continue playing. He flashed them three fingers, which signaled the musicians to switch from the French anthem they were playing to a lively polka. He had found in his past experience that changing to a merry tune sometimes had been an effective pacifying measure in times of crisis. This time it was futile.

Glancing back from the podium, he saw the dining room had been transformed from orderly placed tables around the dance floor to an arena of battle. Tables and chairs were being violently overturned; crockery, china, and glassware slid crashing to the polished floor as the infuriated men and women clashed. The usually moderate, restrained ladies and gentlemen, with whom Franz had frequently shared drinks and conversation, were now caught up in the insanity of the moment. The entire assembled group had become a seething mass of humanity intent upon exterminating themselves, just as their brethren in Europe were currently engaged in doing.

Elena felt the walls and floor shake and tremble with the impact of warring bodies and flying wine bottles. The brass chandelier hanging from the center of the ceiling swayed precariously. She searched frantically for a glimpse of Lorenzo in the crowd, finally spotting his familiar figure in the midst of the throng. When she recognized that he was under attack, she screamed, and, without thinking, started to leave the platform. Max stopped her roughly, and he and Schenck dashed forward to help their beleaguered friend. Franz threw up his hands in disgust as the young men leaped with gusto into battle.

The melee ceased as abruptly as it had started. Madam Streit had called for help from Bangkok's police authorities, and they had stormed into the building, restoring order in record time. As the still hostile patrons were herded out of the dining room, they continued to hurl insulting epithets at each other. The police prodded them with clubs, promising stronger disciplinary measures if they didn't behave. The hotel manager stood in the middle of the dance floor after the room was finally emptied, looking about her in disbelief. The band members silently gathered sheet music and enclosed instruments in their cases. They walked out slowly, exchanging few words; the electrifying events of the evening leaving them stunned and incredulous. Franz stopped before his employer, feeling compassion for her.

"I'm sorry, Madam Streit," he said. "I'm afraid the war has come to us."

"Yes," she said faintly. "It's hard to believe people's emotions can get so far out of control." She waved her hand feebly toward the debris-laden floor, "I don't know who's going to pay for all this." Her normally cool, self-possessed manner had deserted her for the moment; but then taking a deep breath, she straightened her thin, bowed shoulders, and smoothed back the strands of hair that had escaped from hairpins. "We'll have everything back in place and repaired before tomorrow night's performance, Herr Linden, and I'll see that we have some men about, so as not to have a repeat of tonight's brawl." Franz nodded, preparing to withdraw, when she added, an unaccustomed spark of humor in her voice, "And, oh, please discontinue the playing of national anthems from now on."

The three sisters lay on their beds later, too unsettled by the evening's excitement to sleep.

"Papa was absolutely furious with Max and Schenck," Mitzi cackled. "'How many times have I warned you not to become involved in a fight!'" he roared. I thought he would die of apoplexy when he saw both of them with those black eyes. His face was as red as Elena's hair."

"They were only trying to help Lorenzo," Elena said. "Otherwise, they would have stayed out of it."

"Maybe," Lise said doubtfully. "That Schenck is always full of beans; he went and Max followed, like a faithful puppy dog."

They giggled at the picture her words presented in their minds. Aside from the sober side of the fracas, the evening did have some humorous aspects.

"When that French woman fell over backwards into the mess, the whole orchestra got a firsthand view of her lacy Paris underwear," Mitzi said, squealing with laughter. "And she couldn't right herself, her legs were flailing helplessly. Poor Braun's eyes were bulging out of their sockets at the sight."

"And did you see that man grabbing half-full bottles of wine from the tables, sitting cozily in a corner with them, draining every last drop?" Lise said, giggling. "All this commotion going on, and he was sublimely oblivious to the whole thing."

"I think he was soused, Lise, or soon would be," Mitzi laughed. "Oh, if we don't stop this ... I'm going to wet myself." She wiped away tears from her cheeks. They all felt a release from the evening's tension that had gripped them; laughter was healing. "I wonder if Madam Streit saw the man drinking her liquor."

"I didn't see him," Elena said.

"All you saw was Lorenzo," remarked Lise dryly. "Which reminds me, Elena ... I've been meaning to ask you ... exactly what are his intentions, anyway? He spends a great deal of time with you and it's easy to see that you are mad about him." She had a knack for getting to the heart of the matter.

Elena gasped, her face reddening. Was she so transparent, she thought, that her fondness for Lorenzo was there for the whole world to see? "Really, Lise," she insisted, "we're only good friends."

"Of course," her sister said, raising her eyebrows as she smiled at Mitzi, "only friends."

CHAPTER TWELVE

Prisoners Of War

In the days following the furor in the hotel dining room, news reports from war-torn Europe, coupled with rumors of Siam's declaration of war against Germany, were topics of somber discussions by family and orchestra members at the lunch and dinner table. Franz advised a wait-and-see attitude, attempting to downplay any worries his wife and daughters might be experiencing. He knew, however, that it was fruitless to expect the young men to be calm about their position. Tension was building.

"What's worse?" young Braun asked, the color of his rosy complexion heightened by the excitement he felt. "Soldiering in battle, or internment in a black hole somewhere?"

"Either way," Schenck answered placidly, "death is possible, or maybe even inevitable."

"Nice thought," Max said dourly.

"Then why don't we try to get away from here," Braun urged, "escape to Germany somehow, and rally to the cause!"

"What cause," Schenck snorted. "I only fight when confronted by an enemy, and I have no other choice, or perhaps," he paused to wink at Max, "to help a friend. I don't go looking for a war for glory's sake."

"But ... then you're not very patriotic, Schenck, are you? Don't you see that Germany needs us?"

Schenck rolled his eyes upward impatiently. "Germany needs stupid young fellows like you, Braun, not me."

Braun lunged forward angrily towards Schenck, but Max intervened, saying brusquely, "That's enough; let's not fight each other." He glanced at Deigelmeier who had been silent throughout the heated exchange. They traded strained smiles.

The men had been in the garden arbor, and now separated, Braun taking off in a huff, Schenck ambling along, unconcerned. Deigelmeier kept pace with Max on the path.

"Max," the modest musician said, his eyes darting nervously to Max's face and away again. "I … I think about where we might be imprisoned. Aren't you just a bit afraid of what can happen to us?"

"I'd be crazy not to be," Max said, "but I worry more about what will happen to my parents and sisters, Deigelmeier; they are helpless."

Deigelmeier leaned forward earnestly. "Ask anything of me, Max, I'll help any way I can. Mitzi is a beautiful girl." He quickly amended his slip, "I mean … all your sisters are lovely. Anything I can do, just say the word."

Max glanced curiously at the painfully shy man. So that's the way it was, he thought; the poor fellow cared for his sister Mitzi, and she thought him colorless and uninteresting.

Max had other worries—Camille. She was anxious, complained of having no protector. She was alone. His father advised against making a commitment, and Lise distrusted her.

"Camille embraces and fondles you at every opportunity," Lise said to him, "like a vine that strangles the host tree."

Her words made him uncomfortable; he knew this was not the time to marry in haste, but he was drawn to the girl like no other. She kept him in a constant state of longing and desire. In another time he would have asked her to marry him, but now ….

"We should get married, Max," she urged that very evening. "Then we can't be separated, ever."

"You know I'd like nothing more, Camille … but …."

"Why not?"

"Everything is too unpredictable now."

"Oh, Max," she said provocatively, "don't you want me?" Her breath came in little pants. "Come to the arbor tonight; we can make love." She moved his hand so that it cupped her breast, her eyes promising more.

His pulse quickened at the thought—she had never been as bold before—but he held back. "Camille, I have the family to think of; it's just not the two of us to consider."

"Lise!" she exploded. "It's Lise, she hates me!"

"No, it's not Lise; it's the family, the war."

"All everyone talks about is the war, I'm sick to death of it." She turned and walked away from him, her face dark with anger. He'll come tonight, she thought, and I'll persuade him.

* * *

The world could easily have spun off its axis, careening full throttle into outer space, but it's doubtful Elena would have noticed. Over the past months she had been caught up in an exhilarating romance with Lorenzo. For the romantic young girl, all thoughts of the approaching maelstrom on the horizon were eclipsed by the days and evenings spent with the architect. Dancing with him was a virtual sensual experience; she was intoxicated by the nearness of him, the aroma of his after-shave lotion, the touch of his hand on her back as he guided her about the dance floor. His searching kisses in the dark of the garden sent voluptuous tremors racing throughout her body.

Lorenzo felt her ardor. He had long since surrendered his heart to her. One evening during orchestra break they strolled arm in arm in the garden; soft rays of moonlight filtering through tall palms overhead. He gazed at her fondly, rehearsing in his mind what he was about to say to her. "Elena, I have something to tell you," he said. "These past months have been the happiest I've ever known, and it's because ... well ... it's because of you. I've fallen in love with you."

"Lorenzo!" Elena whirled about to face him, her eyes shining. She kissed him wildly in youthful rapture. "Oh ... oh, I had hoped so much ... I love you, too, Lorenzo."

"No ... wait, let me finish, we must talk. I'm fourteen years older than you, Elena, and your father was at first dead set against the match."

Her face fell. "He didn't say anything to me."

"No ... we spoke after the first time I called on you. Remember ... the ants?"

She smiled. "So now he has changed his mind," she said brightly, " and we can be married?"

He hesitated, frowning. "There's more, my *piccola*, my little one," he said. "Let's sit in the arbor, and I'll explain." He took her in his arms as they sat, kissing her hair tenderly.

"Lorenzo," she began restlessly, "why ...?"

"Listen ... you know what the situation is in Europe now. Under other circumstances we could have married, and I would have taken you back with me to Italy. We'll have to wait. You see ... today I received my commission and I leave in two days to join the army in Italy."

She was stunned, speechless for a moment. "The army?" she croaked, staring unbelievingly at him. "But ... why can't you stay here in Bangkok?"

"It isn't that simple, Elena," he said patiently. "My work here is completed and my visa expires soon. Besides, it's my duty to go and fight for my country."

The guns of war had destroyed her paradise. She mentally reviewed the news stories she had read regarding trench warfare, and her heart sank. It had been so easy for her to blot out from her mind the horrors of battle in Europe. It was so far away—but not far enough. She looked at Lorenzo; his refined and gentlemanly manner was so ill-suited to the rigors and terror of combat, and yet he felt the need to fight. Why were men so eager to put their lives on the line for their countries, as though it were a grand adventure? Naïve young men like Braun she could understand; he might perceive war to be an exciting undertaking. But Lorenzo ... he was older ... and wiser? Her lips tightened and resentment began to build in her heart. She felt anger and frustration sweeping through her body, along with an unbearable fear for the safety of her beloved. Breathing heavily, her bitterness erupted in a passion of released fury. She stood up abruptly.

"Why do you have to go to war?" she blazed. Startled, Lorenzo rose to face her as she continued. "I'm sure you can arrange to stay here in Bangkok with me, if you really love me. Lorenzo, if you go, I know we'll never see each other again." Her face was flushed with a heat that even moonlight failed to dim "I ... I didn't think you'd be like all the others, Braun especially, eager to wear a uniform and march off. But Braun is young, Lorenzo, and you're old!"

Lorenzo blanched at the inference. "Elena, be reasonable," he pleaded, "it's my country, my duty. I must go."

"Well, go! Go then!"

"Elena," he said, attempting to embrace her, but she broke away, blindly rushing to the hotel, tears now coursing down her cheeks. Disconsolately, he watched her disappearing figure. Tomorrow, he thought, I'll see her tomorrow.

* * *

The morrow brought the news all had been dreading to hear. Deigelmeier had torn away a large poster he had spied on the wall of a building during an early morning walk. He unrolled the paper with trembling hands before the gathered group at breakfast in the dining room.

"SIAM DECLARES WAR AGAINST GERMANY!"

It was late July 1917. Those who were able to read English gazed at the bold black letters in horror for a moment before translating for the others; then all spoke at once as the full import of their situation struck them. Marta's eyes first rested on Max, her throat tightening with fear for him, then met Franz's in mutual anxiety. He shook his head, pressing his lips hard together. Hotel patrons caught sight of the poster, and soon the room was humming with excitement.

Elena sat motionless, her face tired and drawn. She had spent a sleepless night agonizing over her quarrel with Lorenzo. The rush of voices buzzing about her ears went unheeded. Only the thought that she might never see him again seemed important at the moment. So absorbed was she in her torment that she started when Lise, seated next to her at the table, poked her shoulder and indicated an agitated Lorenzo standing in the doorway of the dining room. Max rose at the sight of their friend, and both he and Elena retired to the lobby with Lorenzo, the men shaking hands briefly.

"It looks bad," Lorenzo said, voice hushed. "I read in the *Daily Mail* this morning that all Germans and Austrians will be interned immediately. I'm worried about you, Max." He paused, glancing uneasily at Elena. "I'm leaving tomorrow. I wish now that I would be here awhile yet, just to see that Elena and your family will be safe."

"I'll take care of them, Lorenzo. You're the one we're concerned about, being in the middle of things in Europe."

"Yes, but be careful, Max, watch yourself. You've been a good friend, not many men would have jumped into a fight to help me as you did in the dining room scrap." He smiled at the memory, and Max smiled sheepishly in return. "Well ... I must leave, I don't have much time ...." He paused, glancing at the pale-faced girl beside them. "I did want to say goodbye to Elena." The young men parted with a hearty handshake, and Max returned to the dining room where an anxious Camille awaited him.

Elena stood stiffly, awkwardly, her shadowed eyes gazing soulfully at Lorenzo as he turned to her. He put his arm around her shoulders and led her out to the veranda.

"Elena," he started, but she cut in.

"No, Lorenzo; let me say how sorry I am about last night ... I don't know what came over me. First you say you love me and want to marry me, and in the next moment, I hear that you're going to war."

"I didn't think my news would be so hotly received," he said wryly. "I did learn redheads have a temper, a fact well hidden these past months."

"I'm sorry," she said. "Forgive me ... and Lorenzo ... I don't think you're 'old,' I only said that ...."

"No matter ... I wanted to talk to you about that anyway." He took her hands in his, gazing into her anxious eyes. "Elena, you are very young. When we meet again, you may have changed your mind about marrying me, and I understand that."

"I'd marry you right now ... if it were possible ...."

He smiled. "I'm afraid we'll have to wait until the war's over, my *piccola*. Meanwhile we'll write." He paused, his face wistful. "I'd planned to give you this last night," he said, as he slipped a slender gold ring on her ring finger. "Wear it for me."

She burst into tears looking down at the ring, then hugged him tightly. "It's beautiful. Lorenzo, I'll never take it off." She clung to him desperately as he held her close, kissing her lips, her eyes, and cheeks that tasted salty with her tears. "Don't go," she sobbed as he finally pulled regretfully away from her.

"I must," he said, lifting her hand to his lips. He turned and was gone.

She dropped into a chair feeling weak and drained of emotion; sobs still wracking her breast. Oh, Lorenzo, she thought, I don't even have a photograph of you. Rudy would have taken a photo of you if he were here. Where was Rudy? Had he already been interned in Japan? Prisoner of war ... such harsh-sounding words.

By that afternoon, she had the answer to Rudy's whereabouts, but so much had transpired in a short time, she scarcely took notice until late in the evening. The poignant parting with Lorenzo was overshadowed swiftly by grim news imparted by Madam Streit to the orchestra members and other German nationals staying at the hotel. A Siamese official stood alongside the hotel manager, prompting her in his own language, as she spoke to them in the dining room.

"Siamese authorities contacted me this morning," she said, her worn face reflecting the strain she'd been under. Elena had observed a party of men enter her office—stiff, formal, Siamese officiaries, and British officers—carrying a myriad of papers and documents. "They'll be here this afternoon," she continued, "to check all passports; please have all papers ready. All military-age men are advised to pack their belongings, only as much as they themselves can carry, and be ready to leave the hotel tomorrow at four in the morning for transport to an internment camp."

Rushed questions were thrown at her in unison as she paused, but she raised her voice testily. "I don't know where the men will be taken. I presume you'll be told this afternoon. As for the older men … the women and children … for the time being, you will be confined to the hotel premises, along with other German nationals who will be brought here from other parts of the city for internment."

Max attempted to soothe the women of the family. The sight of his mother's tear-stained face, Elena's numbed appearance, and Lise and Mitzi's frantic questions tore at his heartstrings. Camille stood on the fringe of the group, fear and reproach written on her face. His powerlessness and guilt at the thought of leaving them to an unknown fate overwhelmed him, his own destiny forgotten for the moment.

"I'll be fine, Mama," he said, striving to ease her worry for him. "Papa will see that you're all taken care of. Before we know it, we'll be together again in Bucharest," he said, echoing the last words Rudy had spoken before leaving for Japan. Franz nodded in assent, though the expression on his face belied any such hope in the near future.

Later, the family gathered in Max's room after the evening meal, Marta helping him to pack his bag. Her eyes were red from weeping. She tucked family photographs in between layers of underclothes, then hunted frantically for a warm woolen sweater she knew was at the bottom of his wardrobe closet, one she had knitted for him in Bucharest.

They reviewed the day's events gloomily while she worked. Checking passports had taken an interminable amount of time; the lines long in the hotel dining room, as more and more internees arrived to be processed and billeted in the establishment. A heated discussion ensued over whether Max would be allowed to take his bass fiddle. Permission was finally granted with strict orders that he be able to carry the instrument as well as his bag.

Franz had spotted Ethelbert in line and, after a brief conversation, reported to Marta that the engineer was to be taken to a camp in Trial Bay, Australia. "The poor man is still worried about his family, and the unfinished railway he's been supervising," Franz told her. Deigelmeier and Schenck, also slated for departure in the morning, joined the family: Schenck joking as usual, slapping Max on the back companionably; Deigelmeier quiet and withdrawn. Braun was visibly excited as he shook Franz's hand in farewell. Elena sat on a chair, saying little, her eyes following Max as he walked to and fro contributing items for his mother to pack. Seeing the torment she suffered, he patted her shoulder compassionately, murmuring consoling words.

They talked of Rudy. A letter had arrived that afternoon amid the chaos in the hotel. Japanese authorities had deported the red-haired musician, advising him to take the first ship out of Yokohama or be interned.

"So," Franz said, relieved. "Rudy is safe in America, in San Francisco. He writes that he had no difficulty entering the country."

Elena nodded. "He speaks English well."

"But what happens if America declares war on Germany?" Marta asked.

Franz shrugged. "Better to be in America than Japan."

"Or Siam," Lise added glumly. "Rudy advises us to come to America."

They looked at each other dismally, reflecting on the events of the day. They were trapped. Sighing heavily, Franz wrote Rudy's address on a small card for Max to insert into his billfold.

Emotional farewells were said that evening, Elena hugging Max tightly. Franz, ordinarily so stern and reserved, first shook hands with his son, but then embraced him, his eyes damp. Max managed a reassuring smile under his drooping mustache. He took his mother and sisters in his arms in turn as they cautioned him about dangers he might be facing. They gave him one last kiss, and all retired with promises to write when addresses were available. No one slept very much that night; Marta clutched her rosary beads praying for her sons.

Elena wandered through the hotel lobby the next morning, several hours after it had been emptied of Germany and Austria's young manhood, who had left with a minimum of noise or fuss. She had opened the door of her room a crack and noted their serious faces as they walked down the hallway, perhaps as they would look going to war, wondering what was in store for them.

She sat in a chair and contemplated the ceiling fan as it turned, her mind in a turmoil of dread and apprehension after the previous day's events. Lorenzo and her brothers ... gone from her life. The delightful and humorous Schenck she would miss, and also shy Deigelmeier and young Braun. Tears threatened to flow again. Did she pity the men, or herself? Both perhaps. She feared for them, feared the unknown—Lorenzo in Italy, Rudy in San Francisco, and Max, it was learned, to Australia. And what was to become of her parents, sisters, and, mainly, herself?

Well, she thought, back to my room. There would be no orchestra rehearsal ... ever again. As she passed the hotel entrance, she was brought up short by the sight of a uniformed guard, rifle in hand, stationed outside the door.

CHAPTER THIRTEEN

Close Quarters

Several weeks had passed since Max and Lorenzo departed. The family had settled into the stressful life of imprisonment as best they could. A harried Madam Streit strode through the hotel hallways each day, doing her utmost to quell the constant complaints of an unhappy group of internees crowded together in rooms intended to accommodate two or three guests, now packed with military cots barely inches apart. The Hotel Europa was not a large building; the almost two hundred and fifty men, women, and children being housed there stretched the establishment's facilities to its limits, and then some.

Heat and humidity made closeness unbearable. Bathing and toilet facilities, which were of minimum quality before, being akin to the conveniences at Singapore's Grand Continental Hotel, were overtaxed and difficult to keep sanitary. The Siamese government had acquiesced to Madam Streit's pleas for extra servants, but the workers were unreliable, often failing to appear at all.

The detainees were expected to keep their quarters neat and clean; however, mothers with small children found doing laundry an impossible task. They paid native women to wash their clothes in the nearby *klong* out of their limited funds, and others followed suit. No one was allowed outside the hotel, not even onto the grounds. At mealtimes, Marta noted that food served in the dining room was adequate but certainly not the excellent cuisine offered before war was declared.

Lobby and dining rooms were used as lounges for the group. Magazines and newspapers were passed around, as well as books and games for the children. Franz spent afternoons getting acquainted with the other older men. Latest news reports became a daily subject for round-table discussion by physicians, businessmen, and merchants. At other times, card games and chess occupied them. Letters from unfortunate friends and relatives who had lived in Java, China, and Malaysia were shared.

"Let me tell you what happened to my cousin; he lived in Java," said the robust Captain Baumgartner. "I'll read part of his letter ...."

It's hard to believe that something like this can happen to one! I'm prisoner of war here in Australia. I was rounded up with other Germans from Singapore, Hong Kong, Ceylon, Fiji, and the German colonies. Every day there are new arrivals in the camp. I have breakfast in the company of government officials, masters of ships like yourself and their officers, plantation owners, and missionaries. I play cards with clergymen, traders, merchants, businessmen, laborers, and adventurers. I talk to German Buddhist monks in their traditional yellow robes. Last night some Germans arrived who had been visiting friends in Singapore, only to be detained and sent here; they don't know what happened to their wives ....

"My sister, too!" interrupted Vogel, the physician. "She and her husband were on a cruise ship; he was whisked off to Australia, leaving her stranded in Singapore. She wrote to me for help, but all I could do was send her money. I don't know where Marlene is now." He shook his head.

"At least we have our families here with us," one man said, "though there are many young women among us with husbands in Australia. The Siamese brought them all here to the hotel, not leaving them to fend for themselves as the British have done. The British confiscated their homes and possessions, or the women were forced to sell everything just to survive without their husbands."

"Marlene appealed to the Australians to intern her along with her man," Dr. Vogel said. "They claimed they have no facilities for women, but are studying the matter. Can't have all these women and children floating about the South China Sea without any means of support. There is no way for them to get back to Germany. It's just too cruel and inhuman."

Franz listened to these accounts with foreboding. Suppose he was forcibly separated from Marta and his daughters—what would they do?

* * *

Elena felt an aching loneliness in her heart for the absent Lorenzo, for Max. Every morning she waited for mail delivery, hoping for a letter from one of them. There was none. With Madam Streit's permission, she turned to her other love, the piano in the lobby. Lightly stroking the keys diverted her mind for an hour or so. Mitzi and Lise soon pulled up chairs and joined her with their violins, and they played lighthearted selections together.

Franz's ears caught the sound of their music as he sat in the dining room. Marta looked up from the chair she occupied in the lobby, as Franz walked slowly toward the girls, his violin strings singing sweet and mellow. Her eyes filled with tears as murmurs of appreciation arose from the women and children assembled. The concert that followed gave the small, low-spirited audience cheer, and they clapped heartily at its end.

"Well done," Franz whispered to his daughters. "And Elena, you've come far in your playing. We must see that you receive lessons when we return home to Romania."

Elena nodded. Her father chose to ignore the fact that she'd be going to Italy, not Bucharest, at war's end. She wondered whether he hoped she would change her mind about marrying Lorenzo after being long separated. She smiled. It was a crafty move on his part—giving his approval to the marriage, and letting time and events decide the outcome.

A blonde-haired young woman attracted Elena's attention as she played the piano each day. She sat in the lobby listening to the music, two small children beside her. Both the boy and girl had blue eyes and light tresses, but the skin on their chubby faces was colored a golden brown. In subsequent conversations, Elena learned the woman, named Lotti, was married to a Siamese businessman. Lotti was being ostracized by the other German women in the hotel because of her "indiscreet" choice of a spouse.

"I'm suspended between two worlds," Lotti explained. "The Bangkok German community didn't invite me into their social groups, and the Siamese friends and family of my husband avoided me also. Now I find myself interned because I'm German."

"But ... but that's so unfair," Elena said indignantly. "How can people be so narrow-minded?"

Lotti shrugged. "My father tried to warn me, but I was in love."

Elena, though not ignorant of the racial discrimination practiced in Southeast Asia, was yet incensed by the cruel treatment suffered by Lotti. She attempted to cheer and encourage her new friend. "These women, the 'Bangkok elite,' looked down on me and my sisters, too, Lotti," she said. "We weren't worthy of being included in their circle because we were members of the orchestra and danced with the hotel guests. In their eyes we are disreputable."

She paused, her eyes flashing impetuously. "But do you know what?" she continued, snapping her fingers, "I don't want to be in their old circle, anyway. They are a boring lot, especially that fat, sanctimonious Frau Langst."

Lotti was quiet for a moment, then smiled. "You can ignore them because you'll eventually move on. I have to live here, Elena."

"Yes, you're right," Elena said, sighing. "And we do have to get along with them while we're prisoners. I don't know what the answer is, but ... let's not let them bother us now."

When Lotti and her children were unexpectedly released into her husband's custody, she and Elena embraced warmly, promising to write to each other. Lotti pressed a photograph of herself and the children into Elena's hand as she left, saying earnestly, "I hope all will be well with you and your family." She laughed when Elena remarked there were no Germans left in Bangkok to plague her.

Elena felt dispirited for several days after Lotti's departure, but the arrival of a postcard from Max was cause for rejoicing. The girls and their mother pressed close around Franz as he read Max's brief message aloud.

Dear Family,

    I'm sorry we can't be together this coming Christmas, but it can't be helped. Some of the other musicians and Schenck and I have formed a small orchestra. They are very good. It keeps us busy. I hope you are all well. I wish you happy holidays.

                Your loving son and brother, Max

"At least he arrived at the camp safely," Franz said, sighing, and the women nodded gravely. They hadn't even thought about the Christmas season coming soon. No one expected to do much celebrating.

Several days later a card came for Elena. Taped across the written message was printed in English, "Transmission of Postcards not Permitted." Did that mean she wasn't to send a card? She managed to read the words Max had written under the tape, and they brought tears to her eyes.

Dear Elena,

    I miss you very much. Now that you have my address, please write a letter to me. Fond kisses for you. Love to Mama and Papa, and the girls.

                    Your loving brother, Max

The return address was Liverpool, Australia. The face of the card pictured a statue of Queen Victoria in a place called Kings Park, Perth, Western Australia. Elena hastened to fetch her writing materials, starting a letter that very moment.

* * *

The next few months passed excruciatingly slowly for the group of prisoners in the hotel. News reports of European battles kept the men in constant contention with discussions sometimes lasting well into the night. The defeat of Serbia by Austrian-Hungarian forces was debated with particular interest by Franz and Dr. Vogel.

"The Serbs have retreated to Corfu," Franz said, as they traced the route on world maps that had been mounted on the dining room wall, much to Madam Streit's displeasure.

"An estimated one hundred and fifty thousand soldiers were taken to safety," Vogel added. The small energetic man peered through his spectacles intently. "And look here, the Russians have retreated, too."

"They were not really armed, but their spirits were high, Doctor, and they were still a match for the Austrians," Franz said. "Had the Germans not come to the Austrians' rescue, the Russians might have prevailed. Really, I couldn't believe this when I read it; it's reported that two million Russian lives were lost ... two million! And another million taken prisoner." Franz's expression was suddenly contemplative as he continued. "We must never underestimate the Russians; Napoleon made that mistake."

"It's madness, just plain madness," the doctor said, shaking his head in anger, "all those lives lost. The Kaiser's actions precipitated this war with all his blunders." He rapped his knuckles on the map in frustration. "That stupid man raised Britain's suspicion when he built up Germany's naval power and supported Austria's ambitions in the Balkans—all Europe was ready to pounce on him." At this point, Vogel continued excitedly, "There have been food riots in Berlin, I hear. The Allied blockade has been very successful ... and can you believe, gas attacks in the trenches! Herr Linden, do you know what gas will do to a man's lungs? Searing, burning agony, and blindness, too, that's what. Disgraceful! What has happened to honor in war?"

Before Franz could muster a reply, Elena's inflamed voice interrupted suddenly. Her body was rigid, feet planted firmly before the group of men, her face flushed. "From what I've read, Papa," she said, "the men of this world were quite willing—yes, eager—to volunteer to fight in this war, on both sides. They couldn't wait to show their patriotism and honor, without the slightest inkling of the horror awaiting ...."

"Now, Elena," her father interjected, "I think you've been reading too much. I'm surprised at you, intruding this way ...."

"Papa, you must forgive me, but I think this war is a farce," she said hotly, forgetting the usual quiet respect she held for her father. "I've listened to the men talking, they follow the reports of battle as though it were all one big game ... you and Dr. Vogel, too!" Her eyes blazed accusingly, bitterness rising like bile in her throat.

"No ... no, my dear, that isn't true." Franz said cajolingly. "Listen, Elena, I think you're upset, not by the war itself, but by the fact that your sweetheart and brother are unlucky victims of the conflict, as we are ourselves, and I appreciate that. But you must also calm down and try to accept that which we're powerless to change."

Franz's words were kindly spoken, but Elena's eyes filled with tears, and she turned away. How could grown men not see the absurdity of it all? she thought.

Her father watched as she hurried away, frowning. "You must excuse my daughter, Dr. Vogel. She is the most sensitive of my girls ... maybe too much so."

"I think she is a very likeable young lady," Vogel said. "A trifle emotional right now, but none of us are exactly ourselves these days." He filed his habitual medical appraisal away in his mind; she was small, firm, shapely, and healthy, with beautiful hair and complexion.

In a week's time, Dr. Vogel found himself to be a very busy man. Crowding the internees together in the hotel spelled trouble. He'd feared from the outset that to detain so many persons in close quarters would lead to illness among the prisoners. The possibility came closer when the rains came, flooding the Chao Phraya River, the main waterway in the city. Ever vigilant, Lise reported to the doctor in irate tones that she'd observed the kitchen help washing dishes in the overflowing *klong* at the rear of the hotel. He was further disquieted when she added they had blithely used the same cloths for cleaning the lavatory and kitchen surfaces. Cases of dysentery soon erupted among the internees and, unhappily, Elena fell prey to the disease.

Anyone who has experienced the distress of diarrhea can well sympathize with the dysentery patient, but the disease is ten times worse in terms of pain and suffering and, very possibly, death. Elena felt as though her entrails were being torn out from within her. Again, and again, and again. Cramps convulsed her, she vomited up any food offered, and her body became weak and tortured from the unrelenting compulsion to void. Lise and Mitzi nursed her faithfully, cooling her hot fevered face and chest with wet compresses and administering fluids per Dr. Vogel's instruction. "We must avoid dehydration," he warned. Discarded water from cooked rice was prescribed to help bind the intestines.

To the concerned parents, the doctor waxed eloquently on the place of dysentery in world history. "The incidence of dysentery in Europe has greatly decreased because of better sanitary conditions," he said, "but here in Bangkok ...." He shook his head. "When you have so many people packed together ... It's a waterborne disease, human excrement is the main pollutant. Do you know that in the time of the Crusades, the Christian knights were killed more efficiently by dysentery than by Saracen warriors? And both Edward the Ist and Henry the Vth of England died of dysentery." He paused significantly. "Yes, it can be fatal."

"But, Doctor," Franz asked impatiently, "will Elena be alright?"

"Oh yes ... yes, of course, she'll be fine. I'll see to that. Proper care will heal her in no time."

Gradually, Elena began to improve, but not to Dr. Vogel's satisfaction. The ravages of the illness had thinned her formerly sound, wholesome body so that she appeared gaunt. "A ghost of herself," her father lamented. Her family recognized that her delayed recovery was impeded by the depression she suffered—there was no word from Lorenzo. Lise and Mitzi hastened to attribute the lack of correspondence to the wartime delay of mail delivery, but Elena became increasingly despondent as days passed and she had not received as much as a postcard.

"She's literally pining away," Marta deplored. "Her frail body will just fade away to nothing if she doesn't hear from that Italian soon." Her usually bright eyes were clouded with anxiety. "Franz, I'm afraid for her; she doesn't eat."

"He'll write, Marta. Be patient. After all, you can imagine the conditions in a country at war."

Franz visited Elena each morning, his attempts at cheerfulness going seemingly unnoticed by his listless daughter. She smiled wanly at him from her chair, but soon turned her head away to the window, gazing absently into space. Her lustrous, wavy hair that had appeared alive, electric in its crimson beauty before her illness, now fell about her pale, pinched face in colorless strands, as if the locks themselves grieved for their mistress.

* * *

Disturbing rumors circulated in the hotel concerning the fate of the internees. Franz and Marta were troubled at the thought of Elena being forced to travel to another place of internment, when she was not yet recovered from the dysentery.

"Yes, it's true," Madam Streit said to Franz as he sat in her airless office. "Tomorrow the British will inform us of plans to send all of you to camps ... heaven knows where. There are several of them, I think."

Franz frowned. "So soon? We were hoping it would be awhile yet. Elena needs time to feel her old self again."

"Well, there's nothing I can do about that, Herr Linden. I asked you here to advise you that you'll only be able to take a limited amount of your possessions with you when you leave."

He gave her a quick glance, understanding her meaning. What they could not carry with them would be confiscated by the Siamese government. His mind pictured the beautiful gold and silver ornaments, jewelry, and silks they had collected in Singapore and Bangkok, packed in chests ready to be sent to Romania, or wherever they chanced to go when the war was over. They could have sold each piece when necessary—their money was dwindling alarmingly. He had heard that German ships in the harbor had been taken as prizes of war, and all German-owned businesses had been laid claim to and impounded. What a bonanza for the Siamese.

"I'll buy your things," Madam Streit offered. "At a reasonable price, of course," she amended quickly. "I can't buy everyone's items, but you'll need money."

"Yes," he said after a long pause, attempting to determine whether her proposal was a mercenary one, or whether she felt pity for the family. "I'd appreciate any help you can give us."

After negotiations had been completed, they rose from their seats and shook hands. "I wondered, Madam Streit, what will happen to you now?" Franz asked. "You've never revealed your background. German? Austrian?"

"Oh, no, if I were German I'd be going with you, wouldn't I? No, my late husband was German, but I'm French. I have a French passport. I'll continue to manage the hotel."

"I see. How fortunate for you." The wily Madam Streit, he thought, she's German alright, but she's somehow secured a French passport.

"I hope Elena will recover soon," she said, as he left the room. He shrugged his shoulders.

It was time to pack their things. Time to leave beautiful Bangkok. It's time, it's time, it's time. The words ran around Elena's brain like a merry-go-round. She tried to sort out her dresses, skirts and shirtwaists, the underwear, her shoes and hats. It seemed an insurmountable task that she'd never get done; she was still weak and lethargic. Lise and Mitzi helped. They chattered as they worked around her, somehow relieved to be finally going somewhere, to get away from the crowded hotel. Their new destination might be immeasurably worse than what they endured now, but the activity was invigorating, exciting.

Marta and the girls inserted some treasured ornaments in between layers of clothing in their bags. Jewelry they planned to carry on their person, sewn into the seams of skirts and jackets. Elena slowly, lovingly, stroked intricately carved silver napkin rings and a little silver container with its fitted lid before finally laying them between her undergarments. She sighed. Was this all she would have as a remembrance of Siam?

Camille, yearning for the departed Max, meandered into the girls' room periodically, bewailing her fate in frightened whispers. Mitzi was sympathetic, but Lise dispatched the girl with irritated remarks.

"She thinks she's the only one being incarcerated," she said, annoyed by Camille's constant interruptions in their work. "I hope Max forgets about that girl." Elena thought of the absent Lorenzo; perhaps he had already forgotten her.

The morning of departure dawned unusually hot and humid. Camille was not alone in her apprehensiveness and fear; every last one of the internees faced their future with some degree of trepidation, except for the very young children who expected a holiday. Bags packed, the group waited restlessly in the dining room for further instructions. Elena, still drained of color and strength, sat quietly, luggage piled in heaps about her. She had badgered Madam Streit daily about the mail delivery, but here they were, ready to leave, and still no word from Lorenzo. She paid little heed to the conversations circling about her head until voices behind her, two women huddled together, attracted her attention. It was Frau Langst of the "Bangkok elite."

"I heard the Siamese officials asked the British to remove us from this hotel as quickly as possible," she said, fanning herself briskly with a magazine. "They were afraid of more disease with us all packed together like sardines."

"I can understand that," her younger companion said, "but I wish they could have found another place for us here in Siam. First they send my husband to Australia, and now they are sending us to India. India! We'll never see each other again, I know it."

We'll never see each other again, Elena repeated to herself. She closed her eyes. Perhaps Lorenzo would never write, feeling it was better that way. He thought her immature, that she would forget him after a time. "Oh, what does it matter," she muttered under her breath. "With this war, I can't marry anyone, anyway."

A British officer entered the dining room briskly, ramrod straight, swagger stick under his arm, mustache waxed alarmingly to sharp points. He was undaunted by the resulting tumultuous complaints his appearance engendered from the captive men, women, and children.

"Ladies and gentlemen," he said in good-natured, but rather bad German, "we have transportation ready for the trip to the ship. If you'll break up into groups, we'll be on our way!"

Amid the uproar, as everyone scrambled to pick up their possessions, Elena caught sight of Madam Streit scanning the crowd from the doorway, eyes finally alighting on her. Smiling triumphantly, she held a letter up over her head, waving it back and forth.

CHAPTER FOURTEEN

Holdsworthy

That Max gave no inkling in his letters to his family of the hardships he'd endured during his voyage to Australia and confinement to the prisoner-of-war camp was remarkable. On the contrary, his correspondence stressed only the positive aspects of camp life, though loneliness for his parents and sisters was heartbreakingly apparent from time to time. When he learned eventually of their unhappy fate, being shipped to India, he decided he would never give them reason to fear for his well-being; it was he who was anxious for them. He brooded over his inability to help as he was carried far from them over the seas. Eventually, his own perilous state blocked out his continual thoughts of them. Bitterness, resentment, and frustration took their place.

The ocean journey to Australia and subsequent incarceration had been a terror-fraught and demoralizing experience. I can't believe the conditions we're sailing under on this ship, he thought. We suffer just as the Chinese coolies and penal colony convicts suffered in Australia's past.

There were three hundred men in the cargo hold in the forward part of the ship, mostly civilians, all doing their utmost to catch some sleep in the confining hammocks hung eighteen inches apart. Max had never been seasick on the family travels, but no sooner was the ship under way on the day of departure, almost a week previously, when the weather turned ugly. The portholes were closed against the high seas, and fumes from still-wet painted bulkheads soon caused most of the men to be sick. Only a few of the retching internees managed to climb into hammocks during those miserable days and nights. Most had lain on the deck under tables and benches, suffering the agonies of sickness. Max's stomach lurched threateningly at just the memory of the rolling and pounding three-thousand-ton ship. He often assisted those men, still queasy and nauseated in the mornings, to the main deck so that he could carry out the work of cleaning up below.

The faint stench of vomit still permeated the area as his eyes roved about the crowded hold of sleeping prisoners. Most of the space was taken up by dining tables, benches, and luggage of the men. Lighting and ventilation were poor. Deigelmeier, scrunched up in his hammock, looked pallid, his eyes ringed with dark circles. He seemed loath to leave this cradle-like cocoon. Schenck lay next to him, unaffected by the vessel's undulation, snoring loudly as though he were comfortably ensconced in a featherbed in his native Austria. Braun slept quietly, innocently. Max stirred restlessly; he turned from side to side like a cat searching for the perfect fit, finally drifting off to a disturbed sleep.

Once the weather cleared, men were allowed up on the main deck. After the confinement in the dark and dank hold below, sunshine and refreshing sea breezes brought welcome relief. Max breathed in the fresh air, taking note of his surroundings. They had use of the main deck, and also the portside promenade deck. Hatchways and access to other parts of the ship had been blocked off by iron bars. Guards in twos or threes were stationed outside the bars, armed with machine guns and steam hoses.

"Don't you think the English are extremely fearful of us," Schenck said, eyeing the tense and uneasy-looking guards, "considering that few of us are military men?"

"How many soldiers are aboard, do you figure?" asked Braun.

"Hmmm ... I guess about one hundred and sixty or so ... soldiers and gunners. We outnumber them, but they are armed."

"They don't take any chances, do they?" Braun said. "Everything is handed to us through the bars. Everything ... even medical treatment." He swallowed nervously. They had all watched, with cringing awe, as the ship's doctor attempted to dress the wound of a prisoner through the bars as the ship pitched and rolled.

"Yes ...," Schenck drawled, "I advise that none of us gets a toothache; you don't want the surgeon working on you like a tiger in a cage. Evidently that's how they think of us, as dangerous animals." Max noted later, though, that when one prisoner was very ill, the main deck was cleared of all internees, and the doctor entered the barred area to treat him.

"I don't understand why we must be imprisoned," Max said to Schenck several days later. They were seated at a table in the hold eating the midday meal. "There can't be that many Germans in the South China Sea to be a threat to the Allied war effort."

"Well, there are a lot more of us here than you think, Max. Thousands, I figure, and I've come up with some reasons for this wholesale internment."

"Such as?"

"There's been a great deal of public sentiment against 'enemy aliens' like ourselves, reaching proportions of hysteria in the area. And the newspapers are to blame, publishing inflammatory reports of 'bloodthirsty Huns.'"

Max grimaced. "Unbelievable," he said.

"Yes, well ...," Schenck continued, "most importantly, besides rounding up unfortunates like us, German residents of the German colonies and other areas are being removed so England and France can assume control. Including German commercial interests in parts of Asia, Africa, and the Pacific. You'll see ...," he said, pounding the table emphatically, "when the war is over, every last German who has resided hereabouts will be shipped back to Germany—if she loses the war, that is—and England will be the big cheese again."

"You think so?"

"Positively ... and I'll bet you the Australians will get rid of as many German immigrants as possible. Second- and third-generation Germans have been too successful in business and farming."

Max silently digested this intelligence concurrently with the bread and stew he was consuming. Germany, he thought. His father had described the country as a land of castles and forests, but Romania was home to him. He wondered where the family would go after the war.

A week later found the internees rattling along on a train, dingy windows open to the hot Australian sun and dust. About thirty prisoners at a time were being transported to Liverpool, about twenty miles southwest of Sydney, from the Victoria Barracks in Darlinghurst just east of Sydney. Max looked down in deep humiliation at his handcuffed hands lying in his lap. His body was bruised and aching, he was hungry and thirsty, and he felt exhausted from lack of sleep.

The name, Victoria Barracks, would be burned into his memory for all time. The voyage from Siam had been only a prelude to the dehumanizing degradation the men suffered at the hands of the guards at the barracks. The stay there was brief, four days to be exact, but it was four days of whippings, forced labor, disgusting meals, little water, and foul language directed again and again at "you bloody Huns." They were pushed and shoved constantly, especially when English was not understood by some of the prisoners, including Max. Relief finally came when they were handcuffed and herded onto trains bound for a camp called Holdsworthy.

"Why did they treat us like that?" Max complained to Schenck, seated next to him.

"I don't think it's official policy," Schenck answered. "As I told you, the newspapers have pictured German soldiers as blood-thirsty ogres, and the guards treated us accordingly, even though we're civilians. You see how even the Australian citizens sitting in this car with us jeered and insulted us, making us feel like felons. They don't know any better."

Max stared moodily at the passing landscape, speculating on whether the Holdsworthy camp would be another Victoria Barracks. His dejection wasn't lightened perceptibly upon their arrival at the camp. Further evidence of the Australian attitude toward the prisoners was brought home with absolute clarity when each man received a serial number pinned to his clothes and was then photographed.

"We aren't common criminals," mourned Deigelmeier, as his turn came. His offended sensibilities were shared by all; their only crime was being German in a hostile world. Military internees accepted being imprisoned as a part of war, but secretly planned escape as their duty.

* * *

Prisoners arriving with insufficient clothing—whether snatched from their families without warning or German Buddhist monks with only saffron-colored robes for protection—received shirts, dungaree trousers, and a dungaree jacket marked "POW" on the back. Max had brought enough clothes, but gingerly accepted the jacket, thinking it would be useful in the cold of winter. Managing these items plus his bag and bass fiddle became a juggling act while marching to his quarters, followed by Schenck, loaded down with his own bag and violin. Deigelmeier and Braun disappeared into the three-inch-high dust of the track between barracks, billeted elsewhere.

The barracks in which Max and Schenck were to endure tortuous years were long sheds with corrugated iron roofs about 140 feet by 9 feet, divided into compartments housing five prisoners each. Max eyed the three-sided sheds, noting that the fourth, open side was fitted with canvas blinds to pull down at night or provide a bit more shelter in inclement weather.

"Not much protection in the winter," noted Schenck. There was no stove for heat, and only a stable lantern hung in each compartment for illumination.

"Get used to it," one cellmate advised caustically. "When we arrived, there was nothing … only burlap sacks to eat and sleep on. We built bunks, tables, and chairs ourselves. You're living in the 'Ritz,' now."

"Well," Schenck said with some grudging satisfaction the next day, "I guess we won't starve." He patted his stomach after the midday meal, which had not been exciting, but generous. Max was relieved to see the meat, vegetables, potato, and bread piled high on his tin plate, and coffee filled to the brim of his mug. Breakfast had been a spare one, black coffee or tea, and bread with jam and sugar.

Reveille was at 6:30 a.m., then the thirteen hundred internees lined up for roll call. The two roll calls each day caused a great deal of grousing among the men. Max stood uneasily in line the first morning, Schenck directly behind him.

"Here we go again," his neighbor on the right muttered resentfully, "being paraded twice a day. They only do this to humiliate us, keep us humble." He looked straight ahead, speaking out of the side of his mouth. "Ja, that proves to us how helpless we are here."

"How will we know we're still alive," quirkily commented a huge, sturdy sailor on Max's left, "unless the guards call our names each day? I think that's very openhearted of them." Max yielded a slight smile, recognizing him as one of his cellmates named Sperling.

Holdsworthy was commanded by a Colonel Banks, who directed a ruthless and dictatorial camp. Australian soldiers battling in the trenches in Europe soon learned the enemy consisted of human beings like themselves, but the camp guards, without such experiences, regarded the prisoners as subversives, dangerous agents, and threatening. Considering the war hysteria that had pervaded Australian cities, it would have been surprising indeed if they had understood the internees' plight. Max felt anxiety and apprehension in the guards' presence, but it wasn't the only trial he was to endure; dealing with the prisoners themselves in the camp proved to be a life-threatening proposition as well. His indoctrination commenced within a few days after arrival.

"My bass fiddle! Schenck, my bass is gone!" he cried as the two returned to the barracks after dinner.

"Aaah," exclaimed Sperling, the sailor, sitting atop his bunk. "You can't keep anything safe from these thieves." He dropped down nimbly to the floor. "You know the Australians throw jailed criminals of German descent right in the camp with us, Australian citizens or not. They lie and cheat, making life miserable for us all. Most of them are members of the Serbian Black Hand Society, like the Italian Mafia."

"They want money?" Schenck asked.

"Anything you've got … they want it. If you resist, you get beaten up at night … dragged right out of the barracks."

"Don't the guards stop them?" Max asked, disturbed.

"Ha! The authorities do nothing; they should care what goes on in the camp. The *Tsingtao*, the military internees, try to keep order, but they're helpless without the cooperation of the guards and officers."

"Well," Max sighed, "that means I've seen the last of my bass."

Sperling raised his brows speculatively. "I'll try to find it for you. I know how things work here in the camp. Somebody might be holding it for ransom." He adjusted his seaman's cap to a rakish angle and made a rapid exit out of the barracks.

Max exchanged a distrustful glance with Schenck, wondering whether he was being duped, but the sailor returned triumphantly a half hour later, carrying the instrument in his heavily muscled arms with ease.

"Just as I thought, Linden, it seems they were willing to part with it for a fee, but I convinced them otherwise." Sperling handed the bass to Max, a broad smile on his weather-worn face. "Here it is. It won't happen again."

It never did. It seemed as though Sperling magically protected them from the menace of the Black Hand. Max and Schenck wondered whether that was because the seaman was involved with the organization himself, noting his absence from the barracks in the dead of night. They searched his bunk, but found nothing incriminating.

"It's possible, Max, that the man just likes you," Schenck said, giving Sperling the benefit of the doubt. "Not even the Black Hand wants to tangle with our massive giant." The idea seemed logical enough because Sperling unaccountably showed a special fondness for Max, responding almost respectfully to his gentlemanly behavior, his decency and honor. He saved bits of food, delicacies really, for Max, that were not available at mealtimes, also divulging that much could be had from the guards through bribery, including mailing letters outside the camp to avoid censorship. Intellectually, the two men had little in common, or so Max thought.

Weeks passed slowly, and the Black Hand continued to control the camp, terrorizing the prisoners into parting with their money and valuables, newly arriving internees becoming a special target. Max knew that without Sperling's protection, life would have been a desperate struggle for him; he might not have survived the beatings and thievery so common-place in the camp.

One pastime helped to obliterate the insanity of life in the camp ... music. Max and Schenck became acquainted with other internees who were either professional musicians or talented amateurs. Deigelmeier and Braun were recruited and an orchestra was formed under the direction of Gustav Schubert, a small energetic man, bespectacled and mustachioed. His eyes glared resolutely from below a high forehead and receding hairline at the musicians as they practiced, putting Max in mind of his father. The erect posture and sure precise movements of the leader's arms and hands were plaintively nostalgic.

One day, a surprised Max spied Sperling sitting close by, paper and pen in his burly hands, listening with rapt attention as the orchestra practiced. He was present every day thereafter, attentive to the music, and busily sketching, but, as Max approached, he hastily put the materials aside, a sheepish grin on his face.

"What are you doing?" the curious Max asked, this artistic side of Sperling intriguing him.

"Nothing, nothing," the sailor said, evading any more questions.

* * *

Increasing unrest became apparent in the compound as the months passed. The Black Handers preyed unmercifully on new arrivals, intensify-ing their robbery and clubbing, not only at night, but brazenly carrying out their terrorizing in broad daylight. Colonel Banks did nothing. The guards were indifferent ... but trouble was brewing.

"Max, be careful," Schenck warned. "Something is up."

Then it happened. The pent-up rage and fury building against the bul-lies in past months suddenly boiled up and overflowed one afternoon like a volcanic eruption, spreading throughout the camp like wildfire.

A gigantic roar erupted from a crowd of prisoners milling about before the mess hall. Max saw thirty or so men he recognized as Black Handers begin to run frantically toward the camp gate, *Tsingtao* soldiers armed with clubs and pieces of timber close behind. Hundreds of prisoners followed, urging them on with encouraging shouts. "Get them, kill them!" Max and Schenck were swept along with the vengeful crowd, and watched in horror as the Black Handers were battered and bludgeoned by the mob, now in a fury of retribution. Lifting the limp bodies of their tormenters, the internees threw them over the blood-spattered seven-foot-high fence, cheering lustily as they fell at the feet of Colonel Banks and his officers, who had calmly observed the melee from outside the gate. No effort had been made to maintain order.

Max saw the colonel at close range for the first time. No colder-looking face had he ever encountered—eyes that viewed the carnage before him unconcernedly, lips pulled into a slight, smirking smile. A man without pity, he thought, carrying out his duty as he saw it … commanding a camp of criminals.

Schenck sensed Max's abhorrence, his bitterness, as they returned to the barracks. His only comment was, "He will get his, Max." Max stopped and picked up an object from the ground, stuffing it inside his jacket. Out of the corner of his eye, Schenck saw that it was a bloodstained cap. A sea-man's cap.

* * *

Colonel Banks was replaced by Lieutenant Colonel Allen two months later, and the crushing oppressive regime of the camp began to ease. Of the twenty Black Handers heaved over the fence during the revolt, all were hospitalized and two died, one of whom was Sperling. The Black Hand was effectively disbanded because of the purge.

Max missed the sailor. Others who had evidently suffered at his hands thought differently, having never seen the man's gentler side. A newly arrived detainee, claiming Sperling's bunk, discovered a notebook of astonishing drawings hidden there. Each page contained a portrait of an orchestra member, an expert likeness with their individual musical instrument in hand. The final page depicted the director, Schubert, clad in evening dress, baton raised, his eyes gazing solemnly at the viewer. The splendid representations were duplicated later for a program cover for a concert performed by the orchestra. Sperling would have been proud.

CHAPTER FIFTEEN

Sholapur

The sea air helped to revitalize Elena. She walked the decks of the cargo ship each day as it plied its way into the Bay of Bengal and then into the Arabian Sea—destination, Bombay. Her appetite and color had improved; the meals aboard ship were plain, but good-tasting, and her spirits elatedly buoyed with the receipt of Lorenzo's long and affectionate letter. Unlike Max's nightmarish voyage to Australia, the approximately sixty men, women, and children internees found accommodations on the vessel to be crowded, but treatment not insensitive.

Passage was slow; cargo was loaded and unloaded in various ports along the way. The children, released from the confinement of the Hotel Europa, raced, jumped, and played on the decks, their young voices shrill with joy and excitement. The detainees could forget for a short time that they were prisoners, perhaps pretend they were on a cruise and the world at peace. The lonely expanse of sky and water helped to foster that fantasy.

Intruding on those idyllic days and nights were newspapers brought on board by a friendly guard, for a fee, whenever the ship was in port. Elena searched the pages for reports of Italy's involvement in European hostilities. The Italian army had pushed a series of offensives toward Trieste, and the Austrian line rested on the Isingo River. There were many casualties in Italian towns called Tolmino and Goriza, and she wondered whether Lorenzo had been there. He'd worried that his country was ill prepared for war. Nights she dreamt of him, his face intermingled with Max's at times, like an ever-moving panorama.

* * *

Bombay was hot and humid, an unwelcome change from the refreshing breezes aboard ship. Elena remembered little of the city from when she was a tot, only a hazy recollection of her fright at the break-in of her hotel bedroom. She saw less this time around. Lorries were waiting for the group as they disembarked from the vessel, and British military guards lost no time in transporting them to the railway station, Victoria Terminus.

The station was overflowing with humanity when they arrived; a chaos of noisy, pressing crowds of Indian travelers and military personnel. As the prisoners, over-burdened with bags and valises, plus children in tow, were herded through the crushing throng, eager beggars scrambled alongside them as they walked, hands outstretched, voices pitiful. The guards pushed the unfortunates aside gruffly, and led the group to coaches reserved especially for them.

"I thought I would faint, Franz," a pale and exhausted Marta said as they sank with relief into their seats. "That awful heat ... and all those people."

Franz nodded. "We're not young anymore," he said, "but once we get to the camp, I'm sure things will be better." He smiled wanly in an effort to raise her spirits.

After what seemed an interminable delay, the narrow-gauge train, hissing steam and blowing warning whistles, finally pulled out of the station. Freight cars in the rear were packed to the rafters with chattering Indian travelers of slender means, surrounded by piles of baggage, huge bundles, crates of squawking chickens, and all manner of sundry items. Others not fortunate enough to find room inside the cars clung precariously to the roof and sides as the train chugged sluggishly through towns and villages.

At first, the passing landscape was diverting. Sun-dried, mud-brick houses with flat roofs of mud-coated grass stalks, with buffalo byres—or cow barns—and chicken houses in the rear, kept the prisoners' interest. Children waved gaily to them from the rooftops. Occasionally, glimpses were caught of houses' interiors, often showing a kitchen with a separate cooking enclosure, a flash of pottery and polished brass utensils on molded shelves over a small hearth. Indian women moved about inside, no doubt preparing for the next meal. The main streets of villages featured teashops, fruit and vegetable stalls, sweetmeat shops, and thoroughfares alive with bullock carts, cows, goats, mules, donkeys, plodding camels, and huge lumbering elephants.

Scenery turned arid and bare of trees and vegetation. Oppressive heat and dust inside the coach took a toll on the occupants. Children whimpered and whined, men loosened their collars, and the elderly napped, their heads nodding from side to side in tandem with the train's motion. Late in the afternoon, stale Indian bread, fruit, and a beverage were distributed by the guards. The journey continued into the night, incessant repetitious clitter-clatter of steel wheels on rails becoming like the drip, drip, drip of a Chinese water torture device to the internees.

Marta moved her legs restlessly; her body ached from sitting on hard, uncushioned seats for hours on end. She thought of her little son, Emile. The motor lorry taking them to the railway station in Bombay had passed the old cemetery where he had been buried fifteen years earlier, stirring grief-filled memories. She shook her head sadly; India was not a lucky place for the family. How ironic it was that they were returning under such bizarre circumstances. Emile would have been seventeen now, old enough for the British to send him to Australia with Max.

The following morning, close to noon, the train pulled into the Sholapur station. Motor lorries were waiting. Indian soldiers—*sepoys*—helped the exhausted, soot-begrimed prisoners into the vehicles, and a half hour later herded them into a large quadrangular-shaped courtyard. Surrounded by one-story, dun-colored buildings, the courtyard, bare of trees or grass, had a waterless fountain in the center. A seven-foot-high wooden gate barred the one entrance and exit, guarded smartly by two sepoys.

"Line up," a British officer ordered.

"Sir," young Lieutenant Morrison went inside, saluting his senior officer. "The prisoners have arrived."

"Hmmm ... so they're here."

"Yes, sir."

Major Adams rose slowly, and rather stiffly, from the chair behind his desk. A stocky, middle-aged man with twenty years of service in India, he had looked forward to retirement well before the war but, of course, every soldier was needed now; there was a job to do. Someone at headquarters, he surmised, had discovered he had a working knowledge of the German language; hence his assignment to this post in Sholapur. Rather degrading for him, really, playing wet nurse to such a group ... old men, women, and children. He sighed. Well, someone had to do it.

"Let's go, Morrison," he said. "Do you have them lined up?"

"Yes, sir."

Outside, Adams briefly outlined the camp rules as the prisoners stood in the broiling sun. They are a bedraggled-looking lot, he thought. No sense in keeping them standing there; the children appear weary and frightened.

"All the rules will be posted in the dining hall," he said in conclusion. "Lieutenant Morrison will call the roll and assign you to your quarters."

"It looks like this place was just recently built," Elena said, surveying the stark, white walls of the dining hall. She and her sisters were eating a breakfast of tea, jam, and bread the next morning.

"A hospital, I hear," Mitzi said. "That's why we have electric in our room."

"One small bulb on the ceiling," Lise said, "and that was turned off at nine last night."

"Well," Elena said, "everything looks better in the light of day, doesn't it?"

And so it did. Fatigued by the journey from Bombay, the sisters had gazed at their new quarters the night before with drooping spirits. The room was bare of anything more than Indian rope-type, wooden-framed beds with one sheet, flat pillow, and threadbare cotton blanket on each. Pegs on the wall served as hangers for clothing. Two small windows were positioned so high on the wall, one couldn't see out of them or possibly fit a body through them—even if there was any thought of escape. No one entertained such a notion as there was nowhere to go. After using the group washing facilities and visiting the latrines at the east end of the building, the sisters had lain down on the beds exhausted and close to tears.

Reveille sounded at seven in the morning. Refreshed by a surprisingly sound sleep, the girls rose immediately to organize their belongings and clean house, as did the rest of the German community, living up to the image of cleanliness the world attributed to Teutonic folk, but not much could be accomplished without tools. After roll call and breakfast, a meeting was called; a visit to the major was in order.

"Sir," Lieutenant Morrison said, "two of the prisoners wish to speak with you."

"Eh? What about?"

"It has something to do with brooms, sir, among other things."

"Brooms? Well, send them in."

Franz and Captain Baumgartner were ushered in, and stood before the major. Checking papers, he deliberately kept them waiting for a few moments before looking up from his desk.

"Yes?"

"Major Adams, my name is Franz Linden, Kapellmeister, and this is Captain Baumgartner, late of the impounded ship, *Brunnen*. We come as representatives of our group."

"Yes, what is it you want? You understand I'm limited as to what I can do for you. This is a prison camp, not a hotel."

"We don't ask for much, sir, only a few things to keep our quarters clean, and also perhaps make it more comfortable for the women and children."

Major Adams drummed his pencil on the desk. "What do you have in mind?"

"The ladies would like plain, straw brooms. They can share them, not one for each, you see, and perhaps an area where they are stored for all to use."

The major wrote briefly on a paper. "I'll see what I can do. What else?"

"Major Adams, we would like to build shelves and cabinets to store our things in the rooms; they are sitting on the concrete floor, as we ourselves are, too. Therefore, we would also hope to build chairs or benches."

The Major's face colored and he leaned forward, continuing to drum his pencil on the desk. "That would require tools and lumber, rather expensive items."

Franz and the captain exchanged glances. "For the ladies, sir; they are not military, only helpless civilians," Baumgartner pleaded.

"I know, I know," the Major said briskly, "however, it's not in my power to grant your request. I'll pass it along to headquarters for review in my next dispatch."

Later, Franz related the conversation with the major to Marta and his daughters. "I think he's a fair man, and will do what he can," he said.

"It would be good if we had some chairs to sit on, and shelves for our things," Marta said. "It wouldn't seem so much like ... like prison."

"It *is* prison, Mama," Elena said, "no matter how cozy we try to make it."

"I know, but we must make the best of it."

The internees wasted little time in putting their world in order, organizing schooling for the children, instituting a library that incorporated books and reading material contributed by the prisoners, including British newspapers. Chess and card games were popular, and though rules posted in the dining hall forbade gambling, the edict was ignored. Coupons of one rupee and five rupees were issued within the camp to purchase daily necessities. Lumber and tools arrived within a few weeks, and those who were handy went to work building chairs and shelves. Soon women sat together in the courtyard into the late afternoon, gossiping and mending clothes. Card players were surprised and pleased when a round table was laboriously fashioned for their games.

Eventually, as the months dragged by, monotony and the confinement of camp life caused discord, especially among the women. Entire families carried on vendettas against other families, sometimes over minor squabbles concerning dining hall seating or imagined insults regarding deficiencies in behavior. Some, like snobbish Frau Langst, fancied themselves superior to others. Elena avoided the "Bangkok elite," and they, in turn, made snide remarks concerning the "shameless Linden sisters." Lise sometimes deliberately "misplaced" brooms from their accustomed location, and watched, innocent of face, as women darted fretfully to and fro, like squirrels hunting for buried acorns. A committee had been formed to arbitrate disputes, but unresolved problems were often laid before the major.

"How do I deal with these petty women?" growled Major Adams to Lieutenant Morrison. "Now they're complaining about the food."

The subject of food was indeed a sore point with the prisoners. They claimed the Indian cooks served inferior meals and pocketed the money saved.

"Mutton, mutton, and more mutton!" groused Lise. "They give us foul-tasting stews and curries, with vegetables as old as Methuselah. And if there's ever any fruit, it's practically inedible." She was further enraged by the sides of mutton hanging in the kitchen storage area, the flesh crawling with weevils, flies, and maggots. "See!" she said to her sisters, "that's why it tastes so terrible, and that's why there are long lines in front of the latrines. Everyone suffers from cramps and diarrhea."

"Why can't we cook for ourselves?" suggested Elena. "Many of the women have volunteered."

Mitzi shook her head. "Papa tried that. The major admitted there was a problem, but he refused to allow us to take over the kitchen. He reminded Papa there was a war on, and we were fortunate to have this much to eat."

Lise grumbled, shrugging her shoulders. Elena's vitals gripped her in a spasm of revulsion. She feared so much the return of the dysentery she had suffered. For a short while, she resolved to eat only bread and perhaps vegetable or lentil soup, but an encounter with a feathered foe changed her mind.

One day she had taken an extra slice of bread with her into the court-yard after the noon meal. When she raised the bread to her mouth, a large crow, flapping its huge wings threateningly, suddenly swooped down under the blazing midday sun, raked her cheek and neck with sharp claws, and absconded with the coveted prize.

"I've been in a fight for survival with the avian world," she told Dr. Vogel later, as he tended to her wounds. She giggled, but the doctor nodded absently.

"You must eat, Elena," he said seriously. "You're still not sufficiently recovered from the dysentery."

* * *

Despite efforts toward cleanliness, the internees battled another enemy. Insects. Clouds of flies buzzed around them incessantly. Ants and roaches scurried about in droves, searching for the smallest speck of sustenance. Windows and doors were closed a half hour before and after sunset to discourage mosquitoes from entering their quarters. Scorpions hid under rocks in the courtyard, a danger to playful, scampering children. It seemed the insect world was winning the war against humanity.

Elena usually rested on the rope bed in her room during the midday heat. One afternoon she lay there listlessly, observing the beige-colored geckos plastered on the walls. They were harmless little lizards, but there were so many of them. Eventually, she dozed off. Lise, who had brought in a mug of tea after the noon meal, let it sit on the floor near her bed awhile, before drinking it at her leisure. She sipped the beverage slowly, reading her favorite novel. Suddenly she uttered a strangled cry, gazing into the mug in horror. Elena sat erect, half awake.

"What is it, Lise?"

"It's ... a bug!" she screamed, thrusting the mug high into the air in loathing. "A huge bug in my tea. All its insides are out ... and I drank it. I DRANK it!" She screamed again and again, her shrieks bringing the passing Dr. Vogel running into the room. Elena rescued the mug from the floor, indicating its contents to the physician.

"Aha," he said calmly, "I think it's a dung beetle, that's all." He winked at Elena. "Dung beetle ...," Lise repeated. "The beetle that feeds on cow dung? Oh, my God!" She rushed headlong into the courtyard, her fingers reaching deep into her throat. She retched uncontrollably in a desperate attempt to vomit the disgusting contents of her stomach.

Elena witnessed her sister's efforts with sympathy, but then couldn't help giggling at the sight of Lise gasping and gagging—eventually managing to bring up some liquid—gurgling and choking until exhausted, her breathing labored, and then abruptly stopping. She had become aware of Elena and Dr. Vogel's amusement.

"You must cover the tea with something, Lise, when you keep it to drink later," the doctor advised.

She pursed her lips in quiet fury and marched back into the room, not answering. Elena raised her brows. "Now I've done it," she said ruefully.

Elena later described the incident to the inquiring Mitzi and, at first, Lise sulked in their presence, insulted by the humorous reaction her experience had evoked. Mitzi, as usual all sympathy and understanding, was charming and winning. When the sisters sat together in the evening, Lise thawed and began to recognize the comic aspects of her nauseating encounter with the insect.

"If you could have only seen yourself, Lise," Elena cackled.

Lise's shoulders shook, she chuckled, then grinned. "I must have been a sight," she said, "but that bug was so horrible, I thought I would die."

"You … you looked so … so …." Elena, unable to continue, dissolved into peals of laughter. She jumped to her feet, whooping, and imitated Lise's attempt to throw up, so that Lise and Mitzi couldn't help but join her in helpless, hysterical mirth. They laughed until the tears came, and Mitzi was forced to make a mad dash for the latrine. When she returned, still smiling, the sisters embraced. All was well. They elected to walk round the perimeters of the courtyard, arms intertwined companionably, and started to sing.

Thomas Carlyle wrote that "music was the speech of angels," an apt description of the strong voices soaring into the dark Indian night. A lively operetta tune, a sad ballad, a sprightly waltz, and then a serenade—they varied their repertoire that evening, and every evening, having an ample wellspring of music to draw from. The internees, sitting outdoors until lights out, sometimes joined in enthusiastically when the tune was familiar, sometimes tearfully when it reminded them of home or a loved one imprisoned in far-off Australia.

"Listen to the girls," Major Adams said to Morrison as they worked late in the office. "They're plucky and cheerful ones, eh?" He stroked his mustache reflectively. "I wonder how my daughters would fare under the same circumstances."

"I'm sure they would do quite well, sir," Morrison said. "They're British."

"Hmmm … maybe. Don't really know them, actually, with them in school in England."

Morrison was positive. "They'd do fine, sir," he said, hoping he didn't come across as a tufthunter, or bootlicker.

* * *

By the close of 1917, the prisoners' day-to-day existence grew as weari-some and frustrating as tigers pacing their cages in a zoo. For the children's sake, the group created as happy a Christmas celebration as possible. Toys were crafted for them from wood the Indian sepoys donated and, with a little bribery, a small, sparse fir tree was smuggled into the compound. A mystery, considering the tree grew only in the higher mountainous areas of India, it was imaginatively decorated with ribbons strung with colorful buttons from the ladies' sewing boxes. Major Adams contributed candies sent to him from England. On Christmas Eve, carols were sung accompa-nied by the plaintive strings of Franz's violin.

Some letters and cards had miraculously arrived in time for the holi-days. Elena was overwhelmed with the receipt of four letters—two from Lorenzo, the others from Max and Stephanie. She treasured the words of love and longing in Lorenzo's letters. "Absence makes the heart grow fond-er," Mitzi said, teasing Elena as she watched her read her letters, her face glowing.

Stephanie's letter admonished Elena for failing to write more often. "After all," she wrote, "you have nothing but time on your hands, whereas I have responsibilities of husband, a child and business." Max lamented the fact that another Christmas was passing without the family being together. He was well, and missed her very much. He hadn't heard from Camille in a long time; was she ill? "Oh, Max," Elena sighed, "what has happened to us all?" She wasn't surprised to hear that Max's love hadn't written to him. Camille had distanced herself from the family over the past months, mak-ing friends with others in the camp. Obviously, Max's absence hadn't made *her* heart grow fonder.

* * *

By the beginning of 1918, three-and-a-half years of war had dragged on, totaling millions of deaths and casualties, and featuring horrors that had never before been experienced on such a broad scale. Elena found the complexity of global warfare—that held the Linden family in captivity—mind-boggling, and struggled to make sense of it all. A sometime listener to what her mother termed, "men talking politics," she sat in on the male conversations around the fountain each morning, careful to hold her tongue after a warning stare from her father. Furious disagreements were the norm over the causes and effects of world hostilities.

"The Kaiser was wrong," said Dr. Vogel, as usual expounding on the German leader's failures and follies, his favorite theme.

"No, no, why should the great powers like England and France have colonial possessions all over the world," insisted Captain Baumgartner, "and Germany should be satisfied with their leavings? Then she has little in the way of overseas markets. Germany is a highly industrialized nation; she needs raw materials just like the other countries. No, it was England that started the war."

"In a way," Franz said, "you are both correct. I've had time to think about the war while penned up here in camp." He leaned back in his chair, slowly twirling his mustache. "I think each country was concerned with their own power and commerce, with ambitions to extend their territory, wealth, and military strength. The powers were watching each other, building up armies, ready to counter any undue strength of the others.

"I agree the Kaiser made mistakes that swung the balance of power against Germany, thereby setting off events that culminated in one crisis after another. Mounting tensions eventually just exploded into a worldwide war. It wasn't all Germany's doing alone, though; it was like a 'Pandora's Box' waiting to be opened, a rivalry of armed camps that burst into an unholy, bloody slaughter." He paused, shaking his head. "I don't think any of the countries participating realizes the magnitude of the desolation they have unleashed on mankind. God help us all."

The group fell silent, finding Franz's eloquence profound. Elena mulled over his words, especially "unholy bloody slaughter." Would Lorenzo be a victim of magazine rifles that delivered fifteen shots a minute or, worse yet, machine guns that pumped out ten bullets a second? She shivered and walked away, not wanting to hear more that day.

* * *

A new abomination was to strike an already desolate and ravaged planet, like the calamitous floods that follow torrential rains. Spanish influenza. By 1918, it had felled twenty million victims worldwide. Dr. Vogel and Major Adams made plans to counteract the viral disease attacking the internees well before it was actually brought into the camp by Indian workers.

Due to swift and competent action, the flu flashed through the compound with little impact, considering the concentration of prisoners, and only two died. Internees with even the slightest of symptoms were immediately isolated from others and treated promptly. The Indian population on the outside was not as fortunate; the native death count from influenza eventually totaled six million. Dr. Vogel credited his success to the major, who wisely disregarded the rules forbidding physician internees to attend ill prisoners. The doctor was allowed to ply his profession in tandem with the British resident physician, burdened with several other civil camps in the area.

Dr. Vogel was mystified. "I've never seen anything like this influenza before, Herr Linden," he confessed. "The young patient who died yesterday, Behrens was her name, was a healthy woman. Yet her lungs were completely filled with bloody fluids when she expired, just three days after the onset of the disease. It was as though she had drowned."

* * *

A letter arrived from Rudy with stunning news. "I've done the unthinkable," he wrote rapturously. "I've fallen in love. Angela and I were married last month, and imagine, she was in a choir group that narrowly missed being taken prisoner of war in Russia. She managed to get here to San Francisco just as I did." He went on to describe his bride as a beautiful, hard-working Austrian-born girl. A photo enclosed displayed a full-bosomed young woman, with large expressive eyes, sitting in a hammock. The sisters studied the photo with interest.

"Her eyes and hair are dark," Mitzi said. She shook her head dubiously. "I can't believe Rudy is married. Somehow it doesn't seem real, especially since we couldn't attend his wedding."

"I wonder if we'll ever meet this Angela," Lise said, "I suppose it's unlikely. Who knows where we'll be after the war."

"Anything is possible," Elena said. "Who would have guessed a few years back that we would be prisoners of war in India?"

CHAPTER SIXTEEN

Day ... By Day ... By Day

Despite prisoner efforts to occupy themselves in the Holdsworthy camp, the months crawled by at a funereal pace. With the replacement of Colonel Banks by Lieutenant Colonel Allen, the atmosphere had changed markedly in the huge compound, now comprised of almost four thousand internees. Allen was responsible for easing restrictions that led to the erection of small private buildings where enterprising prisoners operated businesses.

Max and Schenck could choose to eat meals in any of nine restaurants established on the grounds, or enjoy pastries with coffee or tea in six cafés. At that time, all food preparations in the camp had been turned over to the internees. Vegetables and fruits, animals and chickens, were all raised on the compound. Shops and factories flourished. The prisoners were eating better than the guards.

Other improvements and activities were organized as the weeks wore on. Hot showers and baths, a welcome alternative to the primitive cold-water outdoor installations provided by the Australians, was a moneymaker. Formerly, Max and Schenck had been forced to walk a quarter of a mile from the barracks, and then wait in long lines for their turn to perform ablutions; a cold, shivery trek in wintry weather. Sporting clubs had been founded: gymnastics, track and field, weight lifting, and soccer. In addition, chess and bridge clubs developed, and a library was instituted.

What had started as a theater in a big army tent had by now become a large building, erected by the prisoners, seating four hundred persons. Entertainment of all kinds was presented daily. Choral societies and the orchestra, in which Max, Schenck, and Deigelmeier participated, contributed to the cultural activities. Max benefited when classes were organized—English for him; art, professional training, and lectures for others. Circumstances were considerably improved from the time of the Black Hand.

Of course, these were diversions that could only distract the prisoners for brief time periods. The dark side of their lives considerably outweighed the light. Their activities were a desperate attempt to divert their minds from the miserable, crowded conditions under which they lived.

Deigelmeier, the shy, timid, and modest man that he was, seemed to be the most affected by the strain of long internment. His efforts to adapt came to naught, even when, using a little bribery, Max and Schenck had managed to move him into their barracks. Thick yellow clouds of dust covered the camp in the summer. The air teemed with swarms of blowflies, and the barracks were invaded with insects, mice, and, even worse, lice. In the cold of winter, slimy, ankle-deep mud surrounded the barracks. The three thin wool blankets issued gave scant protection from icy winds penetrating their unheated quarters. These physical discomforts caused Deigelmeier misery, indeed all the internees, but the mental torment he suffered was by far more worrying to Max. The man appeared to be gradually withdrawing from reality.

Few of the prisoners could ever accept what fate had ordained, but most persevered. Even more than in Sholapur, melancholy, despondency, complaints of unceasing monotony, resentment connected to losses of homes or possessions, and grievances of being imprisoned surfaced. Most difficult were the tension and psychological friction between the internees themselves.

"With all these nationalities lumped together, there are bound to be scraps," Schenck said. "We've been placed in the same camp, but are a house divided. Germans against the Austrians ... and there are the Slavs, Croats, Bosnians, Serbs, Czechs, and Slovaks; they all spit on each other."

He shook his head, disgusted. "On top of that, we have the *Reichsdeutschen* from Germany. They are arrogant, look down on the Austrians, the Slavs, Australian-born Germans. On everybody ... us, too."

"Like von Trapp," Max said."

"Yes, like Baron von Trapp, right here in our own barracks. He treats Mussotter, the Australian, like dirt."

"He told me that Mussotter shouldn't have been quartered with him, a titled German officer," Max said. "That he should speak only when spoken to, and take off his hat, if he is wearing one, in his presence."

"Ha! What rubbish."

"Mussotter doesn't deserve to be detained, anyway," Max mused. "He's a natural-born citizen, but the Australians don't trust anyone with a German name, citizen or not. He's bitter."

Schenck sighed. "Whoever said life was fair? Everybody's bitter about something here ... lost homes, lost savings and businesses. Also separation and worry about families. Just like you, Max."

Schenck's reminder of the Linden family's misfortunes served to renew the festering, gnawing ache Max felt whenever the well-being of his parents and sisters came to mind. A letter from Rudy had arrived announcing his recent marriage. Optimistic, he urged Max to come to America when the war was over, saying there was great opportunity. Max was skeptical, yet idly fantasized that Camille would join him there. They could be married; his heart was hers.

That she hadn't answered his romantic letters didn't deter him at first. She was ill, he reasoned. He envisioned all manner of excuses for her. She injured her hand and wasn't able to write, or she was nobly nursing the flu victims Elena had written about. He imbued qualities in her beyond imagining. When the months passed with no response, he had to admit she was lost to him. It was a devastating realization for a man cut off from the world, with only the harsh life of a prison camp to dwell on.

The resulting dejection Max felt wasn't helped by the grim realities of the camp. He busied himself as much as possible by playing in the orchestra and playing cards, but stayed in the barracks to read on weekends, as everyone else did.

"They're at it again," Schenck grumbled, flipping the pages of a tattered magazine. Shots had been ringing out all day, as the guards fired their guns indiscriminately into the confines of the camp.

"Every weekend it's the same," Max said. "Why can't they find other ways to impress their lady friends? Listen to them shrieking."

"The guards are as bored with the monotony as we are," Schenck said, shrugging his shoulders. He turned his head to glance at Deigelmeier curled up in his bunk, and lowered his voice. "Deigelmeier is petrified, thinks one of the bullets will find its way right through the wall to his heart. Everything the guards do terrify him ... the sight of prisoners in handcuffs and leg irons, or in canvas straitjackets, especially."

"He said devices like that should be relegated to the Dark Ages," Max said. "I told him all he has to do is obey the rules, and he'll be fine, but ...."

"He needs to have something to do," Schenck said, "be active." He moved over to Deigelmeier's bunk, tapping him on the shoulder. "Hey, friend, listen. Come with us tomorrow. We go with a work party to cut down gum trees along the gully. New barracks have to be built for incoming prisoners, and drainage ditches have to be dug. We get paid for our labor, a shilling for four hours' work."

"The exercise is good, Deigelmeier," Max said, flexing his arm muscles. "Too bad we can only work two weeks at a time, but there are thousands of us in the camp; they all want a turn."

"You're not forced to work?" Deigelmeier had paid no attention to their comings and goings.

"In 1914, yes, when the camp first opened, but after strikes and protests it became voluntary. Join us tomorrow?" Max pleaded.

"No."

"Here, try this," the stocky, robust Mussotter said to Schenck one day, offering a tin of "sly grog" he had manufactured. His still, made of jam tins, was located in a small place under the barracks. Schenck took the alcoholic drink from him gingerly and tipped the fiery liquid to his lips. He swallowed some with a gasp, then exhaled noisily, his eyes watering.

"Whoosh!" he wheezed, his voice rasping. "This is even stronger than the last batch. We'll all go blind!"

Von Trapp was contemptuous. "The guards will find your still again, and confiscate it. Why do you insist on building another one?"

Mussotter shrugged his shoulders good-naturedly and smiled. "They find it, I build another one. They find it again, and I build another one. It's a game ... they enjoy it as much as I do. I think they drink it later in their barracks, so help me God."

"That's one way of maybe getting rid of them," Max said under his breath, but then warned, "You'll get your smoking privileges taken away again, or perhaps worse. You might be put on bread and water, like Wagner was in the next barracks." Prisoners and guards alike called the separate prison compound within Holdsworthy, where some internees were sent for special punishment, Sing Sing.

"It's worth it," Mussotter cackled. "Building a still is a challenge I can't resist. Sometimes the guards don't find it for a long time." He paused reflectively. "I never drank alcohol before coming to this camp; never smoked, either."

Von Trapp lit a cigarette with his slim, tapered fingers. "I have something to say," he said. "It's about Deigelmeier ... let me say this before he returns from the latrines." His usually arrogant posture was cast aside momentarily as he continued, "I like the man ... wouldn't care to see him hurt."

"Well, what is it?" prompted Schenck, for the first time seeing von Trapp in a different light. From their first meeting he had considered the man to be a pretentious, monocled snob; landed German nobility without a Deutschmark to his name.

The baron cleared his throat uneasily. He drew smoke from the cigarette, exhaling slowly. "I have friends ... the rumor is that another escape tunnel has been dug, and Deigelmeier is involved. Perhaps you've noticed how unusually dusty he has been looking lately ... his clothes, his shoes?"

Max's face fell. "Oh, my God," he moaned. "I can't believe it."

"He's been terrified since the day he first stepped into the camp," Schenck said. "We know that. Von Trapp, when is the break planned? Who told you about it?"

"Braun told me. They go in two days."

On the night of the planned escape, Deigelmeier stealthily climbed from his bunk in the dark, gathered a sack of his belongings, and made his way to the barracks exit. The others had feigned sleep, Schenck snoring loudly. Von Trapp rose swiftly and grabbed Deigelmeier from behind, giving him a sharp clout on the head. Max winced as his friend's form collapsed to the floor. The men easily lifted him onto his bunk. He weighs so little, thought Max

"Why?" Deigelmeier wailed when he regained consciousness. "Why did you stop me? I'll go out of my mind if I have to stay here another day."

"It would be suicide," von Trapp said. "You are untrained in survival tactics."

"I don't care ... I don't care."

The next morning, news of the escape flashed throughout the camp. Of the twenty-five escapees, two were shot and killed by the guards. The rest made it into the countryside, but were rounded up, returned to the camp, and confined to the prison compound.

"Braun got a nine-month sentence," Schenck said, " the stupid ass."

Deigelmeier said nothing, only withdrew within himself, participating less and less in camp life. He slept in his bunk during the day, stirring only for roll call and meals. He appeared disheveled and unshaven. Although Max and Schenck, with the help of von Trapp and Mussotter, did their level best to keep watch on him, he was found one afternoon hanging from the rafters of the barracks. He had eluded them, escaping from his terror-driven existence in his own way.

"As the Arabs say," commented von Trapp, "it was written. He was headed for extinction no matter how much we tried to save him."

Heavy-hearted, Max sat down to write to his father, informing him of Deigelmeier's demise, but withholding the details. He would tell him when the family was reunited, he thought, but then demurred; there was much of camp life he would refrain from divulging to anyone. It would remain solely in his mind and heart, the good and the bad.

* * *

China had declared war on Germany in 1917, and new barracks had been completed for the expected arrival of additional German civilians. When they failed to appear, authorities decided to restructure the main compound by separating the constantly quarreling Germans and Austrians from each other. A barbed wire fence was constructed between the two compounds.

"I don't understand their thinking," Schenck said. If they're going to separate them, then separate them. But no, the stupid Australians allow visits between the two camps, with gates being closed at five in the afternoon. That's going to keep them from fighting?"

In addition, five hundred internees from Trial Bay had been moved to Holdsworthy, making up a third compound separate from the Germans and Austrians. Max, recalling that the engineer friend of his father, Ethelbert, had been sent to Trial Bay, attempted to visit, but was turned away. "Only the elite allowed there," remarked Schenck.

Each compound had its own clubs, activities, and theater. Max and Schenck continued their musical labors, accompanying the plays and operettas the internees presented. The actors were dressed in well-made and sometimes elaborate costumes sewn for them. Female impersonators were the most amusing to watch.

"Ha!" Mussotter exclaimed one morning after roll call. "Did you hear that two of the prisoners, part of the escape last night and dressed in borrowed costumes from the theater, got as far as the railway station? It seems the stationmaster was suspicious of the one dressed as a woman, and turned them in."

"Probably his beard gave him away," laughed Max. "Pretty hard to cover that up with stage makeup."

"It was more likely those knotty, masculine-looking legs sticking out from under the dress," quipped Schenck. They were able to jest; none of the escapees had been killed during the escape attempt, and so far, several had actually gained their freedom. All in the camp reveled at the news, a triumph of the spirit.

* * *

The Holdsworthy camp's population reached six thousand by 1918, and soon it became apparent that Germany and Austria-Hungary were losing the war. Schenck translated news reports in the Australian papers for Max and von Trapp.

"American troops have entered the war in Europe, totaling fifteen divisions, and by September there was a succession of German losses." He paused, his voice sounding pained as he continued. "It seems they were unable to halt the rapid tide of numbers and materials against them. The Austrian Empire is disintegrating, and the Germans retreating."

The German home front soon collapsed. Some German naval crews mutinied. The new Soviet regime's ideology made inroads among the peoples of northern Germany. Misery caused by the Allied food blockade and the influenza epidemic, plus losing all hope of victory, brought the country to the brink of revolution. When the papers stated the Kaiser had abdicated and fled to Holland, after seeing his troops fraternizing with angry mobs in the streets of the capital, the morale of the internees sank.

"A new German republic has signed armistice terms," Schenck said gravely.

Max's feelings were mixed. He felt sorrow at Germany's fall, but at the same time knew it was because he was a member of a German-speaking family. He had no love for the country. He had never lived there, never called it home. Where was home? Romania was in ruins. The words of Rudy's letter flashed across his mind. "Come to America." The more he thought about the idea, the more exciting it became. His spirits revived, he searched for the English grammar book in his bunk.

CHAPTER SEVENTEEN

Waiting It Out

t was November 11, 1918, a date the prisoners would forever remember. An overshadowing sense of doom hung over the group as they stood lined up in the courtyard. They'd not been dismissed after roll call, an event usually signifying an imminent address by either Major Adams or Lieutenant Morrison.

Elena wished she'd worn a hat. Morning sun radiated shimmering waves of heat across the compound. She watched as a lance-sergeant placed a small wooden platform on the ground before them. He saluted briskly as Major Adams appeared and stepped onto the stand. Adams seemed tense; he cleared his voice several times before speaking.

"I must advise you that Germany and Austria have been defeated by the Allies, and the war is now ended. An armistice has been signed by a new German republic." He paused as a groan of dismay erupted from the internees.

"You're to be repatriated to Germany when ships for your passage are available," he continued, "which should be somewhere between six and eight months." As a murmur of despair rose from the group, he said, "You must understand there are many such camps as this one in India and Australia; therefore, transportation will be slow. In the meantime," he said to appease them, "you'll be allowed visits into the town of Sholapur for religious services, shopping, and the cinema. A guard must accompany those who choose to go."

So, the war is over, Elena thought. She had anticipated a feeling of wild delight at the news, but, instead, a heavy weight lodged in her chest. She saw tears in her mother's eyes and in the eyes of others. Freedom would bring an uncertain future.

Gates opened. Years of imprisonment were at an end as Elena and her sisters walked out of the compound, bound for Sunday morning church services in Sholapur. They felt exhilarated, like caged birds suddenly released from an aviary into the bright blue skies above. Elena's gladdened heart reached out to all about her. She smiled cordially at Indian women they passed on the road, but as the women attempted to speak to her, the two sepoys accompanying the sisters stepped between them.

One of the soldiers, a *havildar*, or sergeant, apologized. "The ladies can be rude," he said in English. "My people are that way; they take it for granted that everyone knows each other's business, and they can ask anything. The women will ask—excuse me for mentioning it—but they will ask you what you are wearing beneath your dresses. And the men, you must be careful of. They will 'accidentally' brush close against you. Do not answer questions, or they will never leave you alone."

"But I hoped to be friendly." Elena paused. "What is your name?"

"Kumar, *memsahib*."

"Kumar, I'd like to learn more about your country."

"I will tell you what you want to know," he answered matter-of-factly.

"Well," she said, pausing to think of a subject for conversation. "Alright, tell me about the sacred cows we see here on the road." The animals meandering along the road beside her had *bindi* spots painted on their foreheads, horns adorned with sweet-smelling jasmine, and bells tied about their feet that caused a tinkling as they moved.

"Oh, yes," he said, "The cows wander where they please, eating everything in sight. Their religious and mythical sanctity is drawn from the many nourishing products that can be rendered from their bodies. You see, we are a largely vegetarian country, so we rely on the cow for protein in the milk, also dung for fuel, and their strength for plowing our fields."

Elena's eyes widened as Kumar spoke, impressed not only by his knowledge but by his command of the English language as well. Continuing to probe his intellect as they walked, she found that he was just as informative when they passed a formidable-looking Muslim fort and a lovely temple she admired, situated in the midst of a large blue-tiled pool of water.

The church the Lindens attended was Anglican. Lise and Mitzi were unfamiliar with the service conducted in English, but very much aware of the stir their presence caused among the British military personnel across the aisle. No attempt was made to speak to them, but glances and stares aimed in their direction were enough to make it evident that few eligible ladies were in the small town. The sisters were amused, discussing their experience with relish on the return trip to camp. Being in the company of gentlemen again after their long sequestration was stimulating.

During the week, they made another foray into town to attend the cinema, shown in a makeshift stucco-faced building in the middle of town. Inside the theater, they seated themselves on mismatched wooden chairs arranged in rows, while Indian youngsters sat giggling and wiggling on the floor close up to the screen. An odor of curry, onions, and garlic permeated the air, wafting in from a restaurant next door. This time around, the sisters didn't attract attention from British military in the audience; the lights dimmed minutes after their arrival, and a Charlie Chaplin film soon had everyone laughing. A second film featured American Indians and cowboys. Elena wondered whether Rudy was threatened by Indians; he hadn't mentioned them in his letters, but he was in the "West," wasn't he?

Whenever Kumar accompanied the girls on subsequent jaunts into Sholapur, Elena absorbed his accounts of Indian life like a dry sponge soaking up water.

"Tell me today about your marriage customs, Kumar."

"Well ... marriages are arranged. Groups of families exchange potential spouses from more distant clans. Companionship and love are of minor concern." Elena made a face, and he smiled. "The bride and bridegroom do not know each other; the primary obligation of the couple is not to each other, but to their families, especially the groom's."

"Do they set up housekeeping?"

"No .... The bride must spend the rest of her life in her mother-in-law's house, under her tutelage. The groom owes his mother respect, just as he did as a child, and the bride must be subservient to both."

Elena rolled her eyes, and he smiled again. "I know this is far different from your customs," he said. "The bride only gets her revenge when *her* son marries, and she rules the household."

They were walking past vegetable gardens. She heard the distant "miaow, miaow" of a wild peacock in the meadow. Kumar identified this tree as a banyon; those were papal trees, he said; and the black-trunked, square-crowned tree was an acacia, bristling with white spines. A young girl passed them, smiling shyly, a small bowl in her hand.

"Where is she going, Kumar?"

He seemed embarrassed, and avoided her gaze. Elena smiled, waiting for an answer. Finally he spoke. "Houses have no sanitary facilities. Each farm has a latrine territory, or 'patch,' which the inhabitants use. The water bowl is for cleansing."

"I see."

There was silence between them for several minutes. Lise and Mitzi trailed behind them, deep in conversation.

"Memsahib?"

"Yes."

"Your red hair. It reminds me of someone I knew briefly years ago. In Bombay. There was a little girl. I was about ten years old, working in a hotel."

A glimmer of remembrance flashed through Elena's mind. "It couldn't be, could it?" she asked excitedly. "You worked the *punkah*! I remember the turban you wore."

"You had lost a brother."

"Yes," she said gravely. "Emile. He died of cholera. I guess the experience has stayed in my memory because I was frightened by an intruder in my room." She searched his thin face, attempting to recapture some reminder of his young self, but there was nothing. "How odd that we should meet again in this way."

"It is destiny," he said quietly.

They were entering the town proper where there was much activity to engage the sisters' interest. Dusty streets were crowded with horses and mules, bullock carts and donkeys. Crossing the street was chancy; they evaded the paths of galloping camels, followed by a lumbering elephant. Beggars crouched by the fruit and vegetable stalls, eyes on the sepoys who guarded the ladies from their appeals, as they selected bananas to carry back to camp.

When they returned that day, the compound was in an uproar; Franz looked stricken, appearing old and unnerved. He was sitting in a chair in the courtyard. A calm Marta stood nearby in earnest conversation with several ladies, their faces tearstained.

"I've never seen anything like it," their father said. "First there was a violent shaking, I thought it was an earthquake. My ears were popping, and there was a sound like a train approaching. Dr. Vogel shouted that he saw a funnel cloud dipping down before us, that we should get to shelter. The wind was so strong, dust was flying everywhere, and I couldn't see two inches in front of me ...."

"A cyclone!" Mitzi exclaimed

"We were fortunate, girls," Marta said, joining them. "The doors to our rooms were closed. The others ... well, the force of the wind just scooped out all the possessions in their rooms, high up into the sky and out over the countryside. Everything went—tables, chairs, clothes, books, papers. It's lucky the buildings are made of stone, or we would have been hurt. Most of us were in the dining hall. Papa and the men in the courtyard just made it inside before the cyclone struck."

The imperious Frau Langst complained loudly to Major Adams as he approached the group. She was inconsolable. "Major, this is the absolute worst! It wasn't enough that we lost almost everything in the war," she wailed. "Now a wind comes along and scatters what we had left for miles on end. I can't believe it."

This was the first time that Major Adams had condescended to speak to the internees on their level. Information had previously been posted on the bulletin board in the dining hall, or addressed after roll call. The catastrophe they had just suffered, plus the fact the war was over, evidently influenced his decision to offer compassion and understanding to the group.

"The sepoys will accompany those who wish to search for lost belongings outside the compound," he said. "They'll help carry whatever is salvaged back to camp."

Frau Langst was mollified to some extent by the Major's offer, but the search proved to be fruitless. By now, thought Elena, Indians are picking up the pieces as far away as Bombay.

Grist for the gossip mill began the next morning. The rotund Frau Langst, her troubles temporarily forgotten by a juicy bit of news, waddled over to the ladies' sewing circle, her eyes bulging as she unloaded the latest scandal. Marta listened somberly to her melodramatic tale.

"What dirt is the old witch spreading about now?" Elena asked.

"It's Camille. It seems she's been carrying on with one of the sepoys, and now she is ...."

"Oh, no," Mitzi said, closing her eyes in dread. "How could she be so foolish?"

Lise's expression was one of vindication. "Didn't I always say ...," she started.

"The girl doesn't need criticism, Lise," her mother said. "Then we'll be just like Frau Langst. No, Camille needs help." She paused for a moment, mulling over her next move. "Since she was Max's sweetheart," she said, "and a member of the orchestra, I feel responsible for her. I'll have a talk with her." She fixed her eyes thoughtfully on Elena. "You know Camille better than your sisters, Elena. You come with me."

Camille was despairing. "Oh, Frau Linden, you must help me. Please talk to Major Adams." Her eyes were shadowed and red with weeping, her voluminous hair in disarray.

"Tell me what's happened, Camille."

Camille's words spilled out one over the other in her haste. "We are in love. He wants to marry me, but Major Adams said I must return to Germany. That means if we don't marry, and I have the baby in Germany, I may never get back to India." A fresh burst of tears and sobbing ensued before she continued. "Oh, Frau Linden, please help me."

"Now, calm down, Camille, and tell me what the Major told you, exactly."

"He ... he said that Indian marriage customs are very different from ours, and that I would be very unhappy. He said that it's better that I go back to my own family." She moaned hopelessly. "He doesn't realize that I ran away from my father because ... well, if I go back now, he'll call me a whore, and throw me out on the streets."

Marta sighed. "Which of the sepoys is the father? Major Adams may transfer him away before anything can be arranged."

"His name is Kumar."

Elena gasped. Marta glanced at her speculatively, her eyes narrowing, then said, "I'll speak to Major Adams, Camille. I'll see what can be done."

Kumar was gone the next day. No communication with Camille permitted. Marta regretfully spelled out the rules to her. Despite her pleas for compassion, Major Adams had stated that all German nationals were to be repatriated, regardless of complications or predicaments. He was sorry. No exceptions. Camille took his final word stoically, never disclosing whether it was she or Kumar who had initiated their intimacy. Marta declared that no one was to inform Max of Camille's indiscretion in their letters to him. She hoped the girl would not do so, out of a sense of shame and betrayal. Max, being the kindhearted gentleman that he was, might propose marriage, if only to give the expected child a name.

* * *

Elena's receipt of Lorenzo's letters suddenly ceased. The days passed. She grew uneasy. She had followed accounts in the British newspapers of battles between the Austrians and Italians along the Isongo River in Italy, surmising he was involved. His censored mail precluded any indication of his whereabouts. After an Austrian victory at Corporetto in 1917, where over 260,000 Italians had been taken prisoner, her heart had practically stopped beating until Lorenzo's letters continued. Now ... nothing ....

Ultimately, a letter arrived, but not from him. Addressed to Elena in a fine feminine hand on a gossamer-thin envelope, its contents were written on lilac-scented paper.

> My dear Elena,
>
> I had planned to write a letter to you soon after the war end-ed, welcoming you into our family as my son Lorenzo's intended wife. His letters were full of lovely descriptions; your beauty, especially your remarkable red hair, and your sweet nature and accomplishments. I'm sorry to have to advise you that we both have lost a wonderful young man; your sweetheart and my loving son. It grieves me that you and he will not ever have a married life together, and I, the joy of grandchildren in my old age. The accounts of his death are described as accidental; another soldier mishandled his weapon. Lorenzo survived the battles but lost the peace. He will always live in my heart, as I know he will in yours.
>
> Yours in Christ,
> Carmela Martini

Mitzi found Elena sitting on her bed, tears coursing down her cheeks. She read the letter that had drifted from Elena's limp fingers, then sat down beside her, holding her in a tender embrace. "I'm so ... very sorry, Elena," she whispered. "Lorenzo was a fine man."

The years of inferior and non-nutritional food served in the prison camp eventually brought a relapse of the dysentery Elena had suffered in Bangkok. Dr. Vogel did his best to relieve her with the limited herbal med-icines he possessed, but her rapid weight loss was of great concern to him.

"The longer the disease goes on, the more difficult it is to cure," he said to Franz. "Perhaps when we get to Germany ...." His voice trailed off bleakly. They both knew conditions in Germany were grim.

Franz had written to relatives in his hometown of Erding, describing the family's predicament, and asked for help in finding lodgings for them.

Cousin Karl Kohler answered that he would be pleased to do so, not to worry. Although the German government was doing its best to accommodate returning soldiers and prisoners of war, times were hard. Food was scarce, the black market flourishing, and jobs almost non-existent. Yet Kohler's family would do what they could to assist the Lindens when they arrived.

Marta noted that her husband had aged greatly during the years of confinement. Now in his late seventies, a good deal of Franz's zest for living, which had kept him looking for new horizons, had ebbed. She was cheered when notification of the internees' impending departure was posted on the dining room bulletin board and Franz threw himself vigorously into preparations for their journey, again giving directions to his family authoritatively. They couldn't guess what perils might still lie before them, but at least they would be together again with Max.

CHAPTER EIGHTEEN

A Parting Of Friends

There was a stillness in the Holdsworthy camp initially, as at a wake for fallen comrades. Conversations among the prisoners were subdued, activities forgotten. Anxiety and doubt soon surfaced as the internees questioned their fate. Could they return to their homes or businesses, if they existed, in Singapore, Ceylon, Fiji, and other British colonies, or would they be compelled to go to Germany? The Australian authorities procrastinated. Weeks passed with no clear announcements made regarding their intentions.

"There's going to be trouble," von Trapp said, "if they don't tell us what's to become of us. I feel a riot brewing."

The first indication of an infraction of rules came by the refusal of prisoners to appear for roll call. Max and Schenck, wary of participating in any revolt that might endanger their immediate chances for separation from the camp, attended each roll call. The intransigents, however, were duly punished. The next tactic consisted of strikes and protests that resulted in a new hardship, one that Schenck resented with a vengeance.

"Two days now," he snarled, "with no food, only water. When will Allen decide to enlighten us, tell us where we stand?" He was grumpy and uncommunicative until meals were again served.

Repatriation information was ultimately posted on bulletin boards. All prisoners, with the exception of Australian-Germans, were to be repatriated to Germany. By 1920, Holdsworthy would be a ghost town. Max saw that he and Schenck were slated for embarkation on a transport ship sailing from Sydney in several months' time.

* * *

The tremendous death toll from influenza in Europe and the rest of the world had been a distant occurrence to the internees. Australian newspapers, however, presently commenced reporting an alarming increase in cases in Australia, countrywide.

"They're keeling over in every town, every farm," one guard said to Schenck. "If it hits this crowded camp, it could be a disaster."

Relentless, death-dealing disease penetrated the compound with unbelievable speed. As in Sholapur, interned physicians were asked to help to avoid a major catastrophe. A small timber house located outside the camp had been previously used as a hospital, but was now overwhelmed by the number of prisoners being felled by the influenza. Other locations were quickly set up for patients, and volunteer internees assisted with nursing.

It wasn't long before someone in Max's barracks began showing symptoms; Mussotter complained of headache and all-over malaise. A conversation with him a few days before had disturbed Max.

"Linden," Mussotter had confided, "I've been very hurt and disillusioned by Australia's treatment of me and my family. My poor wife had to sell our farm; she couldn't keep it going by herself. She's living with friends and our little son has had to grow up without me. Some wives and children were interned, so I guess she's lucky. We are third-generation Germans, naturalized citizens, and yet they did this to us. Now my wife writes there are newspaper campaigns urging that all German-Australians be sent to Germany, and, to tell the truth, I'm thinking of doing just that. I'll never trust this government again."

"Things are bad in Germany, Mussotter," Max said doubtfully. "I'm going because I have to, but I'm considering going to America later." He stopped, an idea popping into his head. "Why don't you do the same? My brother lives in California, and he describes it as a paradise. You could buy yourself a little farm there."

"Maybe," Mussotter said thoughtfully. "I'll think it over." He smiled, "Thanks Linden."

Several days later he was hospitalized. Three days after, he was dead. Max and Schenck thought it inconceivable that such a hearty and powerful man could be taken so rapidly. Fear gripped all the prisoners in the compound. Some took to wearing protective gauze masks in a desperate attempt to ward off disease-bearing germs. It was all the more terrifying when realization came that the influenza targeted young men in their twenties, not the old and very young of other epidemics. All camp activities were cancelled. Quick, determined efforts, however, by doctors soon had the pestilence well under control.

"You Germans are efficient, alright," a guard commented to Schenck, when the end of the siege was in sight. "Only 104 deaths out of six thousand men. I heard in other military installations, the men were dying five hundred at a time. There weren't enough caskets; corpses were piled sky high."

* * *

Max was impatient. He could scarcely endure the roll calls, breakfasts, teatimes, and camp activities that now seemed fruitless and uninteresting. The weeks stretched ahead interminably. Like a fretful schoolboy marking time restlessly until the long-awaited holidays arrived, he feverishly paced the small enclosure that was their cell, packing and unpacking his belongings over and over.

"Will you settle down?" an irritated Schenck said. "Go take a long walk, or a bath, or something."

"Sorry, Schenck, I can't seem to concentrate on anything; guess I'm excited."

He unpacked his bag again, fingering several wooden animal sculptures carved for him by a talented prisoner, which he would give as gifts to his family. He would also include a few watercolors of his own, and the sketches the ill-fated Sperling had executed. Gazing affectionately at the family photographs his mother had packed for him so many months ago, Max sighed. How he had missed her warm and loving ways. He imagined himself happily embracing her when they were again reunited. She would be so relieved to see him safely returned. He could almost smell the lilac fragrance of her perfume.

The men were packed, ready to leave. As they finally walked through the gate and climbed into waiting lorries, Schenck growled, "Goodbye, you miserable, godforsaken pest-hole."

"Amen," breathed Max fervently.

In Liverpool, the internees boarded the train for Sydney, feeling a mixture of excitement at the prospect of going to Germany, and misgivings regarding the reception they could expect. The transport ship waited in the harbor. After being assigned quarters, approximately a thousand internees settled down, eager to be on their way.

"I heard the ship had been held up here in Sydney for several weeks, because of influenza on board," Max related to Schenck. "But all is well now, we sail tomorrow morning."

Three days out at sea, Max complained of headache. His illness soon progressed to chills and fever, and he was immediately sent to sick bay. Schenck haunted the adjacent gangways, accosting orderlies at every opportunity for news concerning Max's condition.

"How is he? He's my friend; I want to see him."

"You can't see him. If we let everyone in to visit, the flu would spread all over the ship. All I can tell you is that he's very sick."

Schenck became frantic when another day passed, and the orderlies ignored his pleas to see Max. He sat in the gangway obstinately until, finally, one of the men, either tiring of constantly stepping over him or truly showing some kindness, pulled him aside.

"Linden is dying," he said. "You want to see him, go ahead; it's your funeral."

Max's breathing was labored; his fluid-filled lungs struggling mightily to cling to life. Schenck stroked his face affectionately, noting with pity the skin that had turned bluish from ear to ear. Max barely recognized him at first, but then smiled.

"Schenck," he whispered faintly. "I ache all over."

"I know ... I'll stay with you."

"No ...," Max shook his head weakly, "You'll get sick, too."

"Who cares ... I'm as strong as a horse. I'm staying, they can't make me go, now that I'm in here."

Wracking coughs convulsed Max. The orderlies approached, but Schenck drove them away with a menacing glare. The camaraderie that had developed between the two friends during their internment made the prospect of a final separation a grievous one for Schenck. He did all he could to make Max comfortable— bathed his feverish brow, offered sips of water for thirst, murmured words of encouragement and support—passionately wishing he might fuse his strength into Max's failing body.

The hours passed. Schenck held Max's hand, remaining at his bedside until his brief life had ebbed away.

The next morning Schenck watched, along with some of the ship's complement, as burial services were conducted and Max's body was slipped into the calm Pacific waves. We almost made it, Max, he thought wistfully, tears welling up in eyes that had never before wept for anyone.

CHAPTER NINETEEN

Ending

The Germany that the Linden family was now destined to experience was a vanquished one—crushed, humbled, dispirited. The Allied powers had designed provisions in the armistice that would ensure Germany's complete fall, with no possibility of ever again rising. Wilson of the United States, Lloyd George of Great Britain, and Clemenceau of France, in order to restore peacetime stability quickly, worked to form new states on the ruins of the Austrian Empire. Thus were born Yugoslavia and—from Russia's lost areas—Finland, Estonia, Latvia, and Poland.

Franz was amazed when reading of Germany's heavy territorial losses, including—what was especially galling—the possession of the entire overseas empire, "mandated" to bordering victor states and League of Nations supervision. Coal mines and the Alsace went to France. In addition, five thousand guns, twenty-five thousand machine guns, and seventeen hundred planes were relinquished. Five thousand railway engines, one hundred and fifty thousand freight cars, and the bulk of the German navy, including all submarines, were also surrendered.

Demands for Germany to pay for losses and damages resulted in excessive reparations. The country did not have the massive sums called for; it had no gold. A blame had been laid that would have dire consequences for the world in the years to come. Unemployment and hunger were widespread. Now, the mass migration of German nationals returning each day from all over the world had to be coped with.

* * *

Bone-chilling cold penetrated the unheated railway car. Though the ancient coach was crowded with returning prisoners of war and military veterans, the congestion did little to warm them. Strong odors of sausage and a particularly pungent-smelling cheese permeated the stale, smoke-filled air.

Marta averted her gaze from the shimmering snow-covered landscape rolling by outside, which was barely visible through the frosted windows of the train. She instead gave her attention to the passengers seated nearby, feeling a sense of pity and compassion for everyone. The reception given the returnees by their homeland seemed as cold as the below-zero temperature outside the train. Marta wondered what would become of the military veterans in their midst. They looked so disillusioned. Subdued, with vacant eyes, their frayed, threadbare uniforms and bandaged limbs gave full testament to the pain and suffering endured in battle. Next to them sat desolate internee women burdened with clinging, fretful children. Where were their prisoner-of-war husbands? Alive? ... or dead?

Only the younger, returning male internees laughed and joked, exulting in their new-found freedom. Marta searched their eager faces, seeing Max in every smile and gesture. When the young men had first boarded the train, she had hoped that by some divine circumstance she might recognize her son in the group, and that he would greet her in surprise and joy, hugging her tightly. Wishful thinking.

"I'm so cold, Mama," Mitzi said, interrupting Marta's thoughts.

"Oh, how we could use the winter clothes that we stored at Oma's house in Bucharest," Lise said morosely. She shivered uncontrollably and pulled her light-weight cotton jacket more closely about her.

"Yes ... Elena needs a coat badly," Marta said. Her eyes rested on her daughter's slight figure seated opposite. She was huddled in a blanket a kind young soldier had draped over her, her eyes closed in misery. The stalwart infantryman had smiled in sympathy at the sight of the girl's sickly appearance. He approached the family again carrying a bundle. "I have extra bread and cheese, and some wine," he said. "Perhaps you would like some?"

Franz's eyes lit up. "Well, the wine would certainly warm us up a little, thank you. Here, come sit with us," he said, making room for the soldier on the seat. "What's your name, and where are you going?"

"My name is Kurt ... Kurt Fischer. I'm going to Erding. That's a small town ...."

"Ah ...," Franz interrupted, "that's where we're going! I come from Erding ... I was born there. Have you by any chance heard of the Linden family?"

Kurt hesitated a moment. "Hmmm ... the watchmaker? I think I know your cousin, Karl Kohler."

"Correct, though the watchmaker was my father. I'm the musician."

"Oh yes," the soldier said, light dawning on him now. "The venerated Kapellmeister. Your relatives speak of you with pride."

Franz beamed, and the two men began to converse animatedly, forging a warm friendship as the long hours dragged by. The train's progress was agonizingly slow. Again and again they were forced onto sidings as faster trains sped by. What normally would have taken a day and a night of traveling had now lengthened to over six days before they reached their destination. Elena's condition worsened with every passing kilometer—she became oblivious to her surroundings. When the train finally came to a stop in the Erding railway station, she was unconscious.

Disembodied, blurred faces floated in Elena's field of vision; they were encircled with snow-white auras of radiant light, like halos. Soft comforting voices soothed her. Gentle hands bathed her. Linens were changed and fluids administered. In her semi-consciousness, sounds were muted, distant .... Her mind and body seemed to dissolve into blissful, serene acceptance. She was released from stress and torment, as though she drifted painlessly and weightlessly amongst airy, feathery clouds.

Gradually, she returned to awareness and could now discern that the ethereal faces and halos of her dreamlike state belonged to nuns in white habits, but she still felt disoriented.

"Where am I," she murmured, "in heaven?"

A chuckle. "No, dear girl, you are in hospital."

"But ... how did I get here? I don't remember."

"You were brought here from the train station, but you mustn't try to get up yet. You're very weak."

It wasn't long before she realized how very weak she was. Her first effort to rise from the bed sent her head whirling.

"You've been very ill, Elena," her mother said on one of her many visits to her bedside. "You'll be coming home soon, but will have to rest in bed each day. No solid foods, yet, only the discarded water from boiled rice."

Several days later, an ambulance took her to the family's new lodgings. The rooms of the apartment were large, almost palatial. Most of their belongings sat on the floor, still packed.

"Herr Kohler, and some of Papa's other cousins, rented this place for us, obviously under the delusion that we were wealthy," explained Mitzi. "I guess because of our travels in exotic countries. They were impressed with the glamorous life we led, before we were interned. Papa was reluctant to admit that being musicians didn't pay that much, especially when board was included. Anyway, he and Mama are out now looking for a less expensive rental."

Elena's prescribed bed rest depressed her. While ill, thoughts of Lorenzo had receded to the back of her mind, but the long hours of solitude, with little to do but read, brought the memory of her loss vividly into focus again. She lay on the bed amid abundant pillows, listening to the sounds of the household. A clock ticked loudly in the quiet of her room. Her father practiced the violin, a habit whether or not he played professionally these days. From the kitchen, a kettle boiled on the stove, and pots and pans clattered and banged as her mother and sisters prepared meals. Lise and Mitzi were unusually interested in food preparation, she thought, but then surmised that Kurt Fischer's invitations to Lise for social gatherings were furthering a romance between the two. Mitzi was also invited to participate in skating parties and dances; both girls were marriage-minded. Elena yearned for the nearness of Lorenzo. His touch ... his kiss.

She heard Lise's voice raised in complaint as she energetically swept the kitchen floor. "I'm getting so tired of having to eat rice every day because Elena needs the water for her bowels. When will she be getting better? It's taking forever." Her mother shushed Lise reproachfully, and Elena turned her face into the pillows, tears welling up in her eyes. Feelings of guilt and worthlessness assailed her. I'm a burden to everyone, she thought.

Another apartment was located, and the family moved the first of the month. The final blow came for Elena when official notification of Max's death was received. Marta and Franz were devastated, unbelieving. His sisters mourned his passing with quiet tears. Elena's tears were ones of hopelessness. The one heartening event she had looked forward to, after Lorenzo's death, was Max's arrival, bringing her understanding and sympathy. The loss of the two men she loved most in the world was cataclysmic. She wept for days, refusing to leave her bed.

"There's no grave I can visit, Mama," she cried," Max is at the bottom of the sea. He's lost to me forever!"

"Elena ... Elena," Marta said, holding her daughter in a tight embrace. "You must calm yourself, you'll make yourself sick." When Elena became hysterical, a physician was summoned.

"Your daughter is very near a breakdown," he said, after an examination and consultation. "I'm not surprised ... her illness and all she's suffered these past few years. I'll give her a sedative, but only time can heal her heartache."

When Max's bag was received, Marta asked Franz to bring it into their bedroom. "Elena mustn't see it," she said. "It will only start her crying again."

"It will make you cry, too."

"We've lost many children, Franz, but I think this is the worst of all. Max had grown to manhood; he had so much ahead of him yet. The others were still babies. I felt that God wanted them. If I didn't think that, I guess I would have gone insane. But as the doctor said, time heals. You don't forget, but you accept." Her voice broke. "Oh, Franz, he was so good, so loving."

"I know, Marta, I know."

It was early spring, and the winds were still bitingly cold in Erding. Elena and Mitzi walked daily about the Schranennplatz, a picturesque square in the middle of town. The seventeenth- and eighteenth-century buildings boasted a quaint tower clock and small shops. Elena was following doctor's orders, walking every day, but the fresh air and exercise failed to bring color to her cheeks. Her figure was spare, her lack of appetite kept her looking worn and frail. As it was, food was scarce, prices high. Kurt Fischer brought small tidbits occasionally to tempt her

"I'm afraid she'll get tuberculosis," Fischer said to Marta, "as so many did during the time of the Allied blockade. The only thing that kept people barely alive was the turnip."

* * *

"I've received a letter from Rudy," Franz announced to the family in May. "He urges us to come to San Francisco. Food is plentiful, and the climate warm. It would be good for you, Elena."

"Well, Papa, I guess this is a good time to tell you that Kurt and I are getting married," Lise stated.

"You're telling me?" Franz was indignant. "He hasn't asked me for your hand in marriage. That's the way it's usually done, isn't it?"

"Oh, Papa, that's old-fashioned," Lise said, for the first time boldly daring to voice her sentiments to her dictatorial parent, "but if you insist, Kurt will talk to you. We love each other and plan to marry. You and Mama, and Mitzi and Elena, can go to America, but I'm not going with you." Now that she had started her emancipation declaration, she continued heatedly.

"I don't ever want to travel again, or ever play in an orchestra. I've had more than I can bear of staying up all hours, never getting enough sleep, and always being on the move. Look how we ended up." She paused, her face flushed with bitterness. "It's because of your damned orchestra that we lost Max!"

"Lise!" Marta cried.

"I'm sorry, Papa, but that's how I feel," Lise said as she swept grandly from the room.

Franz looked pained. He closed his eyes and shook his head. "She's right," he said faintly.

"No, Franz, no," Marta said consolingly. "It isn't true; the world was at war and Max could have died anywhere." She patted his hand briefly, her eyes moist.

Mitzi rose from her chair and knelt before her father. "Papa," she said gently, "I don't feel as Lise does about the orchestra and our travels. I'll always remember those years as the happiest of our lives, but ... I don't want to go to America, either. I feel at home here in Germany, even though times are hard. Herr Kohler has offered to let me live with his family and help out in his clock business for my board."

Franz nodded, resigned. He fixed his gaze on Marta and Elena. "Well," he said, "what do you say?"

Lise's harsh outburst had distressed Elena; she struggled to restrain the nervous tension threatening to overcome her. Tears seemed to flow at the slightest provocation of late. She choked back the lump she felt in her throat. "I ... I say yes, Papa," she answered. "There's nothing here for me."

Marta smiled at her husband. He knew without saying that she would follow wherever he led, though she had personal misgivings about making the journey. Did the wanderlust still burn in his breast, or did he feel America was a better place to live out his waning years, rather than the destitute Germany? She suspected the reassuring proximity of a son nearby played a role in his decision. He felt the loss of Max deeply.

* * *

Lise, looking uncommonly angelic and dainty in her white lace gown, married Kurt in a small, rustic, country church. At a quiet, outdoor reception hosted by Karl Kohler, friends and relatives gathered to celebrate the marriage and also wish their fascinating kin another farewell. Lise, blooming with happiness, embraced her mother and sisters joyfully. Elena pensively recalled Lise's wish years before at Stephanie's wedding in Egypt. The family was, sadly, not altogether as she had hoped.

To her father, Lise said apologetically, "I'm sorry, Papa; I hope you have forgiven me my outburst a while ago … I do want us to part friends. I hope you'll be very happy with Rudy in America."

Franz smiled, and nodded. He patted her on the shoulder. "You be happy, too," he said.

Alexandria, Egypt 1920

Dear Family,

Good news, and bad news, all in one letter. It doesn't seem possible that we will never see dear Max again! There he was, on his way home, the worst of his trials behind him. I just can't believe he's gone; we are grieving so for him.

We were relieved to hear you have arrived safely in Erding, and that Elena is recovering from her illness. We have sent our warmest felicitations to Lise and her new husband, Kurt. That was a nice surprise. We wish them much happiness.

Our news is not happy. We lost our restaurant business; we had to close. Alexandria is a dead city. No one has money to vacation here after the war. I am doing sewing and alterations for wealthy Arab families until André gets on his feet again. Life is so unpredictable.

Received a letter from Rudy this morning. Papa, is it really true that you and Mama and Elena are joining him in San Francisco? If so, I am lost. Will we ever see each other again?

Love to all, and God bless,
Stephanie

Elena read Stephanie's letter solemnly. She wondered if there was to be no end to separation for the family. Rudy's letters were bright with the anticipation of their arrival, but there was no letter of welcome from his wife, Angela.

Part Three

THE WEST

CHAPTER TWENTY

America

"How bad can it be?" Franz said resentfully. "We must economize." He'd just returned from the travel bureau and was irked by Marta's complaints.

"I realize we must economize," she said, "but booking third class ...."

"It won't be as though we're going steerage, Marta. It's just that we don't have a private toilet and sink." Her face fell, and he hastened to reassure her. "The agent said the ship was built in Bremen in 1914. It was one of the passenger liners ceded to the Royal Holland Line," he continued, "replacing neutral ships sunk by German submarines during the war. I'm sure it's very clean."

"I hope so," she snapped. Immediately regretting her ill humor, she softened her tone of voice. "I'm sorry, Franz, I don't mean to be difficult, but ... ever since our internment, I find myself less able to cope." She smiled. "When do we leave?"

Franz's face brightened. "In two weeks. We sail from Rotterdam to New Orleans." He unfolded a map before her, his hands trembling in anticipation. "Look here. New Orleans is in a state called Louisiana in the southern part of the country. We travel by train from there to California."

"It's a long way, isn't it?" She noted the vast expanse of land depicted on the map.

"Yes, but imagine all we'll see!"

She smiled faintly—the thought of a cabin without a private toilet troubled her. She was suffering incontinence lately; no doubt the result of bearing twelve children during her lifetime. Franz hadn't noticed that she rose several times each night to visit the bathroom. It would be embarrassing to be obliged to climb out of a berth and turn on the lights several times a night, then disturb Elena and Franz again as she returned from the lavatory. She sighed; it couldn't be helped. Franz was set on saving money, and rightly so, even if it was inconvenient for her.

* * *

Elena sat in a deck chair, gazing out over the railing of the ship to the gray Atlantic beyond. Angry gusts of wind whipped heavy seas into white-capped waves, the aftermath of two days of stormy weather since leaving Rotterdam. Shivering, she drew a lap robe more closely around her legs and sighed heavily. A miserable voyage, she thought. One that had begun badly right from the first day.

Her mother, at the outset, had been repelled by the dingy, unscrubbed condition of the pocket-sized cabin the family had been assigned. "It's just as I feared," she said reproachfully, eyeing Elena's unconcerned father. "Dirt everywhere. The sheets and pillow slips look as though they've not been changed for months, and the blankets smell musty and foul. It's so damp in here, the paint is peeling from the walls."

"Bulkheads," Franz corrected.

"What?"

"Not walls. They're called bulkheads on a ship."

"Oh!" Marta exclaimed, exasperated. "I'm just too old for all this."

"It's only for a few days, Marta," Franz said impatiently. "We'll be in New Orleans before you know it."

"It can't be too soon for me!"

Elena retired that evening wondering what had caused her usually gentle mother's wrath. In India, she had been the one to make the best of things while others fretted and fussed. But the strained atmosphere was to worsen considerably by morning. Elena, collecting her toilette in preparation for a first visit to the washroom, glanced at her mother lying in her berth.

"Mama!" she screamed. "What's happened to your eyes?!"

Marta was startled. "What? .... What is it?" She sat up slowly, half awake, fingering her eye area.

"Look in the mirror, Mama. You look terrible!"

Franz, aroused from his sleep, climbed hastily from his berth as Marta rose to look at herself in a small wall mirror. He paled at the sight of her.

Marta stared unbelievingly at her image in the glass. She caught her breath in horror. "Oh my God!" she wailed. The soft flesh of her eyelids had been almost entirely eaten away. It gave her the appearance of a dead person, like a hideous, frightful-looking ogre with gaping red-rimmed orbs. She began to cry.

The ship's physician was summoned. He introduced himself as Dr. Merwede, a middle-aged Dutchman who spoke German.

"It was cockroaches," he said as he carefully examined Marta. "They had a tasty treat on your eyes last night, Frau Linden."

"I didn't feel a thing," whimpered Marta.

"I'm afraid it's not an uncommon thing to happen here in third class," he said matter-of-factly, as he applied an ointment. "On this ship, anyway." He paused, glancing about the dismal cabin and its immaculate-appearing occupants. A spark of interest flashed in his eyes when he saw Elena, whose red hair gleamed warmly in the overhead light. Clearing his throat, he asked, "You haven't used the washing facilities yet?" When they shook their heads, he continued, "They're not fitting for the ladies. You may use my cabin for washing, if you like. I'm on duty most of the time."

"That's very kind of you, Dr. Merwede," Franz said, "but ...." He cast a furtive glance at his wife and whispered, "Are the washrooms really that bad?"

"Yes," the doctor whispered as he exited the cabin. "They are infested with lice."

Later in the afternoon, Elena walked the decks of the ship. Her mother had been sedated and was resting in the cabin. Her father had somehow wheedled an invitation from the captain to visit the bridge. She suspected that the friendly Dr. Merwede had arranged the meeting. The doctor himself soon materialized from a gangway exit and joined her, adjusting his longer gait to her shorter one. He looked down at her, tall and lean in his blue uniform.

"How is your mother, Fraülein Linden ... or is she your grandmother?"

She smiled. "My mother is resting, thank you, Doctor. It isn't the first time my parents have been mistaken for my grandparents. I'm the last of the brood."

"Especially since you look so young," he said. "I imagine it's because you are so thin, way too thin, I might add. Your father said you'd been ill. I'm happy to see you're taking the air; it will whet the appetite."

His words struck a sore spot. She gazed up at him, sniffing disdainfully. "How can I have an appetite when the passengers we are seated with in the dining salon eat like animals? Their table manners are atrocious." She paused, her mind picturing the offending group at the table. "Do you know that scraps of food from their meals lie in the men's beards for days? And how appetizing can it be," she continued heatedly, "to see soft-boiled egg dribbling down those beards when I try to enjoy my meal? It's easy to see the lice have found a home there, too." She was suddenly ashamed of her outburst. "Oh, I'm sorry, I know there's nothing you can do about it."

The doctor was silent for a moment. "You're referring to the Russian Jews. I can understand your distaste, you have good reason, but ...." He sighed and said, "I feel sorry for them. When you've sailed on these ships as much as I have, you see things. Things you'd rather not think about because they're cruel and inhuman."

"What do you mean?"

He studied her face intently. "We've only just met," he said, "but I feel you're an intelligent young woman, and will understand the ways of the world as you get older. If I asked you why you're going to America, what would your answer be?"

"Hmmm ... I guess I hope to find a home; we've traveled so much."

"And you have someone to sponsor you?"

"My brother."

They stopped walking, leaning their arms on the ship's railing. The doctor gazed seriously into Elena's eyes. "The Jews are looking for a home, too, you see, but with no one to sponsor them, they wander from country to country without success. This particular group is victim of pogroms in the Ukraine, and is hoping for admittance into the United States."

Elena was contrite. The doctor had compassion for his fellow man, despite outward appearances. She had yet little understanding concerning political and historical implications involved in the Jewish heritage, but she identified with their plight.

"I'm sorry, what will happen to them?"

He shrugged his shoulders. "Who knows? The doors to Jewish immigration in America are slowly being closed."

Immigration procedures went smoothly in New Orleans. A taxi took Elena and her parents to the railway station, and they boarded a train bound for California that same day. On the morning of departure, the Russian travelers had lined the railings of the ship. Elena felt their haunted eyes following her passage down the gangplank as she disembarked. She remembered Dr. Merwede's words to her as they said their farewells the night before. "The Russians have been denied entry. Let us hope they'll have better luck in our next port, Brazil." She wondered if the Rosenbaums were still in Singapore.

* * *

How strange and different this new world is, Elena thought. She watched a constantly changing landscape from the train windows as they journeyed westward. Louisiana, Texas, New Mexico. Louisiana had been hot and humid, favored with an abundance of trees and greenery. Subsequently, the land turned arid and barren as they traveled on. Monotonous, treeless, broad open spaces continued mile upon mile. Like India, and yet, not like India, she thought.

Hot, dry wind blew a gritty dust through partially raised windows. Her father napped, his head comfortable on her mother's plump shoulder. Marta looked up from her crocheting and smiled at Elena. Although her eyes were not completely healed, she was in much better humor since leaving the ship. "Papa can sleep anywhere," she said. "Even if the world were coming to an end, I'm sure. A true traveler." She paused a moment, her expression contemplative. "Elena, when we rode through, where was it, Louisiana? You saw the black people?"

"The Negroes? Yes, there were many."

"I thought they seemed sullen, their faces expressionless. Looking into their eyes ... I had the feeling they hated us. Whites in general. Not at all like the friendly natives of Siam."

Elena reflected a bit before answering. "The Siamese were jolly and humorous, alright. It must be the influence of their Buddhist religion, and also the fact that they are a free people. Blacks were slaves until fifty years ago ... and still oppressed, by the looks of them."

Marta clucked her tongue and, shaking her head, returned to her crocheting.

"I have a question, Mama," Elena said after several minutes had elapsed. "I've been watching and watching ever since we started on the train, but I haven't seen one single cowboy. Where are they? We saw so many in the films at the cinema. No Indians or buffalo, either."

A passing conductor, obviously amused by her questions, gave her the answer. "No, no," the wizened-looking fellow explained, "the day of the cowboy, like you see in the movies, is over. You won't see any. And the Indians are all on reservations now." He smiled impishly. "Don't worry, they won't be attacking or robbing us."

Grinning at him, Elena sat back in her seat, translating his words for her mother. Then she became contemplative; her mind had been assailed by so many new ideas and impressions in the past days. The Jewish refugees loomed large in her conscience; the blacks in Louisiana, also. It is an imperfect world, she thought. Even her mother's uncharacteristic behavior on the ship perplexed her. People changed, she decided. Was she now on the road to maturity, observing life with more grownup eyes? She smiled to herself, though she still felt acute disappointment at not seeing cowboys and Indians.

* * *

California. Land of sunshine and orange groves. Home of soaring, gigantic redwood trees and rich black soil that yielded abundant crops year-round. Since the gold-mining days of 1849, settlers had journeyed across prairies, seas, and mountains to reach the promised land. Elena and her parents now found themselves before the Golden Gate.

They were totally unprepared for the beauty of the San Francisco skyline. Shining in the crisp early morning sunshine, it burst into view as the ferry plied its way across the bay from Oakland. The three stood at the railing, gaping at the tall buildings and hills rising spectacularly from the water's edge.

"It's difficult to believe that only sixteen years ago the city was devastated by earthquake and fire," Franz marveled.

"Breathtaking," Elena murmured.

"And remarkable that it was rebuilt so quickly. Such confidence and vitality you don't find everywhere."

"I can almost feel that vitality now, Papa. Just look at the harbor; have you ever seen such energy and activity anywhere else we've been?"

Franz and Marta nodded as they surveyed the scene. The bay was crowded with vessels of every type—freighters, ferries, fishing boats, steamers, and naval ships. All either rode at anchor or were being busily loaded and unloaded at docks and piers. Small boats steamed in all directions, whistles blowing jauntily. Muscles straining, sailors, longshoremen, and dockworkers could be seen laboring vigorously at their various tasks.

Our new home, thought Elena. She felt heartened. For the first time since Lorenzo's and Max's deaths, she felt uplifted. The fresh winds that swept across the decks of the ferry on that clear, sunny morning helped dispel the clouds of tragedy and heartbreak that had enveloped her like a shroud.

The boat docked before the Ferry Building, a 240-foot-tall, impressive steel-and-concrete structure, topped by a Spanish-Moorish-style clock tower. Serving at least forty ferryboats, and proud survivor of the earthquake of 1906, it far outclassed any train terminal of the Industrial Age.

Rudy waited inside the terminal, his lively three-year-old daughter, Marianne, hopping and jumping expectantly by his side.

"Is that Oma?" she asked as passengers started streaming into the large waiting room.

Rudy searched the faces of the crowd, his gaze finally alighting on those of his parents as they walked slowly into the room. How they've aged, he thought with a shock, and could that be Elena with them? She looked so pale and thin, an incredible contrast to the warm-complexioned, wholesome sister he remembered in Singapore. He felt a pang of guilt; the war had left its mark on them.

His mother caught sight of him and waved. "There he is, Franz; there's Rudy!" She smiled, and soon they were embracing and all talking at once, glowing in the happiness of their reunion.

"Oh, Rudy," Marta exclaimed, "what a beautiful little granddaughter we have." She hugged and kissed Marianne. "Just look at that blonde hair!"

Rudy beamed with fatherly pride. "She's clever, too," he said.

"This is a beautiful city," Franz said, as Rudy picked up their bags and led them out to the street. Marianne clasped the hands of her grandmother and aunt, prancing along between them. She giggled delightedly as they lifted and swung her back and forth several times as they walked.

"My machine is parked here on the Embarcadero," Rudy said, motioning his head towards a wide road built atop a sea wall. Docks and wharves spread out on both sides of the Ferry Building, stretching for miles on end. He stopped before a shiny black vehicle, a Ford, he said proudly, and after finally deciding who should sit where, they were off.

"Angela didn't come to meet you because it would be too crowded with all of us and your baggage in the machine," Rudy said as he maneuvered the automobile through heavy traffic on a broad thoroughfare. "She is waiting lunch for us. This is Market Street that we're riding on now; you can see how wide a road it is. There are four sets of streetcar tracks in the middle." He shouted over the din of honking auto horns and jangling trolley car bells.

"It's an exciting city, Rudy," Elena said, her eyes bright with interest as they passed a profusion of shops and businesses.

"Sorry about the bumpy ride," Rudy said, smiling as the auto rattled and jounced. "I read somewhere, though, that vibration is good for the liver."

* * *

When Rudy had invited his family to immigrate to America, he had been motivated by genuine good-heartedness and also some guilt—they had been interned, and he had gone free. When he began making final arrangements, his wife, Angela, could still not believe his intentions were serious.

"You don't really plan to have your parents and Elena come live with us, do you, Rudy?" she asked, an underlying tension apparent in her voice.

He glanced up at her warily from the chair he was refinishing. "I didn't think you'd mind, Angela; when he finds work they'll be on their own."

"What work can he do? He's an old man, and he doesn't even speak English," she said scornfully. "Besides, you know they'll have to live with us, he couldn't earn enough to live separate from us."

"He's an excellent violinist ... or he was. He can arrange music ... and there are his own compositions we can try to get published."

"This isn't Europe, Rudy," she countered derisively. "American music is all popular tunes, not waltzes and polkas. And securing a position with the opera or symphony is just about impossible. You've tried."

"We'll work it out, Angela," he said, striving to placate her. "They're my family, and they need help."

"Oh?" Rudy's words kindled an explosive response in her. "I have family, too!" she cried, her face flushed with fury. "I'd like my sister, Louise, to come from Germany; she's starving over there."

"Now, stop," he snapped. "We can't bring everybody in Germany over. If Max were still alive, he would've helped support my parents, but he's dead."

"Oh, yes," she said bitterly. "So now *we* are supposed to support them. Where is the money going to come from? That's three extra people. Thank God your other sisters decided to stay in Germany."

Provoked, Rudy shouted heatedly, "That's enough! My parents are coming, and that's that. You'll just have to get used to the idea."

She turned from him, taken aback by his outburst. In the ensuing weeks she prepared the cold-water flat they occupied with a furious intensity, scrubbing floors and buffing windows until everything shone like mirrors. When all was ready for the family, she surveyed her handiwork with satisfaction. Outwardly she would welcome, but inwardly she seethed with resentment.

CHAPTER TWENTY-ONE

San Francisco

Rudy fairly burst with pride as he drove the family about San Francisco's terraced streets and steep hills, pointing out various attractions each day with great enthusiasm. It was very evident, Elena thought, that the scenic city had captured his heart, and his fascination was infectious. The energy and animation he had displayed in the weeks since their arrival had drawn her irresistibly toward a healing of the spirit. She gradually began to experience stirrings of a rebirth. Step by faltering step, she entered the world of the living again.

Angela seldom joined the family's sightseeing jaunts, pleading duties that required her attention. And, usually, Marianne needed her daily nap; however, when the tot clamored to be included in the outings, her mother sometimes relented. One sunny morning, they all squeezed into the Ford, Marianne seated happily atop her Tante Elena's lap.

Rudy was a mine of information as he drove. "This is a cosmopolitan town," he said. "The gold rush of 1849 brought immigrants as far away as Australia, Peru, and Chili. Even China and Mexico, too."

"Unbelievable," Marta said, shaking her head. "All hoping to become rich."

"Many went home when they didn't find gold, but stories had spread about sunny California. Irish and other European immigrants from the East Coast arrived, and now, lately, Italians, Portuguese, Greeks, and Russians."

"And Germans," added Elena, smiling.

"Hmmm, yes ... Germans. We weren't very popular here during the war."

"We weren't popular anywhere," Franz said.

"It's over now, Papa," Rudy said, reaching over to pat his father's hand consolingly.

Angela sighed audibly at Rudy's words. Elena peered at her sister-in-law from behind Marianne's continually bobbing head. Angela, staring listlessly at the road ahead, had become a puzzle to Elena, friendly one minute, then distant the next. Oh, she made a great effort to be kind and gracious most days, Elena thought. Yet there were moments when an expression of hostility crossed Angela's face. A fleeting, pained smile was quickly hidden again by pleasantries and good cheer. Elena had an uncomfortable feeling that the real Angela was concealed behind a mask, like the mirror-and-smoke illusions of an artful magician.

They drove through the perennial green of Golden Gate Park to the white, unspoiled beaches of the Pacific Ocean.

"Oh, how beautiful, Rudy!" exclaimed Elena. "The water is so blue, it glitters like jewels in the sunshine."

"Pretty today," Rudy admitted, "but this is exactly where the fog rolls in, especially in the summer. To get the sun, we go inland across the bay— don't we, Angela?—to Marin County. There we swim and hike."

"Well, I think San Francisco will suit me just fine," Elena said, nodding her head firmly. "I've had enough sun in India to last me a lifetime."

"Ah-hah!" Rudy said brightly. "Look to your right, then. We're passing the very spot for you to swim without worrying about the sun."

Elena saw a sign on a nondescript building that read Sutro Baths and Museum. "What's that," she asked, giggling. "Do people swim in a museum?"

"No, the museum is just an added attraction. Inside is a huge salt-water swimming pool, with slides and fountains and a glass-windowed roof. But what is especially intriguing are six side-by-side smaller pools featuring temperatures from hot to ice-cold."

Angela smiled. "You should see Rudy. He starts from the cold pool, swims across each to the hot pool, then turns around and swims through each one back to the cold one."

"Stimulating!" he said, chuckling.

Marianne was suddenly all ears. "Oh, Papa, let's go swimming there now!"

He ignored her, next pointing out a building perched precariously on the edge of a cliff. "That's a restaurant appropriately called the 'Cliff House.' It looks like a French chateau and serves food to match."

"Papa, can't we go there to eat now?" Marianne wheedled, leaning forward to tap her father on the shoulder. He took little heed as Angela spoke. "Look there, below the cliffs," she said, as Rudy slowed the auto. "You can just make out the sea lions lounging on the rocks. We really need binoculars to see them clearly."

Marianne was beside herself by now, bouncing about on Elena's lap. "I want to see the sea lions!" she cried. "Can't we stop and look at them, Papa?"

Elena saw the look of impatience crossing her father's face as he glanced back at his granddaughter. Ever since their arrival he had taken it upon himself to correct the little one's behavior, unaware that he was incurring Angela's wrath. Elena cradled Marianne in her arms quickly before Franz could voice his disapproval.

"We'll see the sea lions another time, Marianne," she cajoled. "Where are we going next, Rudy?"

"Playland at the Beach, it's an amusement park. There's a ride I want Papa to try." He turned to his father. "I know you've never experienced anything like this, Papa."

"What a monstrosity," Marta said, as the family gazed open-mouthed at the tall, wooden structure before them.

"It's a roller coaster, The Giant Dipper, it's called," Rudy said.

Franz's eyes sparkled with anticipation. "Very interesting," he said.

Marta turned to him. "You're not going to ride on that horror?"

"Why not?"

"Because you're too old." From the moment Marta had uttered the challenging words, she knew she had spurred her determined husband on. He and Rudy strapped themselves into a sleek red car, and sped off in a roar of clanging metal to dizzying heights and stomach-flopping descents. Marta closed her eyes, lips moving in silent prayer.

"He'll have a stroke," murmured Elena.

Though Franz's face was a pasty white upon their return to earth, he smiled in keen enjoyment. "Exhilarating!" he gasped. "Takes one's breath away."

"Once more, Papa?" Rudy teased.

"No, no! Enough."

"Hot dogs!" Marianne squealed in English as the family passed the food stands.

"No, Marianne," Angela said. "We have a picnic lunch, and we're going to the beach now."

"Hot dog? What is that?" Franz asked.

Rudy smiled. "That's sausage on a roll, Papa. Do you want to try one?"

"But we *have* a lunch, Rudy," Angela urged.

"That's alright. Papa would like to try one."

Angela walked ahead as Rudy placed a frankfurter piled high with sauerkraut in his father's hands. Elena detected a slight flush on her face, lips drawn into a hard line.

They walked along the paved promenade that stretched for miles along the beachfront. A spot was selected for the picnic, and Angela spread an old coverlet, saved for such purposes, on the sand, setting out sandwiches, potato salad, and some fruit from a basket.

Marta gazed out at the breaking surf, her hand shading her eyes from the sun. "Is that fog out there over the ocean?"

Rudy studied the gray mist blanketing the waters. "Yes. It gets cold and damp in the fog, we'd better ...." He was interrupted by Marianne as she made forays onto the coverlet and back to the sand again. "Stop prancing about, Marianne," he said. "You'll get sand all over the food."

"I want a sandwich."

"Sit down," Angela directed, "and I'll give you one."

"No," the little one whined, "I want to eat the sandwich while I wade in the water." She wriggled her tiny body and hopped vigorously from one foot to the other, sending grains of sand in all directions.

"The sandwich first."

"No, Mama ...."

Franz's voice thundered out suddenly, giving everyone a jolt. "Sit down, Marianne!" he roared. "Eat your sandwich! Do as your mother says!"

Marianne plopped down onto the sand, staring up at her grandfather in surprise and fear. Her lower lip curled and tears welled in her eyes as she watched him select a sandwich and raise it in the air.

"This is what you do," he said, taking a bite and starting to chew. "You sit down, and ...." A look of disgust spread across his face and he spat out the mouthful of sandwich. "Sand in it," he said to Marta.

Angela's entire body seemed to tense, as though rigor mortis was rapidly setting in. She held her breath, lips pursed for a moment, before confronting Franz. "Papa Linden," she said, "this isn't the first time you've scolded Marianne."

Elena saw that the resentment and anger her sister-in-law had harbored in past weeks was about to overflow like rivers swollen with heavy rains.

Rudy recognized the danger. "Angela," he warned.

"Only *I* tell Marianne what to do, not anyone else!" Angela hissed, her face now flushed and contorted in righteous indignation.

"Papa didn't mean to discipline Marianne, did you Papa?" Rudy said quickly.

"Oh, yes he did!" Angela declared before Franz could open his mouth. "Rudy, you've told me time and again how your father ruled with an iron hand ... how he beat you and Max. You still have scars to prove it! He's not going to do that to Marianne."

"Of course he won't," Marta said swiftly, attempting to smooth things over. Marta glanced at the slack-jawed, startled Franz. She knew he had no inkling of the reasons behind Angela's outburst. A father, and now grandfather, he had acted as he always had, correcting children's behavior when he thought they needed it. It would take some effort on her part to explain to him why Angela was upset. "You must understand, Angela," she continued, "there were many children in our family; strictness was necessary."

Angela didn't answer. She shook her head and proceeded to gather the food together. The picnic was over.

Franz, after some urging from Marta, attempted to ignore Marianne's precocious behavior, and, on the surface, other than that day at the beach, Angela was again helpful and considerate. Her face betrayed little of her embitterment, but her underlying dissatisfaction manifested itself in small ways. There were sly insinuations. Her sugary, innocent-sounding voice began to rasp on Elena's nerves like the scratching of fingernails on a slate board.

"I try to cook good meals," Angela said one day, smiling brightly, "but you know how high food costs are these days."

On another day, she shook her head in puzzlement. "Our electric bill has risen. I don't understand it. I know you don't leave the lights on late in your room."

She apologized while aggressively scrubbing the kitchen floor. "I try to keep the flat clean, but it's hard with so many of us living together like this."

Marta sought to understand Angela's plight, urging the still frail Elena to help as much as she was able. Elena tried, but was skeptical. "I think she's trying to impress us with how hard she works. Do the windows really need to be washed every week?"

"To be honest, Elena," her mother said. "I'm sure if she lived in a matchbox, she would still clean house like a whirling dervish. It's compulsive with her."

"Yes, but she makes us feel guilty about everything—the cost of food, the electric, and the extra work we cause her. Papa gives her board money, doesn't he?"

Rudy, ignoring the domestic conflicts buzzing around him, went ahead with his future plans for the family. "Angela and I have been saving to buy a house, Papa."

Franz's jaw dropped. "A house? Isn't that expensive?"

He and Marta were sitting in what Angela referred to as the "living room," though no one did much living in it. Usually the family sat around the kitchen table, the living room door closed to save on heating bills. Sparsely but tastefully furnished, the room showcased Rudy's second-hand and antique shop finds he had refinished. His cello was propped up against one elegantly transformed chair, ready for practice later in the afternoon.

"I know it sounds expensive, buying a house, Papa," Rudy said, "but the banks make it easy. They issue mortgages. We make a small down payment, and pay so much a month toward the principal, plus interest. After twenty to thirty years, we own the house."

Franz looked dubious. He'd always rented. Only royalty, the very rich, and business people owned houses in Europe.

"Everyone is doing it here in America, Papa," Rudy continued warmly, stimulated by the vision of his very own house and garden. "We hope to buy an older house, one I can fix up. You know how handy I am."

Realizing for the first time how he must now depend on his children for help and support, Franz suddenly felt very vulnerable. "And Mama and me, what happens to us?"

Rudy paused, attempting to find the correct words for what he was to propose. "If we can find the right house," he said, "I'll build an apartment for you and Mama, and Elena until she marries. You'll be private, with a small cooking area and bath." He hesitated a moment. "Of course, the house will have to be a little larger and would cost more."

"I see," Franz said, nodding. "You'd need us to contribute financially."

"Yes," Rudy said guardedly. "Then Angela would be ... well, more agreeable to the idea." He rushed on. "We have friends living down the peninsula, the brothers Neuhaus. They have this type of arrangement with their parents, living together with their wives and children. It works out very well."

"I'm sure they don't have a daughter-in-law named Angela," Marta murmured under her breath."

"What Mama?"

"Never mind, Rudy. Papa and I will talk it over and let you know what we think."

On a dreary Saturday morning, several days following that conversation, Franz and Marta left the flat for their daily walk. It took some urging on Marta's part to get Franz out the door.

"It's raining," he complained, stretching his hand, palm up, into the mist

"It's just fog. It'll clear soon. Come." She took his arm firmly in hers and they started walking. A small park close by had benches they could rest on, and, more importantly, a place they could talk privately. "Here, let's sit down," Marta directed when they reached the park.

"The bench is wet from the fog."

Marta sighed. "Stop your kvetching. I brought some newspapers to sit on." She spread the papers and slowly seated herself, wincing from the ever-present rheumatic pain in her bones.

Franz sighed deeply, shaking his head morosely. "I didn't realize how hard it would be, living with Rudy and Angela."

"Rudy's kind and thoughtful," Marta said, "but Angela ...." She rolled her eyes, pausing as another thought came to her. "What happened when you took your music manuscripts to the publisher yesterday? Rudy looked unhappy when you returned to the flat."

Franz avoided her gaze, his eyes darting away from her. "He said I would be charged with assault."

"What?"

"Well, it was the clerk's fault," Franz blustered self-righteously. "Imagine the idiot saying my music was ethnic-sounding, and I should take my work to New York. It would be better accepted there, he said. What quatsch! My music is classical, like Mozart and Chopin!"

"But what did you do?"

"He was rude," Franz said, his mustache bristling with indignation, "and I told him so."

"And?"

"I ... well, I grabbed his cravat and punched his chest, I was so angry. These Americans don't know good music when they hear it. All they like is something called jazz."

"Oh, Franz," Marta said. "What possessed you? I was hoping your music would bring us financial help. We could have had funds to invest in Rudy's house."

He grimaced. "What good is that? Angela would still be unfriendly. She doesn't want us here."

Marta was taken aback. She had believed, except for that day at the beach, that Franz hadn't noticed Angela's resentment and veiled insinuations. "It isn't easy for her, Franz. I suspect Rudy invited us here without first discussing it with her."

He shrugged his shoulders. "We're not wanted anywhere, are we? The world is passing us by. When we walk these streets, I feel so alien, like a visitor from another planet." He took his wife's hand in his. "Marta, I never felt this way before ...." His voice broke as nostalgia overwhelmed him. "If only we could go back to Singapore or Siam."

Tears of pity welled up in Marta's eyes. "Oh, Franz, that world has vanished for us, like a puff of smoke in the atmosphere. It was the war." She sighed deeply. "What are we going to do?"

Their eyes met in a cloud of dejection. Had it been a mistake for them to come to America? On the other hand, would it be any better living with Lise and Kurt in Germany?

* * *

That evening, they announced their decision. They would return to Europe. Rudy, unaccountably feeling relief mixed with guilt, said quickly, "Elena must stay with us." He disregarded Angela's black look. "Her chances for marriage and a good life would be much better here than in Germany."

"What do you think, Elena?" her father probed gently.

Elena looked in turn at her parents, then Rudy and Angela, searching for an answer to her dilemma. Go to Germany where life would be hard, or stay in San Francisco and suffer Angela's unpleasantness.

"I'll stay," she said finally to her father and mother. "The cost of my passage would be a burden to you." When they demurred, she continued, "Besides, you know Germany is strange to me, I wasn't happy there." She paused, turning to Rudy. "I'll look for work, I understand I'll owe you board money."

"Don't worry about it," he said expansively, but Angela was immediately ready with a suggestion.

"Many girls coming from Europe go into domestic service."

"Oh, I don't know," Franz said, perusing Elena's slight figure. "Elena isn't strong enough yet to do housework. It would be too much for her."

"We can check the newspaper advertisements," Angela said. "Elena can be an upstairs maid. She makes a good appearance, speaks well, and the work wouldn't be heavy."

It occurred to Elena that Angela had already been thinking along those lines since her arrival—to arrange for her sister-in-law to work where room and board was included. Nevertheless, the idea appealed to her also—she couldn't be far enough away from Angela.

Farewells are always sad affairs, but, for Elena, this was heartbreaking. The sight of her parents standing on the train platform, looking old and forlorn, grieved her. She struggled to hold back tears, but was overcome with an agonizing sense of loss.

"We'll never see each other again!" she cried, hugging Franz and Marta tightly. Tears flowed as she said impulsively. "Wait another day, and I'll go with you."

"Elena," Marta said gravely, "you must make a new life for yourself. You have Rudy to help you. We are old."

Rudy's face blanched. "Papa, Mama," he began, "I'm so sorry. I had really hoped we could ...."

Marta shook her head. "You did all you could, Rudy. Things don't always work out the way we plan. You must look at it as though we had just come for a visit."

On the ferry back to the city, Elena said mournfully, "This is Papa's last voyage. I know it had to come sometime ... but not like this ...."

Rudy nodded, staring moodily out at the gray waters of the bay. "It was Angela," he said.

Yes, it was Angela, Elena thought. She shivered, suddenly feeling alone and empty. Lorenzo ... Max ... and now her parents ... gone from her life.

CHAPTER TWENTY-TWO

The Beckmans

"You talk funny," the eleven-year-old boy said to Elena.

"Richard, it's not nice to say things like that," Mrs. Beckman said to her son. "Elena learned to speak English in Singapore, and that's why she has a British accent."

"I like the way you talk," his younger sister, Elyse, said. "I think you're the best maid we've ever had."

Mrs. Beckman smiled. "In the two weeks you've been with us, Elena, you've certainly gained the children's loyalty very quickly. Which," she added in a whisper, "is a great relief to me."

"What Mama means," piped up Elyse, "is that the other maids we've had drank beer and danced to the phonograph when she wasn't home."

"Hush, Elyse," her mother said, as Elena's eyes widened. "Elena won't do things like that. She's had a good upbringing, and I can see she's serious about her duties."

Elena smiled faintly. "I try to do my best, Mrs. Beckman." She liked her buxom, talkative employer, who was kind, thoughtful, and undemanding. As upstairs maid, Elena found the workload light. She made beds, dusted, cleaned bathrooms, and hand-washed fine lingerie. Mrs. Beckman's wardrobe required constant attention—pressing, mending, and sending soiled items to the cleaner when necessary. After school hours, Elena accompanied Richard and Elyse to dental visits, social dancing classes, and German lessons.

* * *

On Elena's first day at work, Mary, the downstairs maid, had helped carry her belongings up a narrow staircase to one of two rooms in the attic of the spacious Victorian-style house. It was typical of Mrs. Beckman to provide separate rooms for each girl. Mary sat on the bed watching Elena unpack and hang her clothes in the closet.

"Good thing you don't have many dresses; our closets are tiny," Mary said, noting that Elena's wardrobe was meager and shabby-looking. She shifted her plump frame to a more comfortable position, sighing. "We don't earn enough money to buy a lot of dresses, anyway." She paused as a thought came to her. "That reminds me, did Mrs. Beckman say you'll be expected to serve at dinner when she entertains?" She saw the look of panic flood Elena's face. "What's the matter? Never served before? Don't worry, I'll show you how." Her eyes crinkled at the corners as she smiled reassuringly. "We wear black uniforms with white organdy collars and little aprons, very ritzy. There are a few of them in the laundry room that were used by the other girls; one's sure to fit you."

"I'd be very grateful for your help," Elena said, responding to the girl's friendliness. "This is my first job."

"I thought so. Just do your work, and you'll be okay."

Elena smiled. "I haven't seen Mrs. Beckman's husband yet."

"Ah, yes, Dr. Beckman. He isn't around much. Spends a lot of time at his office on Sutter Street." She gave Elena a sideways glance. "It's better if you stay away from him."

"Why?"

"You'll see. Ta-ta!" She winked and disappeared into her room.

Elena seldom saw Dr. Beckman, only nodding politely when he acknowledged her presence in passing as she fulfilled her duties. Therefore, she was surprised when he beckoned her into the book-lined study one morning, asking her to be seated.

"Good morning, uh ... Elena, is it?"

Feeling apprehensive, she nodded, wondering if this was what Mary had obliquely warned her against. She had been aware of the doctor's dark handsomeness from a distance, and now his keen blue eyes rested on her with what she hoped was a professional appraisal.

"Mrs. Beckman has informed me of your background," he said, "and, frankly, it interests me very much. Perhaps you'd like to describe your family's adventures in more detail. How did it all start?"

Relieved that he wasn't making advances, she told her story, at first hesitantly but then warming up as he asked questions. She began to recognize that her tale intrigued most listeners. It had the glamour of music in exotic locales, as well as the drama of innocent victims being in the wrong place at the wrong time.

"Hmmm ...," the doctor said wistfully, when she had finished. "Your father did what every man wishes he could do, just get away from it all, and the hell with the consequences. I would like to have met him." He leaned back in his chair, clasping his hands over his middle, studying her face and

form intently. She stirred uneasily in her chair. "We've got to get you back
to health," he said. "I can see the dysentery you suffered from has left you
pale and thin. I'll instruct Cook to see that you get plenty of nourishing
food, and I'll bring home vitamins for you from the office."

She smiled, and thinking she had been dismissed, moved to rise from
her seat.

"Wait, Elena, there's one more thing I'd like to discuss with you." He
picked up a magazine from his desk, and cleared his throat before continuing. "I've been reading an article in this medical journal that describes the
trauma many prisoners of war suffer after their release from captivity. For
soldiers in the trenches, it may be something called 'shell shock.' For cap-
tives, there may be haunting memories and uncontrollable flashbacks as
well. Has that happened to you?"

"I ... I don't think I understand," Elena said, suddenly anxious. "I feel
fine now. It did take a while for me to recover, but now I try to forget the
past."

"I didn't intend to frighten you," the doctor said gently. "You should
know, though, that there may be times when small episodes, for instance,
like the sight of an armed guard, or even smelling a hateful odor, may trig-
ger anxiety in you. That happens because these occurrences are somehow
similar to bad experiences you might have had while being interned. In
your case, it may be loss of loved ones and illness."

She nodded, her throat tightening. If the doctor thought she was ill,
she might lose her job. "I'm fine, Doctor, really I am," she insisted.

"Well," he said, smiling, "time usually dims memories, but if you
do have problems, sharing the details of the trauma with someone else
may help." He rose from his chair, rounded the desk and offered his hand.
"We're pleased to have you working for us, Elena."

For the remainder of the day, their disturbing conversation dominated
Elena's thoughts. Painful specters of the agony and grief that had tortured
her in Germany clouded her mind. She thought she had been successful in
suppressing her anxieties, but as she lay abed that night her body shook
convulsively and tears flowed once again. When she finally slept, morbid
dreams ensued. She was falling, falling ... falling like a downed bird in
flight.

* * *

As months passed, Elena settled into the household routine, feeling
a sense of safety in the sameness of the days. The outside world faded in

her consciousness. In the evenings, after work was done, she retired to her snug room in the attic, enjoying the privacy it afforded. The luxury of sitting up in bed, reading books and magazines kindly loaned to her by Mrs. Beckman, gave her comfort and peace. Mary made up for any loneliness she might sustain without the familiar company of her sisters. Some nights, the engaging girl traipsed merrily into her room laden with fruits, cakes, and cookies.

"These goodies are supposed to be for you, as directed by the good Dr. Beckman," she said, "in order to fatten you up." She glanced down at her own full figure. "However ... I think the wrong maid is gaining weight!"

Elena laughed as she watched Mary drop into a chair, seriously munching a cookie while hungrily eyeing the feast she had laid on Elena's bed.

"I've been meaning to ask you about Dr. Beckman," Elena said. "Why did you say I should avoid him? He's been very nice to me."

"Well," Mary said, her eyes shining mischievously, "that kindly man you speak of has a list of conquests in this household as long as the wash line outside. There's been a great turnover of maids since I've been here, and some he's knocked up."

Elena looked blank for a moment. "Got them pregnant?" She was appalled. "Does Mrs. Beckman know?"

Mary shrugged. "If she does, she ignores it. He's a doctor, you know. He can take care of his diddling mistakes at his office.'

Mrs. Beckman supported the idea of self-improvement for all, including the household help. She saw excellent possibilities in the well-mannered Elena.

"Elena," she said one day, "I know you speak English very well, but since you accompany the children to German class each week, perhaps you would like classes in English at the same time to further your knowledge. I'd pay for it."

After a momentary reflection, Elena said, "I appreciate your offer very much, Mrs. Beckman, but I wonder ... you see, a class in arithmetic would be of greater use to me."

"Oh," the flustered lady said, "I don't think that would be appropriate. After all, you're not working in the business world." A better command of mathematics might mean the loss of a good maid, Mrs. Beckman reasoned, so she took another tack.

"I have a niece," she remarked the following week, "who is disposing of some of her wardrobe, Elena. She's just about your size." She tried to be diplomatic. "I know you don't have much money. If you don't mind accepting the clothes, I'll pay for any alterations needed. From what I remember, the colors will set off your red hair very nicely."

Elena couldn't be proud; she took the donation with pleasure. Her own collection was sadly lacking because of the years of internment, the dearth of apparel in postwar Germany, and her own undeniable shortage of funds. Several days later, a veritable bonanza of dresses, coats, skirts, blouses, sweaters, and—even more to Elena's delight—T-strapped pumps in her size arrived at the Beckman residence. Mrs. Beckman immediately sent Elena to Mrs. Johnson, the dressmaker.

Women's clothing styles had changed. Simple lines had replaced the formerly constrictive dresses of the Edwardian era. The new style was more practical, loose-fitting, and hemlines had risen to mid-calf and even higher.

Mrs. Johnson was not a good display ad for the new styles—the plainly designed dress she wore hung on her thin frame like a scarecrow, and her short hair stuck out like pins and needles in a pin cushion. "You don't need to wear a corset with these clothes," she said. "The dresses are supposed to hang in a straight line."

"Oh, no," Elena said. "The corset gives me support; I'd feel too tired without it."

"Well, suit yourself. Many of my clients still wear them, but they aren't necessary. Where do you want the hemline, just below the knee?"

Elena grimaced as Mrs. Johnson lifted the dress to her knees, and she observed the effect it had on her less-than-slender legs and ankles. "No . . . lower, please."

"Longer skirts do cover a multitude of imperfections," the dressmaker teased as she pinned the hemline more to Elena's satisfaction. "You have a nice selection of clothes here."

"I know. They're hardly worn! Imagine what a wardrobe Mrs. Beckman's niece must have to be able to give so much away."

"Hmmm . . . the Beckmans buy new clothes every season but they'll hardly need a dressmaker soon—ready-to-wear clothes have become very popular. I'll be out of business."

"Oh, I don't believe that," Elena scoffed. "Ready-to-wear clothes will look cheap in comparison to tailor-made. Look how beautifully these dresses are sewn."

"I hope you're right."

That evening, Elena penned a letter to her parents, describing her good fortune. "I needed a coat badly with the winter coming on," she wrote happily. "With the money I saved I'll be able to send a little more to you this month." Franz and Marta were living with Lise and Kurt, and it wasn't fair for the young couple to shoulder the entire responsibility for their support. Rudy, she knew, contributed also, but she had hesitated to ask whether Angela was aware of it.

* * *

A grand piano reposed in magnificent splendor in a corner of the Beckmans' traditionally furnished living room. Elena's passion for the musical instrument raged unabated in her breast. When Elyse took lessons on Tuesday afternoons, Elena managed to sit in some nook or cranny of the house and listen with rapt attention as the instructor worked with the little girl. Other days, she dusted the keys with longing, even though Mary had that duty. She became bolder as the months passed, taking the opportunity to play several selections when the house was empty of occupants, save for Ricardo, the Filipino cleaning man. Rich sounds of the piano filled the room, indeed the whole house, with grandeur, intoxicating her. Ricardo popped in at intervals, mop in hand, grinning in appreciation of her efforts. She smiled. Someday ... someday she promised herself passionately, she'd have a piano of her very own.

"It's such a lovely day, today, isn't it Elena?" Mrs. Beckman asked. She was sitting at her small desk in the study, various papers scattered in profusion before her. "Let's see," she said, patting strands of her ash-blonde hair in place. "I'll be at my bridge club this afternoon. Cook said we need more bread, and she has no time to bake today because she's preparing for our dinner party tonight. You can pick some up at the market when you take Richard and Elyse to the park after school." She shook her head. "Imagine, bread is eleven cents a loaf now, and Richard's appetite is growing so. He eats almost half a loaf a day."

"He's a very active boy," Elena said. "I think he's grown a few inches taller since I first came here."

The two children gave validity to Elena's words when they reached the park in the afternoon. Brother and sister unleashed their pent-up energy with a vengeance, running and rolling about with exhilarated abandon on the lush green grass. They shrieked and laughed delightedly as Elena joined them whole-heartedly in a ball game, casting the ball back and forth among the three of them. She found herself, more than once, stretched out flat on the grass after unsuccessfully reaching for the ball as it flew past her.

She collapsed onto a bench laughing and breathing hard. The park setting and the exuberant children had raised her spirits. It's good to be alive, she thought abruptly, startled by the joy of it.

After about an hour of the children's hijinks, she thought to get them started for home. "Oh, dear," she lamented guilefully, "I think it's time to leave. Your mother's going to be very upset when she sees all the green stains on your clothes."

"Who cares? Who cares!" Richard whooped, gasping for breath. "We've had such fun with you today, Elena. Look, you're green, too."

Elyse came somersaulting by, head over heels, head over heels, her blonde hair in disarray. "Elena, Elena, Elena," she beeped with every turn.

"Time to go, time to go," Elena sang out as she began to race nimbly along the path. She glanced back and smiled as the youngsters came scrambling after her like ducklings following a mother duck to the pond.

* * *

Winter passed. A surprisingly mild one, she thought, though there were days when she blessed Mrs. Beckman's niece for the gift of her cast-off coats. She shivered as San Francisco's wet, damp cold penetrated to her very bones. A cool spring advanced into foggy mornings of summer. Mists blanketed the city like a shroud before being dispersed by fresh winds in the afternoons, only to creep in slyly again in the dusk of evening.

On afternoons off, Elena began to explore the city. She visited shopping centers in what San Franciscans referred to as "downtown," not to spend her limited resources, but to mark indelibly in her mind the cosmopolitan atmosphere that was making this town her own. Walking the streets of Chinatown, she felt a rapport with the populace, and Singapore came to mind. At the foot of Powell and Market Streets, she watched cable cars performing their charming merry-go-round on a turntable, preparing to climb the hill again. She hopped onto a car, as everyone else did, marveling as it slowly climbed the incredibly steep hills. Each hill had a name: Nob Hill, Telegraph Hill, Russian Hill, and more, all affording breathtaking views of the surrounding waters.

Mrs. Beckman encouraged her excursions, suggesting various attractions each week.

"Why don't you go to Fisherman's Wharf today?" she offered one morning. "The weather is fine. I'll tell you what trolley to take." Later, Elena would wish she hadn't taken the advice that particular day.

Elena walked along the wharf in the afternoon, admiring the hundreds of colorful, berthed fishing vessels. She breathed in fresh sea air as well as odors of fish and boiled shrimp emanating from surrounding cafés. The smells were tantalizing, and as she debated whether to stop to eat, she noticed a couple sitting on a bench. Faces close together, the man's arm was around a stylishly dressed young woman, who smiled provocatively as he kissed her ear and throat. Something seemed vaguely familiar about the man, and as Elena neared them, she recognized Dr. Beckman. Heart pounding, she wanted to escape before he noticed her, but he raised his head just as she whirled about, catching a glimpse of the unmistakable copper of her hair gleaming in the sunshine as she hurried away.

"Would you please lay out my blue beaded gown, Elena?" Mrs. Beckman asked as Elena came in the door. "The doctor and I'll eat out this evening, then go on to the theater. He'll be home soon from his golf game, I expect. Just see that Richard and Elyse eat their vegetables at dinner and get them to bed after they do their homework."

Elena listened absently, feeling relieved that the couple planned the evening out. She dreaded having an encounter with the physician, hoping fervently she hadn't been noticed at the wharf.

It was a lost hope. She'd just retired to her room after tending to the children's bedtime rituals, when there was a tap on her door. Dr. Beckman stepped into the room covertly and closed the door behind him.

"I don't have much time, Elena," he said hurriedly. "I've come for Mrs. Beckman's wrap."

"It isn't in here," Elena said. "You'll have to go to her room."

"I know, I know," he said irritably. "Elena, I've come about this afternoon. The woman with me is in therapy. It isn't what you think."

"I don't think anything." She had put on her nightgown and had been sitting up in bed, reading. She pulled the comforter up closer about her, feeling compromised by his presence. He moved closer toward her and sat down on the bed, his expression softening.

"You're looking so much better, Elena, now you've gained some weight. Your complexion is blooming with color." He leaned forward to stroke her hair, which was loosened from hairpins and fell down in waves about her shoulders. "Your hair is beautiful; it shone in the sun this afternoon." He paused, a notion crossing his mind. "You know," he said smoothly, "I can make life a great deal easier for you if you'd let me. Nice clothes; jewelry, if you'd like. You're a very attractive young lady; we can go out to dinner on your days off ...." He hesitated as he saw her face flush with displeasure, and he swiftly changed his approach. "All I'm asking, Elena, is that you refrain from informing Mrs. Beckman of my meeting with a certain young lady. She wouldn't understand. I'll give you a nice gift; you can use the money, I'm sure." He lifted a billfold from the inner pocket of his dinner jacket, and that gesture sealed his fate.

By this time, Elena was burning with rage, repulsed and insulted by the doctor's words. Her temper rose to heights even she didn't suspect she possessed. She fairly flew from the bed and threw the door open wide.

"Get out! Get out!" she cried, her voice shrill. "I'll have you know I had absolutely no intention of hurting your wife by telling tales. I could've done that long ago; everyone knows your reputation. And I'm not one of your floozies, or whatever you call them, that you can buy off. Keep your money! You're going to need it." She stood straight as an arrow, diminutive but noble in her nightgown.

The doctor sat frozen on the bed, startled by her outburst. He threw her a dark look and then, eyes flashing, stalked from the room.

Elena dropped down on the bed in a daze as Mary came bounding in from next door.

"You were magnificent!" she howled gleefully. "You really let him have it. What a temper!"

"I can't believe I said all that." Elena said unbelievingly. "Why do men think we'll just fall into their arms? It made me so angry."

"Made him angry, too. You can expect a dismissal. He'll make up some excuse; he's done it before. I'm going to miss you, sweetie ... miss your piano playing, too."

"You heard me?" Elena asked guiltily. "I always thought I was alone in the house."

"Everyone heard you. You know Mrs. Beckman, she was planning to have Elyse's teacher come to give you lessons."

"Oh ...," Elena moaned, tears welling in her eyes. "What do I do now?"

As it happened, Mrs. Beckman had her own plans that would leave Elena, as well as Mary, among the ranks of the unemployed. "The doctor and I are being divorced," she stated sadly. "He's left to stay at the Bohemian Club, and I'll find an apartment for myself and the children."

"I'm so sorry," Elena said bleakly.

"This means, of course, that I'll no longer have need for your services, Elena. I'm sure you understand." Her voice broke, her eyes tearful. "It seems I was the only one unaware of that monster's infidelities."

During the next few weeks, Mary and Elena packed clothes and household goods in boxes for Mrs. Beckman's move into an apartment. Richard and Elyse watched the preparations with bewildered eyes.

"They don't understand," their mother said, heartsick for them. "They're going to miss you so much, Elena."

On the last night Elena spent in the comfortable, friendly house, she lay in the bed, wide-awake, reflecting on her year of service there. She had grown in that time. Her first months in San Francisco, before her parents' return to Germany, had formed the beginning of her recovery from desolation. Despite Dr. Beckman's despicable behavior, she found it in her heart to credit him with her own self-discovery. His description of trauma suffered by prisoners of war explained many things to her. She had previously thought her torment was caused only by the loss of Lorenzo and Max. However, it was more than that—her imprisonment, the breakdown in Germany, all these experiences combined had sparked her anxieties. She'd been numb to feelings of any kind, especially the ability to feel pleasure. She smiled. Dr. Beckman's actions in her room had enabled her to feel something else. Anger. The morrow would bring another challenge, a return to Angela.

CHAPTER TWENTY-THREE

Young And Fancy-Free

The reception Elena received from Angela and Rudy was surprisingly gracious. They had moved into a bungalow in the Sunset district of San Francisco a few months earlier, and were beaming with pride of ownership.

"This is your room," Rudy said, as he led her to a bright, sunny bedroom at the rear of the house, with windows overlooking a small garden. "I finished painting it last week, and Angela put up the curtains. There are shades, you see, for privacy, and here is a closet." He opened and closed the door. "Plenty of room for your clothes."

Elena gazed about the room, noting that pictures had been hung with artistic care on the walls, and a chest of drawers carefully refinished and waxed to perfection. A vase of flowers sat elegantly on a bedside table. "Everything looks so nice and fresh," she said. "I can't thank you enough for taking me in."

"You'll have company in here soon," Angela said briskly. "My sister, Louise, will arrive from Germany next month. You'll have to share the double bed with her."

Elena's mouth dropped open. "Oh," she said, temporarily nonplussed. "It'll be wonderful for you to have Louise here." Glancing at Rudy's expressionless face, she added, "I'm sure she'll be like a sister to me, too." She couldn't help but wonder whether the room would have been so nicely decorated if Louise weren't expected, but then dismissed the thought as unworthy. At the same time, she hoped Louise wouldn't be another Angela.

Elena scanned the newspapers every day with Angela, searching for a new position. No one seemed to be advertising for an upstairs maid.

"Here is something you can do," Angela said. She read an ad aloud from the newspaper. "Delicatessen kitchen helper wanted, six days weekly."

"Elena isn't strong enough for work like that," Rudy said.

"Sure she is," Angela said. "Look how healthy she is now." She turned to peruse Elena's figure as they sat around the kitchen table after the evening meal. "You were well fed at the Beckmans.'"

"But she should be doing something more ... um ... ladylike. A saleslady, perhaps."

Elena was solemn. "My arithmetic isn't good enough, Rudy."

"You could learn. What are you afraid of?"

"I can't seem to do figures."

"She'll have to take what she can get," Angela snapped, annoyed.

Elena started in the delicatessen the following Monday, but on a trial basis.

"Well, we'll see," owner Bertha Wald said. Brisk and robust, she observed the five-foot-two Elena pessimistically. "There are large pots and pans you'll have to lift in the kitchen. If Cook decides you can do it, you can stay."

Mrs. Langendorf, tall and raw-boned, gazed skeptically at Elena as she stepped into her kitchen. "Never worked in a delicatessen before?" she asked. When Elena meekly shook her head, she shrugged and pointed to a gigantic pile of dirty pots and pans in a sink. "You can start with those."

The next week was a blur in Elena's mind of chopping vegetables, peeling an unending amount of potatoes, lifting heavy pots of boiling water from sink to stove and stove to sink, scrubbing counter tops, and washing a continuous array of bowls, dishes, and pots and pans. Staggering home each night exhausted, she dropped into bed soon after eating, too tired to talk to Angela, and seeing Rudy only on her day off, as he worked evenings.

An amazing selection of salads, hot dishes, and desserts was displayed in showcases in the front of the store. Mrs. Langendorf wasted few words in instructions to Elena, preferring to show by doing. Elena learned quickly, watching how every bit of food was used in an economical manner; nothing was ever thrown out. Yesterday's roast chicken was today's chicken salad. Mastering the art of mixing potato salad so it wouldn't turn to mush, she and the cook stationed themselves at opposite ends of the counter, each grasping one end of a long shallow pan, pushing back and forth, back and forth between them until the contents magically melded.

By the end of the month, Elena was turning out tasty little pot pies by the dozen, ready to be baked and sold each day. Fast and helpful, she put forth as much energy as she was capable. There was no praise, nor even a smile, forthcoming from the austere Mrs. Langendorf, but as weeks passed, the women began working smoothly together, establishing a comfortable routine,

Mrs. Wald entered the kitchen one morning and took Elena aside. "Elena," she said, "we could use you up front, waiting on customers. You have a pleasant manner, and I'll teach you how to slice the meats on the machines. We can get another assistant for Mrs. Langendorf. How about it?"

Before Elena could answer, the cook called out from her position before the stove. "No," she said emphatically. "I need Elena here in the kitchen. She's the best worker I've ever had." She turned back impassively to the pots on the stove, slowly stirring her spaghetti sauce, a slight smile playing about her determined mouth.

Elena and Mrs. Wald exchanged astonished glances. "Well," Elena said, grinning, "I think I'll stay here in the kitchen with Mrs. Langendorf." She did feel some pride after hearing the cook's words, especially since living in hotels much of her young life had done little to prepare her for any culinary skills. The work was taxing, but she now had evenings free for socializing.

* * *

Angela's sister, Louise, arrived, looking much as Elena had a year and a half previously. She appeared pale and wasted, another victim of the deprivations of postwar Germany. With some weight on her, Elena theorized Louise would resemble Angela a great deal. Both had the same broad frame, with brown eyes and hair. But there the resemblance ended. Louise's eyes sparkled with good humor, and laugh lines crinkled about them when she smiled. She was prone to giggling at the least provocation.

"I love this room," she said as she unpacked her belongings. "It's so bright and sunny. Angela has outdone herself, fixing it up for us. She was always so … umm … thrifty back home." She giggled. "I guess things are different here."

They laughed and joked together a great deal in the following months, talking long into the night as they shared the double bed in their room. Angela seemed oddly tolerant of the young women's girlish behavior, calling good-humoredly from the marital bedroom for quiet.

"She's the married woman and mother," Elena mused. "We're young and fancy-free, although we're pretty much the same age she is."

"Well," Louise said petulantly, "she's not my mother."

One morning, she picked up a tube of lip rouge she had bought at the dime store and applied it amateurishly to her lips. "Here," she said mischievously. "Try it, Elena." They dissolved into peals of laughter as they observed how garish the orange-shaded cosmetic appeared against their fresh, young complexions. Elena's skin was again freckle-free with the purchase of a new bleaching cream discovered at a nearby druggist's.

Rudy popped his head into the room, box camera in hand. "I want to take your picture in the garden," he said brightly. "The sun is just right."

"Oh, no, wait a minute," wailed Elena. "We have to wipe this mess off our lips."

"No ... that's perfect," he chuckled. "It'll make a great picture, one we'll always remember."

It was Saturday night, and they were going to the German House. Elena had rushed home from the delicatessen in order to bathe quickly before dressing, as Rudy would be playing in the dance orchestra and needed to leave early. Louise curled stray locks of her hair with a curling iron as Elena slipped into one of the Beckman castoff dresses.

"We'll have a good time tonight, Louise," Elena said. "I've been there before when Rudy played in the orchestra. The building is a meeting place for the German community; dances are held in the ballroom on Saturday nights. In the summer, they sponsor picnics, and there are socials and choral groups."

"Sounds wonderful," sighed Louise.

At that moment, Rudy's voice could be heard bellowing in anger from within the confines of his bedroom. "That lousy cat," he roared. "Look at my dress suit! It's full of cat hairs. Angela, I've told you a thousand times not to lay my clothes on the bed, it's like a magnet for her." Angela's reply was soft and unintelligible, but he continued raging. "Where's the clothes brush? No, that won't do it. Get a damp towel. You're going to make me late!"

Louise and Elena exchanged uneasy glances. "The Linden temper," whispered Elena, unable to hold back a smile. "Rudy was always meticulous about his clothes." They collected their coats and crept quietly into the living room, waiting for the storm to cease. Unfortunately for Angela, Rudy's ill humor continued as the couple entered the room. He looked at his wife casually as he prepared to don his coat, then gazed at her more closely.

"What's that white stuff all over your front?" he asked. "Powder? What did you do, pour it all over you?"

"I was in a hurry," she said, attempting to brush the powder particles away with her hand. The resultant smear on her dark-colored dress irked him even more.

"Why do you always look so untidy?" he asked critically. "Look at Elena. She always looks neat and clean. Why can't you be like her? Losing some weight wouldn't hurt, either," he added sarcastically.

Angela's face hardened. She climbed into the car and was silent during the drive to the German House.

The evening had started badly for Angela, but Elena and Louise were soon swept up in a sea of friendly faces in the chandeliered ballroom of the German House. Elena flushed with the pleasure of being on the dance floor again. A popular dance partner, she could well have danced the night through, but as the evening wore on, she began to tire. Her day in the delicatessen had been a busy one.

"I need a rest," she said, collapsing into a chair next to Louise. "That last polka did it."

"I'm tired, too," Louise said. "I'm not used to all this exercise. I don't know how you do it—work all day, then dance all night." She sighed, looking out at the lively crowd. "Uh, oh … look, Elena," she whispered, "there's a man coming toward us."

"Where?"

"He's in uniform; he's going to ask one of us to dance."

"Oh yes, a ship's officer," Elena said. "You dance with him."

"No, you take him."

The young man had eyes only for Louise as he led her out onto the dance floor. They danced through several selections before he returned her to her seat.

"Well?" Elena asked, noting that Louise looked charmed and stimulated.

"He's getting us something to drink." Louise said. "You'll be interested in his story, Elena. He was a seaman on a German ship in Mexico when the war started, and was stranded there when the ship was interned. He made it to San Francisco by a coastal steam schooner, and is now first mate on a ship that sails up and down the coast." She smiled, her cheeks rosy. "His name is Albert."

His name suited him. Calm, reserved, and well-spoken, the stocky seaman entered into a polite and intelligent conversation with the girls. Elena was impressed. His was the age-old tale of a boy running away to sea from a strict schoolmaster uncle in Germany, working hard, and now well on his way to someday being master of his own ship. Even as he talked, his eyes were drawn again and again to Louise. Finally, he rose, and drew her from her chair out onto the dance floor again.

Elena felt a momentary sensation of envy as she watched them. She closed her eyes, remembering the warmth of Lorenzo's arms about her in Bangkok. At that instant, she heard a voice and opened her eyes again. A man of medium height stood before her. She noticed, first, his eyes; they were a deep brown, orbs she could drown herself in. Odd thought, she mused, a little confused. Perhaps it was because they seemed so gentle and kind. His sensual lips drew into a smile as he invited her to dance. "My name is Christian," he said.

CHAPTER TWENTY-FOUR

Christian

When the S.S. *Kronprinz Wilhelm* arrived in New York Harbor from Bremen, Germany, the ship had exceeded the contract speed of 23 knots, delivering 707 first- and second-class passengers to their destination in luxurious splendor. The 1,054 souls in third class sailed less elegantly between decks, but their accommodations were clean, if somewhat congested.

Christian fell into neither of the above categories. Except for a week's layover in Southampton, he had toiled in the bowels of the vessel carving sides of beef, veal, and lamb into fine cuts of meat that were then transformed into delectable entrees served in first and second class. For third-class immigrants, he cubed less tender cuts intended for stews, or ground them for patties.

During his free time, he observed the immigrants, noting that the group was made up of mostly Italians and Slavs. Not many Germans, he thought, certainly none from his hometown of Besigheim. Although his family and friends had always led their small provincial lives oblivious to the great world outside their borders, his eyes had been opened by his two years of compulsory military service.

* * *

Gretel had noticed the change in her younger brother when he returned from the army. He appeared restless, distracted, unlike the hardworking, eager-to-please young man of old.

"Christian, what is it?" she asked as they sat under the ancient apple tree in their neatly tended garden. It was Sunday afternoon. The shop, located in the forefront of the house, was closed, and she had just finished tidying up the kitchen after the main meal. "Ernst and Dietrich have been complaining that your mind isn't on your work in the shop. You've even neglected the vegetable patch out back. I have enough to do waiting on customers without watering and weeding for you."

Christian grimaced, sighing heavily. "I'm sorry, Gretel. You know the way it is. My foxy brothers took over the store while I was away, and now that I'm back, they treat me like hired help. No say in the business; they're the bosses. I'm twenty-three years old, not fifteen!" He exuded frustration and thwarted hopes, his face red with bitterness.

His sister gazed at him fondly. Christian was her favorite. She had protected him—in fact, practically raised him—after their mother had died. His winning ways had endeared him to her; she did all she could to oppose her older brothers as they repeatedly found fault with their young sibling. They couldn't complain about his work, for he had learned his craft well, but his easygoing nature irritated them. He was popular with the village girls, spent time with other youths in beer gardens, and declined to take life seriously. Most of all, they thought it important that the family attend church each Sunday; people in business couldn't afford the slightest tinge of scandal or mistrust attached to their name. And, of course, Christian refused to attend church services. Gretel sighed. She must somehow solve the problem. "Your brothers don't mean to be domineering, Christian; actually, they need you. You make the finest sausage in town ... and who will slaughter the animals?"

"They will. They did it while I served in the army, didn't they?"

Gretel shook her head. "No, they had to hire Johann, the butcher, to do it after Papa died." She smiled. "Papa always said you had a knack for it."

He shrugged his shoulders. "Gretel, I've made up my mind. I'm leaving. They can have the shop, I don't care."

Gretel's face fell. "Listen, Christian, the business is as much yours as your brothers'. Don't give up your share; think of the future."

For a few days, he had pondered over her words, eventually deciding she had given him good counsel. She and his brothers all agreed Christian would go to America and send back a portion of his pay to invest in the business as a sign of good faith. He would be a partner upon his return. "Get it in writing," Gretel urged, but he declined. "I trust my brothers," he told her.

* * *

When the *Kronprinz Wilhelm* had berthed, the ship's personnel were free to go ashore on leave until departure, but Christian would be jumping ship. They'll be returning to Germany without me, Christian thought, as he walked lightheartedly down the gangplank. As ship's crew, he did not have to present immigration papers to any authorities.

He found it almost ridiculously easy to lose himself in New York's 1908 milieu. Armed with an address he had secured from a fellow galley worker, he joined the city's inhabitants on the busy sidewalks. Men and women swarmed past him like an army of ants bent on replenishing their nests. The streets teemed with streetcars, horses and wagons, and automobiles. Christian started nervously as elevated trains roared past on the rails above him. The noise of traffic was deafening.

Fishing the paper with an address on it from his pocket, he stopped several pedestrians for directions. *"Bitte?"* he asked, indicating the address he sought. He neither spoke nor understood a word of English, but nodded his thanks as they pointed north, and then headed in that direction. After walking a while, he became uncertain. Against his better judgment, suddenly uneasy regarding his illegal status, he approached a policeman for help. Almost dropping the paper in his nervousness, he handed it to the lawman, pointing to the address with shaking fingers.

The huge, helmeted, florid-faced officer nodded indifferently. He extended his arm, pointing to the north. "That's in Tompkins Square Park," he said. "Little Germany."

Satisfied, Christian shifted the suitcase, containing sandwiches he had packed along with his few possessions, to his other hand, adjusted his derby hat to a more rakish angle, and set off again. Heat and humidity grew oppressive as he walked; air so close, he could hardly breathe. His bag became heavier and heavier as he progressed. In addition, his feet began to hurt with the pavement radiating summer heat through the thin soles of his shoes. Plus, he was thirsty.

After asking several more passersby, he finally reached his objective, an address located above a mercantile store on a noisy neighborhood street. It seemed an eternity since he'd left the ship. Trudging up two flights of wooden stairs to a small landing, he knocked on the door.

"Ja?" a slim, middle-aged man asked, opening the door only slightly, his eyes wary.

"Otto Holzman? My name is Christian. Hans Sauer gave me your address ... said you would put me up."

"Aaah ... just off the boat." Offering a gap-toothed smile, Otto opened the door wider, motioning the latest illegal immigrant into his shabbily furnished flat "Come in, come in. Ja, I can put you up. You can share a room with the other fellows here. When you find work, I'll expect rent money. Ja?"

Christian sighed. He was relieved to hear someone speak German again. "Ja," he said.

* * *

Otto took his new lodger under his wing, immediately warming to the amiable, dark-haired young man. He quickly introduced him to Little Germany, or *Kleindeutschland—rathskellers*, beer halls, *konditorei*, and, most importantly, the numerous pork stores in the community. Within the week, Christian had obtained work in one of them.

"Do you play cards?" Otto asked one Sunday. "There's always a good pinochle game going at the Palm Gardens every weekend, and for the price of a beer, we get free lunch." He paused, smiling. "I think the young ladies there will be very interested to see a handsome new face as well."

Christian felt at home from the moment he walked into the Palm Gardens. The beer hall overflowed with men, women, and children. Palm tree murals decorated the buff-colored walls and live potted palms were scattered about on sawdust-covered wooden floors. The atmosphere of the hall was charged with the sound of friendly good cheer as well as dense clouds of cigar and cigarette smoke. A round-faced musician dressed in Bavarian lederhosen and felt hat squeezed familiar German waltzes and polkas from his accordion while seated on a platform well above the crowd.

"Let's eat before we play cards," Otto said, leading Christian to the bar where lunch was laid out. Christian's mouth watered at the sight of thick slices of meats, crusty slabs of dark breads, potato and herring salads, cheeses, salted white radishes, pickles, olives, and hard-boiled eggs. "See," Otto laughed. "A feast for poor bachelors. Ja?"

After eating, they were welcomed at one table of card players. Christian quickly learned to play the going game of pinochle, a pastime that held a particular fascination for him, one that would last a lifetime. He could be found thereafter, not only on Sundays, but most evenings, playing cards in the beer halls of *Kleindeutschland*, a cigar hanging limply from his lips as he concentrated on the game.

His dark and lean handsomeness was not, however, overlooked by the young women who frequented the halls. Otto was sitting next to Christian at the table one day when a buxom, blonde-haired girl tapped him on the shoulder.

"Otto, you devil," she said. "Where have you been hiding this charming fellow?" She smiled provocatively at Christian.

Otto was unfriendly. "Go away, Clara," he said. "We're playing cards."

"But Otto, introduce us, at least."

He grimaced, looking up at her from his chair. "Oh ... alright. This is Christian, Clara. He came over from the old country a few months ago. Now leave us. Ja?"

Christian nodded politely, and Clara smiled again before moving on, her blue eyes lingering on his in an open invitation.

"She's trouble," Otto warned. "A flirt."

Christian had had enough experience while serving in the army to recognize when a girl was making herself available, and his sexual reflexes responded. His concentration on the cards broken, he followed her movements about the hall. Smugly aware of his interest, she cast teasing glances at him as she laughed and joked with other patrons. She patted the golden braids on her head, and suggestively smoothed the white ruffled blouse along her bodice and waist. When her eyes met his in a bold look, and her tongue sensually licked her lips, he excused himself from the table. Otto watched as the two met, exchanged brief words, and disappeared through a back exit. "Ja ... she's trouble," he muttered, shaking his head morosely.

* * *

Christian had never met a young woman as fascinating and tantalizing as Clara, nor one as shrewd and cunning. Innocent girls—and, yes, even those in brothels he had visited in Germany—paled in comparison to Clara. She occupied his thoughts day and night. He scarcely managed to get through his twelve-hour day in the pork store, feverishly anticipating the favors she enticingly extended to him in the evenings.

Sundays, instead of playing cards, he explored the island of Manhattan with her. They ambled along 86th Street to Central Park, an oasis of trees and grass, then on to 90th and 93rd Streets where Ruppert's brewery buildings dominated.

"You can smell the hops roasting from blocks away," Clara said, wrinkling her nose in distaste. "Let's take the subway downtown. It's nicer to walk by the brownstone houses and mansions of the rich people."

On 62nd Street, she pointed to a five-story townhouse as they walked. "That's owned by the Vanderbilts," she said. "I know a girl who works there. She said it has a grand ballroom, a music room with an organ bigger than a church organ, twenty fireplaces and eleven maid's rooms." She paused, gazing at the elegant balconied structure in awe. "Someday, I'll live in a place like that."

"Only in your dreams," Christian said, laughing.

Clara glanced at him, her expression enigmatic. "Maybe ... maybe not." She smiled and took his arm. "Come, we passed a jewelry store down that street. I want to show you something."

And so it went. Increasingly, their time spent together was spent shopping for clothes and trinkets. She wheedled winningly and coaxed bewitchingly. "I can't live without this dress, Christian," she cajoled. "You want me to look nice when we go out, don't you?"

He nodded reluctantly, consumed with a hunger for her.

"She's running rings around you," Otto said as he watched Christian's plight.

"I love her,"

"That's not love, that's lust. You owe me rent money, you know, and you better pay attention to your work, or you won't have a job, either."

To top off Christian's troubles, a letter arrived from his sister, Gretel. "Your brothers say they haven't received payments you've promised," she wrote. "Have you been ill?" He sighed. Working six days a week, there was no way for him to make extra money. Sundays he wanted to spend with Clara.

Clara herself solved his problem, becoming suddenly cool towards him. "I have other things to do," she said indifferently, when he approached her at the Palm Gardens one day.

"She's found another fool," Otto said. "One with more money. He won't last long, either."

Christian's emotions were mixed at this turn of events. He felt betrayed and wounded by Clara's duplicity, but at the same time was filled with a sensation of deliverance. In addition, he suffered regret for his treatment of Otto, who had been critical of his madness, but understood it.

"Think of it as a good lesson, Christian," his friend said. "You're not the first man to be taken in by a woman."

The two went back to their pinochle games, but Christian soon felt the urge to move on. In his conversations with Otto and other men at the card table, a picture of the vastness of America began to emerge in his mind. The far horizons beckoned to him. A chance meeting with a stranger sent him on the first of his migrations across country.

"You're going where?" Otto was incredulous.

"Well, this fellow named Walter said the coal mines in a place called ... umm ... I think called Pennsylvania ... need workers. The pay is good, he said ...."

"Ja, that smooth-talking bamboozler always comes around looking for fool-headed immigrants. You didn't sign anything, did you?" Otto warned.

Christian looked blank. "I leave on Wednesday, Otto ... but listen. Others will be on the train with me, and I'll be boarding with a German family."

Otto dropped his head into his hands despairingly. "I wish you'd asked me first about this, Christian. You don't know what you're getting into. You don't need to work in the mines—you're a first-rate sausage maker."

To Christian, the mines would be an opportunity for him to change his vocation. He longed to remove himself from the steamy environment of cooking and curing hams and tongues, stuffing sausages, tending meats in the smokehouse. His greasy work clothes and boots he planned to shed forever.

* * *

Christian's first impression of the colliery was of a gloomy world enveloped in black. Coal dust was everywhere. It settled on the long rows of company housing, the company store, the church, and the schoolhouse. Only when the snows of winter covered the shabby village did the area take on a pretty picture-book aspect. Nature's beauties were otherwise veiled by man's intrusion into the bowels of the earth.

It wasn't long before Christian realized that working in the mines wouldn't be a step upwards for him. The two years he toiled in the caverns of horror were to be the most grueling work he ever experienced. Although he formed close friendships, he developed a burning hatred for the mine owners and operators, recognizing that the owners' one priority was to acquire great wealth, flagrantly ignoring the dismal conditions under which the miners worked.

"Accidents and death happen every day in coal country," Emil Kirchner said to Christian. They were sitting on a bench outside Kirchner's wood-frame, company house.

"I've seen too much already since I came here," Christian said to his host, "especially your seven-year-old Eric working in the coal breaker. I worked at an early age, too, back in Germany, but I went to school, doing chores and garden work afterwards."

Kirchner sighed. "They wouldn't let him work in the mines with his four older brothers as he wanted, so now he works in the breaker with the other boys, separating the culm—the rock or slate—from the coal." He paused, his lined face reflecting his pain. "I know it's dangerous; some boys suffocated when the coal came rushing down from above them.'

"Then why do you allow it?"

"We need the money. Even though we have boarders like you, Christian, it's hard to make ends meet. My wife works miracles, you know, growing vegetables, tending the animals, cooking and washing for our seven children, as well as the boarders ... you can see for yourself how hard she works."

Christian pictured in his mind the gaunt, work-worn Frieda going about her duties. She baked seven days' worth of bread each week in an outdoor oven. There was no indoor plumbing; she and her daughters hauled water for washing and baths from a lone community spigot down the road. She can't be more than forty-five years old, he thought, yet she looks sixty.

On his first day in the mine, Christian dropped down the shaft in an elevator-like cage to what he estimated to be at least twelve hundred feet or more below ground level. The air was clammy and cool, the blackness impenetrable. Only the flickering flame of the carbide lamp he carried lit his way along the gravel floor in the wake of Kirchner and his oldest son, Helmut. Lunch pails swung noisily back and forth as they walked into a tunnel. From there, they branched off into their work chamber and set to work. Kirchner and Helmut drilled holes into the coal seams, pressed in explosives, and fired them. Christian then shoveled the heaping piles of coal chunks into mine cars after the smoke subsided.

"Keep your lunch pail close by," Helmut warned, "or the rats will knock it over and have a feast." His advice came too late as Christian saw the last vestiges of his meal disappear from his toppled pail into the darkness. Sharp, beady eyes gleamed red in the lantern light, then faded. A roar of laughter erupted from the miners.

"Come, Christian," Kirchner said, smiling. "We'll stop for lunch. Helmut and I'll share with you." As their pails opened, the rats came forward into the light, sitting up on their hind legs to beg, like squirrels.

"My God," Christian exclaimed, "they're big as cats!"

Helmut shrugged his shoulders resignedly. "It's bad luck to harm them," he said. "If they panic, that's a sign there may be a cave-in or maybe poisonous gasses in the air." Christian stared at him uneasily, for the first time realizing that this work could be dangerous.

At the end of the workday, the trio joined other miners for a bit of relaxation in one of the nearby saloons. "Drink, Christian, drink," urged Kirchner. "A shot of whiskey and a beer is good for clearing the coal dust from your lungs." After much jovial socialization, they filled their lunch pails with more beer and headed home, where Frieda awaited their arrival with galvanized metal tubs of hot water to wash the black from their bodies. Christian was initially reluctant to cleanse himself in the presence of Frieda and her daughters, but soon appreciated the giggling eleven-year-old Ilse's help in scrubbing his back. Ilse was irrepressibly cheerful and friendly; she reminded Christian of his sister, Gretel, and her ministrations to her brothers after their mother had died. Both had plaited brown tresses that bounced delightfully as they walked.

Dinner was a boisterous, happy affair. Frieda, Ilse, and daughter number two, Heidi, served the men and boarders, who joked and engaged in good-natured banter. Much of the conversation centered about their work in the mines.

"My four sons are good workers," Kirchner boasted, "but Rols there, he takes too many chances." He nodded to one of the powerfully built boys. "He rides the mine cars down the slopes like a cowboy. One day he'll go flying off like a top."

"I love the danger, Papa," Rols said, his eyes shining. "I love the speed."

"Hmph, they'll bring you home dead one day in the Black Maria for us to bury." Kirchner paused, a slight smile on his lips. "We'll miss your pay," he jested.

"That's nothing to joke about, Emil," his wife interjected, visibly upset.

Christian sensed that mine accidents were Frieda's worst fear. "Frau Kirchner," he said quickly, "why don't you sit down and eat with us? You always serve us, but you never eat."

"I'll eat later," she said, with a wave of her hand, but she smiled at him, her eyes thoughtful. He felt great admiration for the courageous and close-ly-knit family. He basked in the warmth and friendliness they extended to him, as though he were one of their very own. His business-like brothers suffered in comparison.

* * *

Frieda approached Christian one Sunday afternoon a couple years later as he sat on a bench outside the house. She sat down quietly beside him.

"I ... I've wanted to speak with you, Christian," she started hesitantly. She shaded her eyes from the warm spring sunlight with her hand, her fingers dry and cracked. "I wondered whether you plan to stay here at the mine ... permanently, I mean." She paused self-consciously. "You're a good man, kind and gentle."

He stared at her uncertainly, waiting for her to continue.

"If you intend to stay, you might consider marriage to Ilse?"

"But she's too young!"

"Oh, no ... no. She'll be thirteen next month. She can cook and clean and bake, all the things I've taught her. And you know she has a cheerful way about her."

"Frau Kirchner," Christian said, straining to find the correct words. "I like Ilse, she's a fine girl. If I were to stay, I might think seriously about your proposal, but ...."

"You're going to move on."

"Yes."

"A pity," she said, disappointment flooding her face.

He almost felt like relenting, telling her he would stay and marry Ilse; but it was sorrow he felt ... for Ilse, for the Kirchner family, indeed for the entire pitiful village. It would make him one of them.

Christian left the mines soon after their conversation. For many months afterwards, his dreams were haunted by flashbacks ... he toiled in a cavernous mine, shoveling endlessly, fueling the fires of hell.

* * *

Little towns, big cities, mere whistle stops, lonely farmhouses set in the middle of flat landscapes, this was the heartland of America that Christian journeyed across. He followed in the steps of millions of immigrants before him, working at odd jobs—or sausage-making when he was lucky. As a result of his hard work in the mines, he no longer thought of his trade as a lowly occupation. He was surprised to discover his skill, or "old country" expertise, was much in demand.

During Christian's years in the mines and his three years of migration from coast to coast, he had learned to speak basic English. His first attempts to communicate had been met with derision and laughter. He felt frustrated and inadequate, noting that others assumed he was uneducated, even simple-minded. Eventually, he managed to make himself understood, though his speech was heavily accented and, worse, sprinkled with profanities he had innocently picked up from English-speaking miners.

When he arrived in San Francisco in 1914, war clouds were gathering over Europe, and he struggled with his conscience over whether to return to Germany. "If I volunteer to fight for America," he said to a card-playing friend, "they'll make me a citizen; but then I may be killed, and what's the difference if I'm a citizen or not? I wouldn't want to fight my own people anyway." He paused, attempting to find a way out of his dilemma. "If I get back to Germany, then I'll have to fight this country, and that would hurt; I like it here." A letter from his brother Dietrich settled the matter. He urged Christian to stay in America, writing that the war was sure to be a brief one.

Christian remained in San Francisco during the four years the war lasted, but at the back of his mind he always thought he would return to the family pork store in Germany. Until, that is, one evening when he saw a red-headed young woman go waltzing by on the dance floor as he played his usual game of pinochle at the German House.

CHAPTER TWENTY-FIVE

When Christian asked Elena to dance that evening at the German House, her world suddenly became a bright and shining place, as though the sun had finally broken through to the last vestiges of loneliness and grief that had lain in her heart. Emotions she had thought long dead surged through her being from the moment he took her into his arms. Her tumultuous feelings were reminiscent of the exhilaration she had experienced with Lorenzo in Bangkok, yet they were different. She found herself responding to Christian's virile handsomeness as a grown woman; no longer was she the naïve young girl of the South China Sea.

For Christian, the sight of the smiling, red-haired young woman on the dance floor immediately took his interest. He was drawn to her not because she was beautiful, for she was not, but there was an indefinable something about her that he was eager to explore further. Sixteen years had passed since he had first set foot on the shores of the United States. Since the time of the scheming Clara in New York, he had met and romanced many women, and was well experienced in his relations with the opposite sex. However, he was unprepared for the rush of excitement he felt when Elena melted into his arms. She seemed unlike any other woman he had ever known.

Looking down at Elena while they danced, Christian admired her clear complexion and dainty figure. There was a friendly, refined quality about her. Neither the typical, farm-bred German immigrant girls he knew, nor the bold, powdered, and rouged American women who smoked cigarettes and seemed to have bathed in perfume could compete with Elena's simplicity and artlessness.

"You smell good," he ventured.

She smiled, "It's just the soap I use for bathing," she said.

"You're different from the other German girls here," he said, knitting his brows. "I can't quite make out why."

"Perhaps it's because I don't come from Germany."

Perplexed, he said, "I heard that you came from Germany not long ago."

"My family was sent there after the war. Before that we lived in Romania."

"What do you mean, you were 'sent' to Germany? From where?"

Elena smiled, enjoying his confusion. "We were prisoners of war in India for two years."

Christian's jaw dropped, and he stopped short in the middle of the dance floor. He gazed at her, incredulous. "How did that happen? Tell me about it."

She rolled her eyes. "It's a long story. Why don't you tell me about yourself first?"

Louise was curious to hear about the man who seemed to have held Elena spellbound all evening at the dance. They were preparing for bed after returning home with Rudy and Angela.

"You look like you're in another world," Louise said, noting the entranced expression on Elena's face. "Who is this fellow, and where does he come from? I didn't even get a chance to meet him; you two were snuggled up in a corner, talking as though you knew each other all your lives."

Elena slowly folded her clothes and placed them onto the back of a chair. She turned to Louise, flashing a deliciously secret smile. "His name is Christian, he comes from a small town outside Stuttgart ... and I'm going to marry him."

Louise giggled. "Does he know about it?"

"Not yet," Elena said blissfully. She sat down on the bed and began to languidly brush out her hair.

Louise sat down beside her. "You can't stop there," she said impatiently. "Tell me more."

"Oh, Louise, I'm sorry," Elena said, shaking her head. "I'm in a dream, I think. What happened with the maritime officer you were dancing with? What was his name again?"

"His name is Albert. I know it wasn't love at first sight with him," Louise said, laughing, "but he said he'll call when he returns from his next run."

"I thought he seemed very interested in you, Louise; his eyes followed your every move."

Louise shrugged. "We'll see."

Christian called the very next day. Was he as smitten as she? Did his heart go off like a fire alarm at the sound of her voice? She thought not. He sounded strangely faint and hesitant as he invited her to lunch. Only later in their relationship did she discover that he was uncomfortable speaking on the telephone; holding the receiver gingerly in his hand, he invariably brought the conversation to a hurried end. His uneasiness mattered little to Elena for she knew Angela frowned on long telephone conversations.

Instead, in the weeks following their first meeting, Elena and Christian walked the streets of San Francisco, seeing only each other. The beautiful city became an enchanted fairyland for them as they shared their hopes and dreams, their angst and pain. Hearts and minds bound together in mutual understanding and emotional involvement. Christian listened as she described her heartbreak, her love, her illness. Taking her into his arms, he gave her, at long last, solace and peace. Elena helped ease his feelings of guilt concerning his non-role in the war.

"If you had gone to war, we'd never have met," Elena commented, thinking of Lorenzo's unhappy end. Sitting on the grass in Golden Gate Park, a picnic lunch spread out before them, Elena felt an inner titillation as she watched Christian cut slices of sausage and place them on slabs of bread. His hands handled the knife with knowledgeable precision, like a surgeon; hands that also caressed her, loved her.

"I was in no hurry to become cannon fodder," he said ruefully. "Besides, why should I kill a Frenchman or Englishman I have no quarrel with, and he no quarrel with me? It was the leaders of the countries who started the whole fiasco." He waved the knife in the air as he spoke.

Elena smiled. "I'm glad you didn't go back to Germany, Christian," she said gently.

"I always thought I'd return," he said contemplatively. He gazed at her intently, and she held her breath, hoping for the words she wanted to hear. "But ... I know I'll never go back now," he said.

* * *

Elena had been certain of her feelings from the start, but Christian was hesitant. The affair had progressed so quickly; he was astonished at the deep passions Elena stirred in him. He worried that despite the obvious pleasure she showed in his company, she still might not accept his proposal of marriage. His age, in addition, might cause her concern; he was fourteen years older. However, as he sat with her that day in the park, the yearning and longing he felt for this lovely woman overcame his indecision. He decided to shave two years off his thirty-nine.

Having been a bachelor until then, proposing marriage didn't come easily to him. He rehearsed his words nervously in the hours before their next meeting, and pocketed the ring he had purchased in his best and only suit. They had planned to meet by a certain bench in the park. Elena was late, and he waited as a heavy fog, that was almost a light rain, drifted into the city.

She arrived, breathless and smiling. "I'm sorry, Christian, I couldn't get away any earlier from work." She glanced at the bench. "I see our bench is waiting for us. A little wet, but that doesn't matter. Let me sit and rest awhile."

He put his arm around her as they sat. "It's cool," he said. "Let me keep you warm," and she snuggled closer to him. Encouraged, he drew her tighter to him and kissed her ear and cheek. She appeared ethereal to him. In the misty glow of a nearby street lamp, droplets of the fog glistened like diamonds in her hair. It wasn't the first time he had held her in his arms, kissed her, but now they embraced in earnest, her kiss returning his with a warmth that told him all he needed to know. He hugged her, elated, and all the romantic words he had planned to say to her went by the wayside. "If I asked you to marry me," he blurted out clumsily, "what would you say?"

Elena's eyes widened and she smiled. "Is this a proposal, Christian? If it is, the answer is yes! I thought you'd never ask."

"Elena is engaged to this fellow? Christian?" Rudy asked Angela once again as she prepared lunch in the kitchen. He hadn't been able to concentrate on cello practice all morning since hearing the news from Angela the night before.

"Yes, I told you," Angela said cheerfully. "Louise and I were having a last cup of coffee when she came bursting in, all smiles. I've never seen her so happy. She showed us the ring Christian gave her ... we talked awhile, and then she and Louise went to bed." She went on as she ladled soup and cut slices of bread. "She asked me to tell you when you came in from your job at the hotel, as she had to rise early for work this morning." She looked up at Rudy, noting his pained expression. "It can't exactly come as a surprise to you, Rudy. Elena's been like one on a merry-go-round these past months."

"Well," he said, seating himself at the table, "I thought she'd at least talk to me before accepting a proposal. Since our father is in Germany, I should be acting as her protector."

"Why? She's old enough. In the times we've seen Christian, I thought he was a fine man, kind and gentle."

"I heard at the German House that he is a card player, and has little money."

Angela shrugged her shoulders. "Elena said he's been sending part of his pay to his brothers in Germany. It seems they lost the family pork store during the war, and are now in bad shape."

"Wonderful!" Rudy exclaimed. "So he's a mere nothing of a sausage maker, with no prospects. Elena can do better."

Angela's face flushed a deep red. She choked on a spoonful of soup, coughing and sputtering into a napkin. "Look, Rudy," she rasped, "if Elena loves him, she should marry him. She's not getting any younger, and she may never get another offer."

"Oh, Angela, that's absurd!"

"I know, I know, you think Elena is a princess, but listen to me." She shook her finger before his nose. "I mean this for my sister, Louise, too. If they have a chance to marry, don't stand in their way. Otherwise, we might have them hanging about our necks for the rest of our lives."

He stared at her for a moment, then rose from his chair and stalked from the room.

* * *

Elena and Christian were married in an Evangelical church several months later. The morning of their wedding day dawned bright and sunny. "A good omen," Louise said as she assisted Elena into her dark-blue, lace-trimmed dress. The choice of a dark gown instead of traditional white was a practical one for Elena. Money was tight, she reasoned, and the dress could be worn again as a "best" dress in the future.

"The color complements your fair skin and red hair," Angela said as she secured a string of pearls about Elena's throat. Her tone of voice was uncharacteristically cheerful. Elena smiled. Angela was ridding herself of the last member of Rudy's family, she thought, but then sighed happily. No one could spoil this special day for her, not even Angela.

The wedding ceremony was brief, Rudy and Angela serving as witnesses. Louise cried softly. Albert, whose ship had fortunately berthed just two days previously, stood solemnly by her side. Marianne, now an irrepressible five-year-old, watched the proceedings with an admirably restrained awe.

Elena's heart was full as she stood before the altar with Christian; God had granted her a second chance at happiness, and she breathed a prayer of thankfulness. She also prayed that He would forgive her sin of entering the state of matrimony in a Protestant church. Christian was not a Catholic, and had little inclination towards becoming one; indeed, he refused to attend any church service after their marriage, for reasons she was to discover later. However, this was her wedding day, and she looked forward to a life of joy and fulfillment.

Nuptials concluded, the radiant bride emerged from the church on the arm of her beaming groom. They laughingly dodged a shower of rice, received congratulatory kisses and embraces, and posed for photos taken by the ever-eager Rudy as he searched for the perfect angle. In high spirits, the wedding party then repaired to a nearby restaurant for a celebratory luncheon.

At the restaurant, Christian and Elena gazed lovingly at each other, paying scant attention to what they ate or drank. He slyly caressed her knee and thigh beneath the table; she shivered in nervous anticipation of the wedding night to come. When the conversation became increasingly ribald and peppered with innuendos, she blushingly escaped to the restroom with Louise. Inside, they embraced fondly.

"Oh, Louise, I'm so happy," Elena said, tears welling up in her eyes.

"You look so beautiful, Elena, and Christian so handsome."

"He was nervous. Did you see he almost dropped the ring?"

Louise giggled. "All men are nervous. It isn't easy to give up the bachelor life."

Elena raised her brows. "Perhaps Albert will take a hint today," she said mischievously, "and then we'll have another wedding?"

"Oh, I don't know," Louise said, shaking her head. "Albert isn't impetuous like Christian; he's more deliberate about making up his mind."

"You look so pretty today, Louise, I don't know how he can resist you."

Rudy was waiting impatiently for the two when they returned to the table. "What took you so long?" he grumbled. "I'm ready to give the toast."

"He's smuggled in some gin," Angela said, looking about the restaurant guiltily. "It looks like water, and no one will be the wiser."

Rudy rose from his seat, water glass of gin in hand. "First of all, I want to say, Elena, that you have chosen a good man for a husband. Not a rich man ... but a good man." Angela kicked his ankle, and he paused, clearing his throat. "We all wish our families in Europe could be with us at this happy time ... but since this is not possible, we must start our own traditions here in San Francisco today."

"On with it," groaned Albert.

Rudy smiled and raised his glass. "We wish you, Christian and Elena, a long and happy life together!" All joined the toast, lifting their glasses high in tribute.

"Jawohl!" chirped Marianne suddenly from her seat, and the company dissolved into laughter. She brightened at the attention as Angela bent over to hug her.

Elena sipped the gin cautiously, making a wry face at the taste. "Rudy," she said, shaking her head, "in all the time I've known you, not even a drop of wine or beer ever touched your lips. Now ... you make gin in the bathtub!"

He shrugged his shoulders, smiling broadly. "I didn't know how sweet forbidden fruit could taste," he said unapologetically, which was the overwhelming attitude of the whole of America towards the Volstead Act ... Prohibition.

* * *

"I'm pregnant," Elena thought, "married one month and I'm pregnant." She sat in the kitchen of the cold-water flat she and Christian had rented shortly before their wedding, a flush of happiness on her face. The kitchen was dark; one window of the room looked out on a drab airshaft. Her heart, however, was suffused with a radiant light of wonder, for a tiny being was growing within her womb. A miracle of love.

"What would you like, Christian, a boy or a girl?" she asked later as they lay together on the bed of their sparsely furnished bedroom.

He stroked her hair, then playfully ruffled it. "Doesn't matter, as long as it looks like you."

"Oh, no, not my red hair and freckles. I hope the baby looks like you." A sudden thought popped into her mind, and she propped herself up on one elbow, gazing steadily into his eyes. "I must have conceived on our wedding night, isn't that so?"

"Hmmm ... possibly."

"After we became engaged, you had wanted to go to bed with me."

"You can't blame me for trying, Elena," he said, smiling. "We were going to be married, weren't we?" Admiring her peaches-and-cream complexion, he paused. "I think because you refused me," he continued, "you became even more desirable to me." Frowning, he asked, "But what are you getting at?"

She sighed. "I wasn't playing games, Christian. I was afraid I would become pregnant. If something happened to you before we were married, I'd be alone with a child." The memory of Camille's predicament in the prison camp had not faded from her mind. "Look how quickly I conceived."

Laughing, he gathered her into his arms. "Nothing happened to me, did it?" he teased. "All those good times we missed."

"For you, yes." She pulled away from his embrace and sat up erect on the bed, her facial expression now earnest. "Christian," she said, "you're not sorry you married me?"

"Sorry?" He slapped his forehead in exasperation and rolled his eyes. "I don't think I'll ever understand women. How can you ...?"

"No, no," she interrupted, "I only say that because you might feel I'm keeping too tight a rein on you ... about our budget, I mean."

"Elena, you're better at managing money than I am. I told you that, and I don't mind giving up card playing ... for money, anyway." He smiled affectionately at her, patting her stomach lightly. "I'm a married man now, with a son or daughter on the way. Which reminds me ... I want you to leave your job at the delicatessen. Lifting those heavy pots is bad for you."

Her eyes filled with tears. How good and considerate her husband was. Later, he proved to be more than considerate; he was generous to a fault, being quick to assure her they would continue sending money to her parents every month as Rudy did. "My brothers know I have other responsibilities now," he said.

* * *

Rudy and Angela had already bought and sold several homes during the first years of their marriage, a pattern they would follow for many years. Rudy aimed to purchase a house in need of repair, renovate and refurbish it, then sell at a tidy profit. The talented fingers that had made him an excellent cellist restored the properties to their former glory with professional results. Elena was intrigued to discover a piano in the living room of his latest Richmond district abode.

"I bargained with the former owner to include the piano in the asking price," Rudy explained. "He didn't want to go to the trouble of moving it, and now Marianne will be able to take lessons."

Elena stroked the dark wood of the piano. Angela had, in her house-keeping zeal, polished the instrument to a glowing finish; it beckoned to Elena like a lover thirsting to seduce her. Rudy noted her wistful expression. "You can play, too, Elena," he said. "In fact," he added, his eyes lighting up, "we'll play together here on Christmas Eve, and that's only a few weeks away."

When Christmas Eve arrived, Elena was six months along in her pregnancy. She felt well, but nevertheless basked in the attention showered on her by Angela and Louise. They waited on her, refusing her help with meal preparation and cleanup later. "I'm fine, I'm fine," she protested, but it was of no use.

"Elena looks wonderful," Rudy said to Christian. "You should keep her pregnant all the time."

"Spoken like a man," Angela said. "You don't have to have the babies." She was in a rare good humor, the usual tone of complaint absent from her voice. Removing her apron, she sat down on one of Rudy's elegantly refinished chairs, breathing a sigh of relief. "I'm tired," she said. "Rudy, why don't you and Elena play for us now."

And so the concert began. Elena and Rudy made music together, cello and piano rendering sweetly the holiday selections of the Yuletide season. Their father, the Kapellmeister, loomed brightly in Elena's vision as she played, evoking memories of Christmases past. Engraved on her mind was the remembrance of his violin leading his family in song, and him as Saint Nicholas, spreading treats and good cheer over his excited children. When they finished playing, brother and sister smiled at each other, each knowing they had experienced the same magic.

Conversation became more and more lively as the midnight hour approached. Albert had arrived late, adding his friendly demeanor to the festivities. He drew Angela aside, whispering in her ear; she nodded, smiling broadly.

"It's Christmas Day," Rudy announced as a clock on the mantle struck twelve. "It's time to open the gifts." He moved agilely toward the lighted Christmas tree he had decorated the day before. "I'm going to play Saint Nicholas tonight," he said, "or Santa Claus, as he's called here in America, and give out the gifts."

Papers rustled as packages were unwrapped, followed by appreciative comments from recipients. Marianne excitedly tore papers aside hoping to find gifts she had asked Santa to bring her. Sometimes she was successful, sometimes not. She threw uninteresting items to the side, finally settling down with games and toys. Then Louise received a tiny box from Albert. Elena thought she would never forget the expression of joy and surprise on Louise's face when she opened the box. She looked at Albert quickly, and he raised his eyebrows questioningly. She nodded her assent. No words were spoken, nor were any needed. She smiled through tears as he took the ring from the box and slipped it on her finger. As they embraced, the room echoed with oohs and aahs of pleasure and delight from the family.

"What a perfect Christmas," Rudy said brightly. "It couldn't *be* any better!"

Elena snuggled next to Christian on the trolley going back to the flat, her mind on Louise's newfound happiness. We both came to San Francisco to recover from the aftermath of war, she thought, and we've been healed of our wounds. Christian's voice, raised a decibel or two over the grinding noise of the trolley's wheels on the tracks, intruded on her reveries.

"I thought Louise didn't look well tonight," he said. "There were deep circles under her eyes, and she seemed feverish. Did you notice how little she ate? She's losing weight, too, and that isn't a good sign."

"Oh, perhaps she was just excited about everything, " Elena reasoned.

Christian was adamant. "No, I've seen it before, Elena, someone I knew ...."

"What do you mean?"

"I think she has TB."

"Tuberculosis." Elena's heart did a flip-flop

CHAPTER TWENTY-SIX

Dreams And Realities

On a Sunday afternoon several weeks into the New Year, Albert came to Christian and Elena's flat, his face set and grim. Elena helped him from his seaman's jacket and cap, her body tense with apprehension.

"I've just come from the hospital," he said. "Louise will be there a few more days."

"Come into the kitchen where it's warmer, Albert," Elena said. "We were just having a cup of coffee."

"Well?" Christian asked as Albert sank heavily into one of the kitchen chairs.

Albert's usually placid brown eyes were desolate. "You were right, Christian," he said. "Louise has TB." He glanced at Elena as a mournful gasp escaped her. "Luckily, the disease isn't greatly advanced, Elena. The doctor is confident she'll recover."

"Poor Louise," Elena said tearfully as she poured coffee into a cup for Albert. "She was so happy making plans for your wedding."

"Plans will have to wait," he said, sighing heavily. "She'll need a year's rest in a sanitarium."

"A year ...," breathed Christian, his eyes widening.

"Well, Rudy and Angela have a less costly solution. The summer house that Rudy has been building down the peninsula is just about finished, and Louise can stay there."

Elena nodded enthusiastically. "Redwood City. They drive down on weekends, takes about a half hour. Much warmer and sunnier there than here in San Francisco."

"Exactly. Louise will need plenty of fresh air and sunshine."

"That sounds perfect, Albert," Elena said, now smiling broadly. "I know Louise will be fine again, and then you can be married. A year isn't such a long time to wait."

Christian wasn't as optimistic. After another cup of coffee, Albert excused himself, citing work to be done on his ship, and Christian walked with him to the sidewalk outside the flat. A dismal fog was rolling in from the ocean, reflecting the misgivings he felt in his breast as they talked.

"I know you love Louise, Albert," he said tentatively, "but don't you think ...."

"You think I'm taking a chance marrying a girl that's sick?"

Christian shrugged his shoulders. "Well, Louise may never be healthy, never live a normal life. You might be hounded with doctor bills."

"That can happen to anyone after they marry."

"But you know ahead of time."

Albert nodded. "True," he said. He paused for a few moments before continuing in his slow, deliberate manner. "Christian, I'm like you. You married Elena knowing about the trauma she has suffered. Maybe she'll be fine, maybe she'll have a nervous breakdown, but you went ahead and married her because you love her. I feel the same way about Louise. I'm willing to try."

The men shook hands heartily, and Christian returned to the flat. He lay down on the bed, intending to nap, but instead stared into space, reviewing his conversation with Albert. The possibility of Elena having a breakdown had never occurred to him; he couldn't take credit for being noble about his actions. She had appeared healthy to him in mind and body. No, he reasoned, she had had an unfortunate experience, being interned and all, the effects of which would pass in time. Confident that his love and understanding would keep her safe, he promptly fell asleep. He was never one to worry unnecessarily.

Every Saturday when Christian returned from work, Elena took charge of his pay envelope, and they would enter into a charming ritual.

"Here it is," he said, laying the unopened envelope on the kitchen table. "I've done my job, now it's your turn." After changing from his work clothes, he joined her at the table, where she had a large cup of coffee waiting for him.

She then spread the bills and coins out, counting and arranging them into separate small piles. Her professed lack of mathematical skills didn't include counting money, it seemed. "This is for your trolley fare and lunches," she said, touching the first pile with her fingers.

"I told you I don't need lunch money," he said, slurping the coffee to his lips appreciatively. "You know I only take bread in my lunch box. There are plenty of meats at the shop for me to make a sandwich or two."

She waved her hand. "Use it for cigars, then. You need some spending money. Now this is for groceries," she said, indicating the second pile

He watched fondly as she went down the line ... money for the doctor, rent, gas and electric, and finally there was one pile left.

"This," she said proudly, "goes in the bank on Monday." Each week it was the same. He was impressed by how well she managed their household expenses. Speculating idly on how much money he might have saved, were it not for the funds he had sent his brothers as well as money spent on card playing and beer, he shook his head. He had counted on living a comfortable life upon his return to Germany, but the war had changed everything

* * *

"Push! Push!" the doctor urged. "Bear down, Elena."

Elena lay in the hospital delivery room, her face perspiring and flushed with pain and effort. "I'm so terribly, terribly tired," she whimpered. "I can't push anymore." She tilted her head wearily to one side, her voice trailing away to a whispering sigh. A sympathetic nurse murmured encouraging words, sponging her face with cool water.

"She's been in labor ten hours," the doctor said, his strained face showing his own fatigue. "The umbilical cord is caught around the infant's neck," he added. "Forceps," he snapped, and the nurse slapped the instrument into his hand.

A full-throated cry erupted from Elena as the infant was unceremoniously drawn, protesting vehemently and indignantly, from the warmth and darkness of her womb.

"Look, Elena, look. You have a beautiful little daughter!"

Elena gazed with lustrous eyes at her baby being held up by the smiling doctor for her to see. She's all arms and legs, she thought tenderly, and she has dark hair, like Christian. No red hair and freckles for this little one to fret over.

* * *

When Elena took her daughter on daily outings to the park and grocery store, the twelve-month-old Trudi's limpid dark eyes and plump, rosy cheeks inevitably drew admiring comments from acquaintances and strangers alike. Seated in the wicker baby carriage, little Trudi responded to the attention with a beguiling friendliness that charmed all about her. The clerk at the grocery store was no exception.

"Look at the poster here on the wall, ma'am," he said eagerly. "You should enter your daughter in the baby contest being held at the church hall next week."

Elena at first dismissed the suggestion as frivolous, but then had second thoughts about the venture. Why not?

She eagerly awaited Christian's arrival home from work a week later, gaily waving a blue ribbon before him as he walked in the door. "Our Trudi won first prize in the contest today, Christian," she said triumphantly.

He smiled. "That's because she looks like me," and he stooped to kiss the little contest winner seated in her highchair. Trudi giggled and gurgled in response.

"Hmmm ... well, she certainly is the picture of you. You couldn't deny that she's your daughter."

"We can make a few more like her," he teased, gathering Elena in his arms and planting a kiss square on her lips.

"Oh, no, not yet," she said quickly, pulling away from him. "I'm still recovering from this one."

The thought of having another child frightened Elena. She wondered how her mother had produced twelve children so easily ... like the family cat. Not only had the length of labor been painfully traumatic for her, she was not yet completely healed from little Trudi's abrupt entrance into the world. A second physician she consulted stated that her doctor had failed to suture her torn vaginal walls at the time of birth, causing normal love-making to be a still tortuous experience for her. She didn't want a baby now, maybe later, when Trudi was older.

Further depressing her during the baby's first months, Christian resisted having their daughter baptized.

"I hate everything about the church," he had fumed. "It's all poppycock."

She was shocked. "But ... you married me in church."

"I did that only for you."

"Then ... why not do it for the baby?"

He waved his hand dismissively. "She can decide when she is older."

Elena shook her head, perplexed. "I don't understand why you feel this way, Christian. You said you attended church in Germany when you were a boy. In fact, you were an altar boy, weren't you?"

"That's just it!" His eyes blazed with remembered injustices. "The pastor of our church whipped the altar boys if they missed services, even if they couldn't help it. I got the worst of it, because when I missed, I was thrashed by my father as well."

Elena's eyes brimmed over. "But you believe in God?"

"I don't know ... yes ... but not the church."

* * *

Elena had sighed deeply at the time, and dropped any further entreaties. Nagging would only irritate Christian, she thought, better to bring it up again later when he was in a good mood. She concentrated instead on Trudi's well-being. The flat they lived in was one of four in a building located in the Mission District of San Francisco. The rent was inexpensive, and Elena had been able to build up a moderate bank account with her penny-pinching ways. She began to think about buying a house.

From San Francisco's beginnings since the gold rush of 1849, the city retained a multinational character. The lure of riches had attracted immigrants worldwide to the area. Even at the end of the nineteenth century, almost everyone was a new arrival, and rigid social structures had not had time to develop. Foreign-born and second-generation residents lived together in neighborhoods of mixed ethnic backgrounds.

Rudy's knowledge of the city was invaluable to Elena as they occasionally toured the Richmond, Sunset, and Outer Mission districts in his auto. "The city of San Francisco is confined to the tip of a peninsula, you see," he said. "So homes and commercial buildings have been densely constructed to make use of every square inch. After the war, homes were designed as two-story, wooden, stucco-faced row houses, with living quarters on the second floor. The bottom story is used as a garage or storage space, or even a spare room."

"Not like the Victorian-style houses," Elena observed.

"No, the demand for housing since the war has been great, and the row houses are being built everywhere."

Elena liked the look of the homes. They were neat and attractive with their small patches of greenery at the front and small yards in the rear. One evening she approached Christian hesitantly.

"Don't you think it's time we consider buying a house?" she asked.

Christian froze. "It's too much money," he said. "We'll be in debt for thousands of dollars." Rudy was at the back of it, he thought. Elena had that look in her eye every time he and Angela bought a new house.

Elena was prepared. "It's an investment, Christian. Every month we pay rent and have nothing to show for it."

"I work hard six days a week," he countered. "I need my rest on Sundays, and besides, I'm not handy and know nothing about caring for a house."

"Rudy has offered to paint and fix up," she said quickly. "I'll do what I can to help, and when little Trudi goes to school, I'll go back to work."

Christian sighed. "Elena, it's more than that. Look ... my job is located close by here, only a short ride on the trolley. I'd have to travel a lot farther from one of the new districts, and I have to be at work at seven in the morning. Rudy has a car, he can buy wherever he wants, but if we buy a house, we can't afford a car, too."

She had no answer for this last consideration, but then put forth her more persuasive arguments. Surely Trudi should have a nicer neighborhood to grow up in, she said, and lastly, the threat of fire from cigarette-smoking tenants in the other flats of the building was very real.

In the end, Christian capitulated, and Elena had, at long last, roots ... a home of her own. After several months' search, she and Christian decided on a stucco-faced, two-story house in the Outer Mission District. Christian seemed satisfied that the trolley ride to work was manageable, even complaining little about the steep, two-block climb up to the house from the trolley stop. "Doesn't everyone live on a hill in this city?" he joked. She saw, however, that his hand was far from steady as he signed mortgage papers that put them four thousand dollars in debt.

Elena was confident they would be able to carry the house. She cleaned and organized, Rudy painted and papered, and Christian cleared the small, wooden-fence-enclosed yard at the rear, surprising her in the spring with a vegetable garden. "That I can do," he said proudly. As the months passed, she diligently cooked, cleaned, and shopped, lovingly tolerating Christian's insistence on teaching her how to make sauerbraten, soups, liver dumplings, calf's brains with scrambled eggs, and sweetbread. To her surprise, even tripe from the cow's fourth stomach simmered in tomato sauce was appetizing to her palate. "Americans don't use every bit of the animal for food," Christian said. "They throw it away or use it in dog food. Properly cooked, the ears, tongues, hooves, and other internal and external parts are delicious." Elena smiled as he went on about how he was going to make homemade sausage, acquire a vat to make wine in the garage area, and bake onion cake, so tasty with a glass of beer. "When Prohibition is repealed," he said confidently.

* * *

Louise was well again. She and Albert were quietly married, and Angela and Rudy hosted a dinner for them in their home after the ceremony.

"The roses are back in your cheeks, Louise," Elena said as they freshened up in a guest bedroom.

"I feel fine," Louise said, her face radiant. "I thought the year would never pass, though. I missed you and the family so much, Elena; Albert most of all." She hesitated, her expression suddenly bleak. "I was so afraid he wouldn't wait."

"Oh, no, Louise. Albert was always loyal and faithful."

"I know that now ... but Angela ...."

Elena bristled. "What did she say?"

"You don't know what it was like all by myself in Redwood City, Elena. Nothing to do but read ... no one to talk to. I had to sleep with the windows wide open each night, no matter how cold it got. I think it was even worse than Germany after the war, where I had to forage for food in garbage cans ... Angela came twice a week with groceries ... and then it would start." She paused, her heart remembering. "Angela thought Albert might find someone else, not wanting to be tied down to a sick girl. She didn't say it in so many words, but I knew ...."

Sly insinuations, Elena thought ... Angela was good at that, terrified she would be saddled with an ill sister. "She was wrong, wasn't she?" Elena said, hugging Louise. "Albert did wait, and now you're man and wife."

Louise brightened. "Did I tell you we're going to buy a house in Redwood City? Albert thinks the climate will be better for me." She hesitated. "Of course, that means we won't see each other that often, unless Christian buys an auto."

Elena shook her head. "He has no interest in driving, even if we had the money. I'm sure Rudy will give us a ride occasionally." She put her arm around Louise's shoulders as they prepared to leave the room. "You know," she said, her eyes misty with emotion, "we've both survived the horror of war, like two neglected flowering plants blooming in the sun again."

They smiled and walked together to the dining room where Rudy waited with glasses of bathtub-manufactured gin. Marianne scurried about serving canapés to guests, her eyes bright with excitement. Now nine years old, she hovered over her two-year-old cousin, Trudi, like a little mother, entranced with the tot's doll-like beauty. In years to come, the pair would be like sisters, both destined to be an only child in the Depression era a few years away on the horizon. For now, though, when Albert and Louise married, prosperity and good times flourished in the land, and hopes for a rich and plentiful future still abounded.

* * *

After several months of deliberation, Elena bowed to the dictates of fashion and bobbed her hair. She felt lightheaded, free of the everlasting chore of washing, brushing, and arranging her long abundant crop. Nevertheless, when the barber carefully wrapped the vivid auburn mane in tissue paper, and handed it to her compassionately, she felt an extraordinary pang of regret. Though no longer a part of her, it represented the world she had left behind. For days afterwards, she periodically unwrapped the package stored away in her bureau drawer, and gazed soulfully at the still-vibrant tresses. They would outlast her, she thought, recalling the photos she had seen of Egyptian mummies with hair as alive as the day they were interred.

Christian bemoaned her action loudly, saying the girl he had married now looked like a "drowned cat." Previously, he had buried his face in the sweet, fragrant-smelling strands of her hair, as they lay abed on Sunday mornings, a prelude to their making love. His fantasy had vanished with the click of an unfeeling pair of scissors. On the following Sunday, however, the lure of her warm body next to his was enough to put to rest any thoughts of lost pleasures.

Rudy was noncommittal as he appraised Elena's changed appearance on a visit one morning. "If you like it, that's fine," he said. "Angela is considering cutting her hair, too. All this hullabaloo over women not being ladies anymore is nonsense." He lifted his eyebrows mischievously. "No matter what you do to your hair, or what you wear, you're all still female underneath. Besides I have no aversion to short skirts."

"Uh, Rudy, don't let Angela hear you talk like that."

"Angela can't wear short skirts. She would look like a battleship on legs." He paused, smiling at the vision his words had engendered in his mind, and Elena giggled to herself. "Well," he added, "I have news."

"Oh?"

"Papa wrote that he's heard from the Rosenbaums. Seems they were interned at the Teutonic Club in Singapore during the war. Guess where they are now?"

"Where? In Germany?"

"No, in Chicago. They have cousins there."

"I'm so glad, Rudy. Mama was worried about them." Elena paused, her thoughts reflecting on their life in Singapore. It seemed so long ago. "What I wouldn't give for a taste of Chang's chicken curry again," she sighed.

Rudy picked up his tweed cap, ready to leave. "Ha," he said smiling. "It just so happens I've been able to collect all the spices needed to make a curry. I thought we could get together this weekend and try our luck."

Elena's mouth watered at the thought. She waved a fond goodbye as Rudy disappeared down the hill in his auto, and sat down to read the afternoon mail before Trudi awoke from her nap. A letter from Lise was full of news and complaints.

Mitzi was getting married in the spring to a small-town newspaperman named Horst, Lise wrote. Franz, their father, spent many evenings with him discussing the merits of classical composers and playing chess. Their mother, Marta, had suffered a small stroke, but was recovering well. Lise was expecting her third child, and therein rose a problem that Elena found intriguing.

"I find it exceedingly trying, Elena," Lise went on, "that Papa takes it upon himself to discipline my little Heidi and Gabriella. He was absolutely too strict with all of us when we were young, and I don't want my children to suffer as we did. I have a right to raise my girls in any way I please. Kurt is a quiet man and doesn't say much about it, but Papa and I have constant arguments about his unwanted interference. Believe me, you are fortunate to live far away in America."

Lise's lament brought to mind Angela's emotional reaction to the Kapellmeister's treatment of Marianne a few years previously. Elena, now a mother herself, had a better understanding of the situation Angela had faced. She had to admit she, too, would be unhappy if her father interfered in her daughter's upbringing, especially if they lived together. She shook her head.

Still, she felt there would never be a true friendship between herself and Angela. The animosity and discontent present in her sister-in-law's nature would always be there, like a great divide separating them forever. Elena suspected Angela was afraid, fearful of any circumstance that would make Rudy's family dependent on him. And it all boiled down to money. Her war experience had frightened her into a desperate search for security. I can see the future, Elena thought. Angela will become a miser. She didn't know how close she was to the truth, for the Depression years would make Angela a skimping, tightfisted penny-pincher. Elena smiled, knowing Christian could apply the same word to his own frugal wife. It was a matter of degree, she thought, comforting herself.

Trudi's chirping from her crib aroused Elena from her meditations. Christian would be home soon from work. It was Saturday, bath night for him, and she was determined to see that he didn't step into his dirty underwear again when he was finished bathing. Each bath night she handed him fresh long johns as he entered the bathroom, only to find the clean underwear still on the closed toilet seat when she came to clean up after him. This night would be different, she vowed. Planning to creep stealthily into the steamy room and spirit the soiled clothes away while he bathed, she giggled. Wasn't it amazing how much subterfuge was necessary for wives to keep husbands nice to be near? Changing Christian's untidy bachelor habits proved to be a challenge she took on with clever diplomacy. She persuaded, cajoled, flattered, tickled, and teased, until soon he was cleaning the tub after his bath, picking up clothes from the floor, and hanging coat and hat in the closet when returning from work, all without a murmur of dissent. Working tirelessly to keep their home in tip-top shape—scrubbing floors, cleaning windows and dusting—one day it all seemed worthwhile.

"I think you are the best housekeeper in the world," Christian said, his eyes admiring the newly scrubbed and spotless kitchen floor. He took her in his arms, exclaiming as she leaned her head on his shoulder and cried.

* * *

During the first year Christian and Elena lived in their new home, the living room had been bare of any furnishings. Elena put aside a few dollars each week towards the purchase of a sofa and chairs and possibly a carpet. Fringed shades hung on the casement windows to provide privacy, though the room was never used. She hoped to eventually furnish the dining room also; invitations from their ever-widening circle of friends meant some kind of reciprocation was in order. At the moment, Trudi slept there; the house had only one bedroom. They would worry about that situation later.

"I've $250 saved now, Christian," Elena said one morning before he left for work. "Hales Department Store has sales on furniture. I thought I'd take a look."

Christian was content to let her do the shopping. He knew next to nothing about furniture, and, of course, from past experience trusted she would make a shrewd purchase. This time, he couldn't have been more wrong.

Early in the morning she walked to the Mission District to save on trolley fare, pushing Trudi's carriage up and down the hills. It was still foggy, the mist almost like a soft rain. If she had time she planned to take in the new Gloria Swanson film showing at the Lyceum Theater. She usually sat in the back row with the other mothers, the carriage by her side, Trudi fast asleep. However, first came the exciting part of her day. Her heart thumped in anticipation as she entered the store and headed for the furniture department.

As she wandered through the jungle of upholstered sofas and chairs, she heard the sound of someone playing a piano. Chopin, she thought idly. She compared the cost of each sofa on the sale tags, striving to visualize the colors and patterns as they would appear against the background of the living room's papered walls.

"That was a Strauss waltz," she whispered to herself, her concentration broken by the vibrant tones of the piano. She craned her neck to get a glimpse of its whereabouts in the store. Then she saw a young man seated before a shiny upright, his body swaying back and forth in waltz tempo as he played. A picture of Schenck suddenly flashed through her mind, and a sweet, nostalgic memory overcame her. Dear Schenck had sat in that very same way before the piano in Singapore, playing for an enthralled young girl. She caught her breath, listening raptly as the player switched to Debussy's haunting "Clair de Lune." Now the music drew her, inching along toward the piano, almost forgetting to pull Trudi's carriage with her. Here was what she had always dreamed of ... and she had the money in her handbag. The years of longing overwhelmed her.

"You're lucky," she heard the salesman say, his voice sounding as if he were a long distance away. "The pianos are on sale today, and we can deliver it this afternoon." She didn't answer, all she saw were the black and white keys ....

Elena supervised the workers that afternoon as they carefully carried the piano up fifteen marble-like steps to the second story of the house and placed it on the fireplace wall in the living room, an upholstered bench sitting perkily before it. After the men left, she put Trudi down for her nap, and sat herself eagerly on the piano bench. For hours her music filled the house with beauty, and she was lost in its glory.

When Christian was due home from work, she began to have qualms. How was she to explain her outrageous action to him? She hardly knew how it happened herself. She peered nervously down the street from the front porch at intervals, watching for his familiar figure to come striding up the hill. His easy-going, sloping walk was so identifiable. When he finally appeared, she panicked, and rushed into the kitchen to busy herself with dinner preparations, her heartbeat drumming in her ears.

Christian, unaware of his wife's folly, hummed an aimless tune as he unlocked the front door. He was fond of music, but had no talent for it. In fact, he was asked to drop out of the men's chorus at the German House because he persistently sang off-key. Indignant, Elena threatened to send a letter of grievance to the men of the chorus, but he had laughingly said that one music lover in the family was enough.

Now he stepped into the living room and, at first, thought the room was bare. Elena had not found a sofa she liked, he thought, or perhaps it was to be delivered the next day. Then he saw the piano standing proudly by the fireplace, as though its mere presence could dress up the room without a stick of other furniture in sight.

Christian stared at it in astonishment. Elena crept in from the kitchen quietly, trembling like a dog that expected punishment for some misbehavior. He looked at her and back at the piano.

"You bought ... a piano?" he asked, more shocked than angry, though the idea of immediately shipping the upright back to the store did cross his mind.

"I'm sorry, Christian," she said weakly, tears welling in her eyes. "I ... I just couldn't help it. When I saw it in the store, so beautiful, so grand ... I just *had* to have it."

The expression on her face was so pitifully remorseful, his heart melted. Money wasn't everything, he thought. It wasn't as though she had bought something *really* expensive, like a fur coat or an auto. He couldn't help erupting into hearty laughter as he realized what she had done.

"And you are the frugal one of the family," he roared, "saving every penny!" She dropped her head and blushed deeply, and he paused. Owning that music box meant so much to her. He put his arm around her shoulders. "Well, let's go in and eat. You know, now you'll have to start saving all over again for a sofa and chairs. How else am I going to sit down and listen to you? Can you play "Moonlight and Roses?"

Acknowledgments

For twenty-two years, I brought my invalid mother breakfast each morning in her room. Over coffee and conversation, this book was born as her remembrances took form in my mind. I decided the book should be in the form of a novel, much more fun to write, and, besides, my mother had passed away by that time.

I want to thank all the friends and family who gave me encouragement along the way as I undertook a tremendous task of research. My husband, Harold, helped in every way, even taking me to the countries described in the book: Romania, India, Egypt, Singapore, and Thailand (Siam). How much more could one ask? My children, Howard and Helaine, were very interested in my activities, printing manuscripts for me to send to the inevitable agents and publishers. Reed Billings and Jay Baluh were wizards with computers. God bless you both.

Joining a local writers' group was the best thing I ever did. They helped to make my book professional. They listened. They became friends. Thank you, Page Faust, Trish Grizzard, Connie Reeves, and all the other great members.

Made in the USA
Charleston, SC
12 August 2010